Dance of the Butterfly

Cris Anson

ELLORA'S CAVE
ROMANTICA PUBLISHING

What the critics are saying...

∽

5 Stars "*Cris Anson* has created an absorbing, exciting story populated by well-rounded characters [...] If you have a [yen] for brooding heroes and tough-as-nails independent women, hot sex and fast paced stories then *Dance of the Butterfly* is clearly a worthy choice." ~ *Euro-Reviews*

5 Cupids "Kat and Magnus are two very likeable characters. The chemistry between them is explosive and the sex scenes are scorching hot and erotic. *Dance of the Butterfly* is a well written, passionate love story of two people who are the complete opposite [and] fall in love, and if they are to have a future together they must both let go of the past and find a middle ground. Sexy, passionate, emotional, intelligent and fun, that's what *Dance of the Butterfly* is. This one is a keeper!"
~ *Cupid's Library Reviews*

"Highly erotic and highly charged with emotional intensity [...] Exciting, loving, and very sensual, *Dance of the Butterfly* proves to be a great sequel [...] a fun story to read but it also covers some very serious relationship issues such as trust, love, and commitment." ~ *Fallen Angel Reviews*

An Ellora's Cave Romantica Publication

www.ellorascave.com

Dance of the Butterfly

ISBN, 9781419952883
ALL RIGHTS RESERVED.
Dance of the Butterfly Copyright © 2005 Cris Anson
Edited by Sue-Ellen Gower.
Cover art by Syneca.

This book printed in the U.S.A. by Jasmine-Jade Enterprises, LLC.

Electronic book Publication May 2005
Trade paperback Publication November 2005

Excerpt from *Dance of the Seven Veils* Copyright © Cris Anson, 2005

Also by Cris Anson

∽

Dance of the Seven Veils

About the Author

∽

Cris Anson firmly believes that love is the greatest gift...to give or to receive. In her writing, she lives for the moment when her characters realize they love each other, usually after much antagonism and conflict. And when they express that love physically, Cris keeps a fire extinguisher near the keyboard in case of spontaneous combustion. Multi-published and twice EPPIE-nominated in romantic suspense under another name, she was usually asked to tone down her love scenes. For Ellora's Cave, she's happy to turn the flame as high as it will go—and then some.

Married for twenty years to her real-life hero, Cris enjoys slow dancing with him to the Big Band music of the Forties. She also plays the piano, nurtures a small garden at their home in eastern Pennsylvania, wishes she had time to bicycle more often, and is known to break out in song (yes, she can carry a tune) when the spirit moves her.

Cris welcomes comments from readers. You can find her website and email address on her author bio page at www.ellorascave.com.

Tell Us What You Think

We appreciate hearing reader opinions about our books. You can email us at Comments@EllorasCave.com.

DANCE OF THE BUTTERFLY

ဆ

Trademarks Acknowledgement

ﾪ

The author acknowledges the trademarked status and trademark owners of the following wordmarks mentioned in this work of fiction:

Armani: GA Modefine S.A.

Bentwood: The Bentwood Companies, Inc.

BMW: Bayerische Motoren Werke Aktiengesellschaft

Crown Royal: Diageo North America, Inc.

Day-Glo (flowers): Switzer Brothers, Inc.

(Dodge) Ram: Chrysler Corporation

GQ: Advance Magazine Publishers Inc.

Guinness: Arthur Guinness Son & Company

Homelite Super 1130G gear drive chain saw: Textron Inc.

Hot Wheels: Mattel, Inc.

Jeep Wrangler: DaimlerChrysler Corporation

Lycra: E. I. du Pont de Nemours and Company

Manolo Blahniks: Blahnik, Manolo

Papa John's: Papa John's International, Inc.

Philadelphia Inquirer, The: Philadelphia Inquirer Co.

Ritz Carlton Hotel: Ritz-Carlton Hotel Company Of Boston

Sam Adams (beer): Boston Beer Corporation

Starbucks: Starbucks U.S. Brands

Uggs: Ugg Holdings, Inc.

Thermos: American Thermos Bottle Company

Volkswagen: Volkswagen AG

XNash Rambler: LLC "Rambler Internet Holding"

Chapter One

🔊

"Do my eyes deceive me or is the panther in that painting licking a naked woman?"

"How perceptive you are, Jules. The artist was so subtle, so clever, yes?" Kat Donaldson smiled with almost proprietary pride. The painting would be the talk of the Philadelphia art world within a week, and Kat's reputation for discovering unknown talent would skyrocket. She tucked a stray auburn curl back into her severe topknot. She'd have preferred to leave it loose for the evening, but her primary rule at work was, Do Not Upstage the Artwork. Unbound, her riotous curls looked rather like a red flag being waved in front of a bull. So she'd pulled it up and worn a long-sleeved black sheath that nonetheless emphasized her tall, svelte figure.

"I must have it. Let me give you a check for five thousand tonight and arrange for the balance from my trust fund within a week. Would that be satisfactory?"

Kat gazed at her friend with tolerant amusement. Seven years younger than Kat's thirty-six, Jules Rubin was tall, charming, rich, and easily swayed, in and out of bed. "Surely you've noticed this little tag in the corner? As an art collector of some note, you know 'NFS' means 'Not For Sale'."

"But Kat—"

"I've already had to turn down two offers. The artist insists *The Oasis* is not for sale. It took me a week to convince her to exhibit it at all."

"If you're angling for a higher price, I'll pay twenty thousand." His dark eyes silently begged her to comply.

The other two would-be buyers were strangers to Kat, but puppy-dog-sweet Jules had enriched the coffers of A

Discerning Eye Fine Arts for the four years she'd been its sole owner. She needed to keep him happy.

"The artist was adamant. I'll talk to her again, but don't hold your breath. Meanwhile, there's another one you might like. A close-up of a rose." As she steered him halfway down the gallery, she leaned close and whispered in his ear, "Looks just like a cunt."

"Really?" Jules' swarthy face brightened as they stopped at a painting done in subtly blended shades of vermilion, pink, mauve, and fuchsia that indeed resembled a swollen, dewy cunt that had just been satisfied.

Jules stared, transfixed, at the painting. "What do you think—was she fucked? Licked? Stroked with a finger?"

Although Kat took no offense at Jules' blunt language, she hissed, "Keep your voice down. Not everyone here is a member of the Platinum Society."

He cleared his throat. "Of course. Sorry."

Unobtrusively, Kat brushed her fingers against the slender silver bracelet on her left wrist that marked her as a member of the Platinum Society, a sex club with strict entry requirements. Kat and Jules both served on the club's Board of Directors, which voted on every prospective member. No one could apply, only a current member in good standing could nominate someone for membership. Kat herself had nominated the artist, Lyssa Markham, after introducing her to the Society at a masquerade the previous summer.

"I'll take it. Shall I write a check now?"

Kat removed a discreet "Sold" sign from the black beaded bag she wore on a chain around her tiny waist and tucked the card into the lower-left corner of the frame. "Let's wait. You might find something else you like." She plucked a flyer from a nearby table. "Here. Keep this handy and browse. And help yourself to the champagne."

"Hey, I know her, don't I?" He was staring at the artist's photo on the brochure.

"Yes." Kat glanced around the room. "There she is, the beautiful blonde in the clingy blue dress. You voted her into membership last September."

Jules' eyes narrowed in thought. "Ah, yes. The voluptuous Salome who took off each of her seven veils. She's the one who got Savidge to participate. God, I've never gotten so horny watching a man go down on a woman. It was almost like watching a tight bud opening up into a..." His voice trailed off as he looked back at the painting he'd just bought. "Self-portrait? I wonder."

Wisely, Kat said nothing at his astute guess. But she felt pride at the way Lyssa, her best friend, had discovered her own sexuality—with a little help from the Platinum Society.

Kat moved on to circulate among the guests, answering questions, offering comments, nudging those who seemed on the verge of buying, introducing the artist to a reporter for the *Philadelphia Inquirer*. By the end of the evening, she had sold four paintings and had "maybes" on three others.

At last Kat released a tired but satisfied sigh. The only person left was Jules, whose dark eyes tracked her as she deftly turned the sign to "Closed" and switched off the spotlights, leaving the gallery in soft, indirect night lighting. Her pulse kicked up a notch. She knew exactly what would happen next, although sometimes she wished he'd surprise her and be the dominant one for a change.

"I do admire the way you work a room," he said as he followed her to her office in the rear of the building. "Women as well as men. Everyone got your undivided attention for a few glorious minutes, as though each person was an old friend."

Kat smiled. The way to sell a piece of artwork was to read body language and then act on it. Jules included. She picked up the last remaining invoice on her desk. "Ah, here's the paperwork Sandy wrote up for your *Unfolding Rose*."

Taking the hint, Jules whipped out his checkbook from an inner jacket pocket and paid for his purchase. "By the way, did you hear about Mrs. Peifer's new acquisition? She was raving about a one-of-a-kind table her husband just bought. Says the guy's going to be the next George Nakashima."

"Ooh. The New Hope woodworker who used claro walnut slabs with the bark still on? He got every design award there was. Didn't he die about a dozen years ago? His resale prices must be off the charts." Kat used her "For deposit only" stamp then slipped Jules' check into her desk drawer. She folded his copy of the invoice and provenance, slid it into an envelope, and handed it to him.

"Yeah. If he's that good, maybe you'll want him to be your next 'discovery'. His prices would certainly be more reasonable." Jules slipped the envelope and his checkbook into his jacket's inner pocket.

"As a rule, I don't handle furniture, but it wouldn't hurt to check him out. Thanks for the tip. I'll call Mrs. Peifer tomorrow." With a sigh of relief, Kat began to remove the pins that held her hair too tight. "It's been a long day."

"Here, let me," Jules murmured from behind her, delving into her hair to retrieve a hairpin.

She spun around and slapped him, open-palmed, on his left cheek. "I did not give you permission to touch me."

Face flushed, eyes glowing, Jules meekly lowered his gaze.

"For that indiscretion," she continued, "you must remove all your clothing from the waist down."

"Yes, mistress." Toeing off his tasseled loafers with alacrity, he sloughed off his trousers and boxers in one swoop. His hand-tailored silk shirt bared his buff ass cheeks as he bent forward to lay the garments, neatly folded, across the edge of a side chair.

With an innate grace, she sat on her butter-soft burgundy leather chair behind the desk and swiveled to the side.

Sometimes he was *too* compliant, she thought then dismissed it immediately. He had a lovely cock, and boy, did he know how to use it once she'd given him permission. "Approach. You may remove five pins."

"Thank you." Jules came to stand diffidently in front of her, his already-hard cock protruding between the edges of his shirt placket.

As his questing fingers gently massaged her scalp, Kat idly scraped blood-red fingernails down both his thighs, from the crease at his hairy groin to his knees, then trailed around to the back, scratching similar tracks up his legs to his ass cheeks. His cock twitched. Nothing else moved except his hands in her hair.

She expelled a soft puff of air at the purplish head then licked the drop of fluid off the tip. A tremor ran through him, but he remained otherwise compliant.

Cupping his ass cheeks in her hands, she opened her mouth and closed it around him.

He let out a choked sound. His fingers stilled in the act of removing a pin.

She sucked him in with more force, gloving the rigid length of him with her inner cheeks, her teeth skimming the velvety skin. *This* was why she liked Jules. He was so responsive, so smooth and hot. She pulled her head back, her mouth and tongue sliding over him in sweet friction. When almost all his cock was visible, she reversed direction and sucked at him, hard, until the engorged tip touched the back of her throat and his rough pubic hair tickled her nose.

With an audible moan, Jules grabbed her head with both hands and held her immobile while he thrust himself into her mouth.

Kat exploded upward off the chair, arms flailing to break his hold on her head. She shoved him backwards to land on her desk. "How dare you! Did you have permission to move?

Did I allow you to behave like a rutting animal, thinking only of your own pleasure?"

Arms akimbo, she watched his Adam's apple bob up and down as he stammered a reply. "N-no, goddess, but your mouth is so delecta—"

"Silence! For your offense, I sentence you to a hard, throbbing, *unfulfilled* cock. You are not to come. You are not to jerk yourself off. You are not to touch yourself in any way, shape or form. Is that clear?"

"Mercy, please—"

"I ordered you to silence!"

Jules stood eye to eye with her, her spiky Manolo Blahniks adding three inches to her five-ten, his chest rising and falling with every harsh breath.

"Take off that shirt. It offends me."

In a flash the shirt lay in a heap on top of the clothes he had earlier folded so carefully.

"Stand in the middle of the room and let me see if there's anything worth redeeming in your worthless, disobedient hide."

He moved to the designated spot, his olive skin sheened with a light layer of sweat. The desk lamp sculpted his body in light and shadow. The darkness of his hair, a heavy mat of it on his chest, stomach, and legs, stood in contrast with the sleek smoothness of waist and hips. She loved the look of a totally buff man in his prime.

As she circled him, she took nips with her teeth on his shoulder, his back, his firm butt, the tender skin just outside the circle of pubic hair. His cock stood almost straight out, straining with need. A muscle in his stomach quivered.

"You do show some promise." Kat turned her back to him, unhooked the chain around her waist that held her beaded bag. "Unzip me."

The susurrus of the zipper was followed by Jules' choked cry as the soft black fabric fell to the floor. She was naked except for her heels.

Keeping her back to him, Kat stepped out of the pool of black. "My dress then my pins."

She heard the swish of silk as Jules bent down to pick up the garment and laid it carefully atop his own clothes. She felt him come up behind her. The body heat radiating from him caressed her bare back, her ass, her legs.

As he delved once again into her topknot, she felt his cock brushing briefly in between her butt cheeks, then out, as he retrieved the pins one at a time and laid them in her upraised palm. Finally he ran his fingers through her tangled hair, searching for any missed pins. Her hair cascaded halfway down her back. She tossed her head. The tickle of the silky tresses on her shoulders raised the fine hairs on her skin.

"Come." She ambled to the burgundy leather sofa, her stride sinuous in her spike heels. She felt just as decadent walking naked in her Blahniks before an audience of one as she did in Lady Godiva mode at a fully subscribed Platinum Society affair.

"Earn your forgiveness, wretch."

Setting the pins on the side table, she sat regally on the sofa, her knees primly together, and watched him edge forward like a supplicant, his engorged cock bobbing with every step, his balls drawn tight to his body. Kneeling before her, he gently pried her knees apart, then slipped his hands underneath them to lift her feet off the area rug and set them back, spaced wide enough for him to fit between them.

For a moment he simply knelt there, his hot gaze raking over her widespread thighs to the swollen pink lips at their center. She was bikini-waxed and smooth, her tiny fluff of pubic hair a shade darker than that on her head. His lustful stare made her pussy twitch with anticipation.

"Do not test my patience," she hissed, moving a leg to bring one spiked heel down hard in his groin-crease, calculatedly missing his balls by less than an inch.

Jules cupped the outside of that delicate ankle, grinding the stiletto tip into his flesh while managing to rub his cock with the black leather. He leaned forward, began licking and nibbling her inner knee, then worked his way slowly up her inner thigh. She could feel his curly hair graze her skin as his head moved. Involuntarily she opened her legs more as his mouth reached the part that was most wet and ready.

His tongue licked her slit lightly then stopped. She withheld a moan, more to make him work for his forgiveness than from any misplaced sense of decorum. She was hot and horny and she wanted more.

"Jew-els," she drew out his name into two syllables, "don't make me angry."

Thus encouraged, he tossed her legs over his shoulders and pulled down her hips so her crack was at the edge of the sofa. He began sucking and licking in earnest, and thrust two fingers into her pussy. She ground her hips into his hot mouth, hands fisting in his hair. Her spikes jabbed into his back as she sought more traction to press her crotch more fully into his face.

His teeth grazed the hard acorn of her clit. She exploded, tossing her head from side to side, muttering incoherent syllables as he kept sucking, sucking.

At length she released her death-grip on his hair and sighed. "That was nice." She slid her legs off his shoulders and plunked her spikes on his thighs, her legs still casually apart to allow him to see where he'd been, what he'd done.

Then as if noticing it for the first time, Kat captured his rampant cock between her shoes and rubbed gently. "If you come all over my Blahniks," she warned, "there'll be hell to pay."

Jules groaned but said nothing, simply stroked her calves and gazed at her glistening pussy.

"Okay, that's enough." She swung her legs to one side of his knees, planted her feet on the rug, and stood. "Get me some champagne."

Bending down to the floor, he kissed her shoe tips. "My pleasure."

He stood as well, six feet of wiry height and eight inches of solid cock, and gave her a burning gaze. Then he did something Kat considered out of character. He leaned forward aggressively and suckled one ripe, turgid nipple as he tweaked the other between thumb and forefinger. The unexpected, provocative action had Kat reaching out to cradle his head closer as she arched her back into him. Yes, at last Jules was waking to what she really wanted, what she needed—to be dominated. But he turned to get her some champagne, making her realize he was only asking for more punishment.

As hard as she could, she smacked one of his lush ass cheeks. "How dare you!"

After a slight hesitation, he continued on to the small fridge to do her bidding. She could hardly suppress her smile as she saw in a mirror that his cock had swelled even further with her blow. And that a satisfyingly red handprint had appeared on his skin.

Returning, Jules handed her a tulip-shaped glass filled with bubbly. Kat took a sip then kneeling before him, tipped the glass and dribbled a few drops on his cock. Then licked it off, relishing the quiver of his muscles as he struggled to remain motionless. "Mmmmm. Warm champagne."

Encircling the base of his cock with her fingers, she guided it until it dipped into the glass then popped the dripping appendage into her mouth, sucking the taste of champagne, of him. "Hot. I like hot."

Jules made a rough sound in his throat.

"Did you say something?" Her mouth still around him, she raised her eyes to his, noting the strong veins in his neck standing out in bold relief. Like the veins in his cock.

He thinned his lips into a tight white line. Closed his eyes.

Slowly Kat got to her feet, sliding her body over his as she rose. "You know what I'd like?" She turned her back to him, knelt on the sofa with her belly pressed against the cushions and her knees spread wide apart, and reached over the top to retrieve the packet she'd stashed on the table behind it. The movement had the effect of raising her ass and spreading her cheeks and her swollen slit wide open. Turning her head to talk over her shoulder, she tossed the packet onto the sofa cushion and purred, "I'd like to pretend I'm a mare in heat, waiting for a stallion to service me."

In a few seconds Kat heard the rip of foil over Jules' harsh breathing, a few more seconds for him to roll the condom onto his cock. Then he knelt behind her. Shoved his cock into her, hard, until he was buried to the hilt. "Oh God, Kat. Oh God." He leaned over her, spooning his chest to her back, and reached under her to fondle her nipples. His hips began to piston, slowly at first, then gradually building up steam to fuck her good and proper.

Kat strained to get closer to him, loving the feel of him ramming into her. She'd learned through the Platinum Society that Jules needed this kind of domination to get really hard, and when he was hard he was good, and she liked good. In fact, he was even better than good. If she had to be the dominant one, it was no hardship if it got such an explosive result.

She felt another orgasm gathering inside her. He must have sensed it too, for he moved one hand from her breast to her clit, stroking it while pumping his cock in and out, and pulling and pinching her other breast. His teeth bit lightly into her shoulder, urging her without words to let go.

She did.

The sofa, the gallery, the man, all faded from her consciousness as she concentrated on the sensations that sizzled through her, the electricity, the contractions, the delirious letting go, the floating to a magical place where only feelings existed.

A moment later she felt a warm cloth being applied to her wet pussy, then to her thighs as Jules endearingly wiped away the track of her juices. He kissed her lightly on each ass cheek.

"Marry me, Kat."

That shook her out of her sensual spell. She turned around to sit on the sofa, idly noting that she hadn't even kicked off her Blahniks in the frenzy of the moment.

"Jules, you're so sweet. But you know that I'm like a butterfly, dancing around in a field of wildflowers. There's too much out there to limit myself to just one flower."

"But we're so good together."

She took his free hand, kissed its palm, and said gently, "I'm not the marrying kind. I'm happy living alone, running my business alone. I'm quite a bit older than you. You deserve someone just learning about life. Both of us are 'good together' with other people from the Society, too. Just because we're good together isn't a reason to get married."

"Kat…"

"Let's stay friends, Jules. I enjoy your company, but I don't want to be exclusive. Okay?"

Shoulders slumped, Jules turned from her and reached for his clothes. She didn't want to hurt him, but she didn't want to marry him, either. She didn't want to marry anyone.

She hadn't found a man yet who could dominate her.

She was her mother's daughter, all right.

Chapter Two

ဆာ

"Easy! Put her down gently!"

Magnus Thorvald watched anxiously as the 'dozer operator lowered the winch wrapped around a swaying eight-foot length of American black walnut that had just been chain-sawed by an expert tree-monkey. The sun had dipped below the tree line and they still hadn't completed the job of dismantling the hundred-foot-tall tree.

At last the precious hardwood rested safely on the forest duff. This was the piece Magnus most wanted, with its massive burl encircling the entire four-foot diameter of the trunk. Squinting, he lifted his head to the sky, holding onto his hard hat with a well-callused hand. About an hour of daylight left, he estimated. The remaining section of trunk could be done without his mother-hen supervision, as his youngest brother, Rolf, had jokingly called it. But an artist was only as good as his materials, and this virgin stand of mixed hardwoods his great-grandfather had bought was not only his primary source of supply, it was his pride and heritage.

Magnus had learned to wield a chisel and spokeshave on his grandda's knee. Knut Thorvald had lived long enough to see some of his eldest grandson's hand-carved bowls and figures displayed in museums. Magnus closed his eyes as a shaft of pain seared him. Five years the man had been gone and still he felt the loss as though it were only yesterday.

After dispensing a few more last-minute directions to the foreman, he strode down the dirt road to his cramped quarters inside the two-level barn. Time to get ready for work. Weekends were the busiest nights in a bar, and at six-five, two-ten, he looked like Central Casting's idea of a bouncer whose thirty-five years of hard living had made him able to handle almost any problem that arose in his brother Soren's establishment.

A quick shower, a short nap, and two huge cups of coffee later, Magnus revved up his battered Jeep Wrangler—a real canvas-top Jeep, not the overgrown, citified SUV with forty thousand dollars worth of trimming—for the twenty-mile trip to Allendale.

Using the employee entrance of Thor's Hammer, Magnus punched the clock, strode through the kitchen and pushed open the swinging door leading to the bar. "Hey, Soren."

"How're they hanging, Mags?" Soren stood behind the bar building a Guinness.

"Loose, man, loose. Any trouble?" A year apart, they were often mistaken for twins, with identically piercing blue eyes the color of an iceberg's interior. Soren kept his hair shorter and less unruly than Magnus, whose blond locks were pulled into a short ponytail.

Magnus' practiced eye checked the premises. Patrons occupied all the booths and most of the tables, the combo was setting up in a corner, and several couples on the minuscule dance floor were shaking their assets to a blaring rock tune from hidden speakers that had Magnus gritting his teeth.

"Naw, it's quiet. They were waiting for you to arrive. No fun fighting without you."

"Bite your tongue."

"Hey, handsome, wanna buy me a drink?"

A slithery platinum blonde in a tight T-shirt and denim miniskirt swiveled on her stool to bat heavily mascaraed eyelashes at him.

"Sorry, ma'am, I'm just the hired help."

He turned his back on her practiced pout and made a slow circuit around the room, taking mental notes. The rowdies at table six would bear watching. A couple of young women—he assumed Soren had carded them—might be drinking a little too desperately fast. He nodded a smile to the sax player limbering up his fingers with scales and riffs. Listening to Dwayne's mellow style was one of the few perks in this job.

When the recorded blare ended, the combo started its gig with a hot, fast jazz piece. After completing his circuit, Magnus ducked into the kitchen for a quick cheeseburger and quart of milk, listening to the short-order cook relate his most recent problems with his perfidious girlfriend.

Women. Magnus had learned to steer a wide berth around them.

Back on the floor, he noted that the four rowdies had encircled the carded women, one of whom was swapping spit with a dark-haired dude with two earrings in his right ear. The pouty blonde was vertically scratching her itch on the dance floor with a biker type.

The decibel level rose at one corner as a couple of tattooed heavyweights began shoving each other around. Magnus sidled over.

"She's comin' with me!" the one with a mustache snarled.

"You're outta your fuckin' mind," Snake Tattoo retorted. "She's mine. You keep your filthy hands off her."

"Yeah? Ask her. Go on. Ask Belle who she wants to spread her legs for."

Magnus hovered in the background, standing on the balls of his feet, arms loosely at his sides but ready to intervene before any damage occurred to the premises. He caught a glimpse of the woman in question. An overly made-up woman in her mid-thirties sat in the booth, long blonde hair as straight as a swizzle stick, cantaloupe-size tits half-spilling out of her scoop-neck sweater. Black wasn't her color, he idly noted. It made her look harsh, cold.

She slithered out of the booth and insinuated her well-rounded body between the two rivals, encircling an arm around each man's waist, making sure a breast nestled against each puffed-out chest.

"Hey, guys, I've got lots of stamina. Either of you ever daydream of a threebie?"

Magnus' lip curled into a sneer. Not only wasn't she picky—both men could stand a bath, in his opinion—she was as promiscuous as his ex-wife.

Dammit, don't go there, he chided himself. That was ancient history.

Snake Tattoo looked leery, but Mustache's eyes widened with interest. "Mmm, bodacious idea, babe. I'm in."

"How 'bout it, Snake? You told me you used to get your kicks watching your sister and her guy getting it on out in the backyard after dark. This way you can watch and do it at the same time. And guess what—" she stood on tiptoe and said in a stage whisper meant to carry far beyond his ear, "I have two holes."

Magnus' stomach muscles tightened. He didn't want to hear any more, but he had to stay until the situation defused.

Snake glared at his rival, striking an intimidating pose. "I'm in charge."

Mustache lifted his hands away from Belle's waist in a conciliatory gesture. "Hey, man, I'll take seconds."

"Hold it, hold it. *I'll* be in charge," Belle said. "It was my suggestion, it's my apartment, and my body you two will be poking. You guys bring the beer and the stamina. And anyway," she crooned to Snake while her hand wandered down his zipper to his crotch, "I always dreamed of having a guy with a mustache go down on me while I'm sucking off someone else."

"Jesus, Belle, you got my balls so hard I can't talk. Let's get out of here."

With a smug smile, she turned to Mustache, stroked the hair on his upper lip. "What's your name, champ?"

"They call me Rod," he said.

"I can't wait to see why." Her vulgar laugh trailed behind her as she led both men between the tables and out the door.

"Good Christ, I need a drink," Magnus mumbled as he wended his way back to the bar.

"Trouble?" Soren said as he deftly mixed a Cosmopolitan and set it on a waiter's tray.

"Just a bad taste in my mouth. Thanks." He lifted the glass Soren handed him and drained the seltzer water without stopping. He gazed unseeing at the now-closed door to the street. "How can a woman let just anyone dip his wick in her like that? She didn't even know his name, for crying out loud!"

Soren wiped the bar in front of his brother's propped elbows and waited.

"That blonde who just left? She's going to do both of them at the same time."

"Magnus." Soren's tone was mild, but the warning was there just the same.

"I know. I have to get over it."

"What Lydia did was unforgivable, but you can't dwell on the past. It's been three years, Mags. You've got to forget it."

"But in our own bed."

"It's done. It's in the past. Let it stay there."

Magnus barely heard his brother. "Why do I seem to pick the ones who hurt me? You think I'd have learned after Angie. I excused her because we were both too young. I was studying too hard and she needed a lot of attention. But Lydia. Hell, I thought we had it made. I thought she loved—"

Without prompting, Soren handed him another ice-filled glass of seltzer water.

He took it, wrapped both massive hands around the glass, and stared into the fizz. Soren moved down a few stools to hand a regular customer a bottle of locally brewed beer.

Magnus didn't notice. He idly wondered how much more pressure it would take for his white-knuckled hands to shatter the glass.

Was any woman loyal? Trustworthy? Monogamous? Hell, even his mother had stepped out on her husband. Magnus had been fourteen before he realized why Rolf didn't look anything like him and Soren. Black sheep indeed. He didn't know how his father was able to forgive her.

Magnus sat straight up. Maybe he hadn't. Maybe he'd died of a broken heart.

One thing Magnus had vowed. He'd never, ever again, let a woman wrap him around her little finger. He would dominate her, or there would be no relationship.

And his aching balls reminded him of it every painful minute.

Chapter Three

೫

Oh man, could the guy live any further in the boondocks?

Following directions from Mrs. Peifer, Kat took the Pennsylvania Turnpike east, got off at 611 north, and drove through the rolling hillsides of upper Bucks County, where sheep still grazed on expansive meadows and corn stubble dotted farmlands on this first day of November. Just beyond a red barn with a hay wagon stashed on its peaked roof, she turned left onto a two-lane road then checked her odometer. One-point-two miles from the turn she looked for a driveway half obscured by a stand of black pines.

"Good grief," she said as she carefully steered the sporty BMW around a series of potholes in the long gravel driveway. "This guy must be a recluse." She pictured him as an aging lumberjack with scraggly gray beard and a nest of thinning hair that hadn't seen a comb in years.

Topping a slight rise, she saw a barn that had to be sixty or seventy feet long tucked into a hillside that sloped down to the road on its short side. The middle of the long wall was broken by a series of French doors.

"Okay, there's a Jeep," she muttered, eyeing what almost looked like an Army-issue vehicle with its canvas top parked on the dirt ramp abutting the glass doors. "But how the heck do you get there?"

With a grimace, she followed the gravel path in a hard right curve around the barn, then saw an offshoot leading to the lower level of what turned out to be a two-story barn from the rear, with a pair of closed barn doors on rollers, probably to accommodate farm machinery. She turned into the offshoot, then killed the engine near a solid oak door.

Good thing Mrs. Peifer warned her to wear jeans and boots, Kat thought. She'd break a stiletto heel walking across this yard, if that's what you could call the bumpy surface.

Shifting her buttery-soft leather attaché case by its shoulder strap, she knocked and waited, looking around curiously. A soft wind stirred the dead weeds around the perimeter of the building. She could hear birds of some sort chirping in the wooded area on the other side of the driveway, and the rat-a-tat of a woodpecker. Kat smiled. She hadn't heard that sound since her childhood, when they'd visit her grandmamma in the summer. City-born and reared, she hadn't thought of woodpeckers in years.

After another knock elicited no response, she walked to the right side of the building. She'd noticed windows there when she drove by. She peered into one, then the other. Both looked to be shuttered from the inside.

"Hell." She returned to her car. Mrs. Peifer was a sweetheart, but she wouldn't make a good administrative assistant. Although her directions were impeccable, she didn't have the woodworker's business card or even remember the man's name so Kat could look him up on the Internet, or at least the phone book.

"There has to be another entrance," Kat reasoned as she backed out and then continued bumping along the uneven driveway.

"Aha! I knew it." Following the path that was little more than two ruts in the grass, she pulled around the far side and parked next to the Jeep. And sighed in relief on spying the simply carved sign that said "Office". Getting out of the car, she took a moment to breathe deeply. She didn't realize how much she enjoyed the smell of autumn in the country. It conjured images of hot mulled apple cider and scuffing through dry leaves underfoot.

Attaché case on her shoulder, she ascended the ramp and stood at the row of French doors, uncertain which one she should knock on. The sun was high overhead, and she realized that whatever room lay behind these doors would be flooded with afternoon sunlight.

"Oh well, nothing ventured, nothing gained," she murmured and rapped on the jamb of a door at random.

The first door on the left—two down from the middle one she'd knocked on—opened to the inside. She strode to the opening. All she could see was the silhouette of a shaggy-haired giant, holding the doorknob and silhouetted against windows on the opposite side of the barn.

She swallowed. "I'm looking for the woodworker."

"You found him."

"Uh, are you coming out? Or can I come in? I wouldn't want to have you heating the entire outdoors." She gave him her most dazzling smile, one that had turned many a man's knees to mush.

"Come in." His formidable bulk blended with the dim interior as he moved back into shadow.

His voice was like low thunder rumbling in the distance, Kat thought, then shook off the fanciful notion and entered. It took a moment for her eyes to adjust to the contradictory blocks of light and shadow. Then she realized why she was confused. There were only the two large expanses of windows, front and back. The large blocks of light illuminating parts of the plank flooring came another source. She looked up. Two massive skylights on the far side of the huge, loft-like room shone lambent light on two large sculptures displayed on pedestals.

Her breath caught. Without a thought to civilities like shaking hands or introducing herself, Kat found herself drawn to a richly hued carving, cherry perhaps, about four feet tall perched on a rounded pedestal. Her artist's eye immediately recognized the exquisite workmanship in the soaring wings, the suggestion of feathers, the strong clawed feet of a stylized bird.

"Is he taking off or landing, I wonder?" she said almost to herself.

"Taking off. See how he's leaning in front of his wings? If he were landing, the wings would be in front to help him brake."

His voice from right behind her sent little shivers down her spine. "Yes, of course it would be a he. The lines are utterly masculine. Is he for sale?"

"You get right to the point, do you?" His voice held a touch of amusement.

"Oh God, I'm sorry. I'm like that. I get carried away when I see beauty of any—"

She had been turning as she spoke, but her throat closed when she got her first real look at the sculptor in the light. At five-ten in her bare feet, Kat hadn't looked up to many men, but this one was at least six inches taller than she. His face and physique could have graced a Viking's ship. Talk about utterly masculine. Talk about beauty.

Holy shit.

She had to swallow twice to find any saliva to moisten her throat enough to speak. She fumbled in the pocket of her waist-length, faux-fur jacket for her calfskin business-card holder.

"I'm Kat Donaldson, owner of A Discerning Eye Fine Arts." She handed him her card, discreetly printed on fine cream-colored vellum, her logo a single brown eye under a gracefully arched brow.

One thick blond eyebrow rose. "Bryn Mawr? A little far from home, aren't you?"

"I go where the talent is. I've made a number of trips abroad to find just the right pieces for my clients. This drive was a piece of cake."

"And your clients are looking for—?"

"They're looking for first-class artwork." Like you, she thought. How she'd love to bring him to the Platinum Society! She could just visualize herself stripping the well-washed jeans, the snug blue T-shirt draped across what must be exquisitely honed pectorals, off that thoroughly male body. On second thought, she'd keep him tied to her bed for as long as it took to bring him to heel.

Realizing the direction of her thoughts, she spun on her high-heeled boot. "And this other one. My God, look at the texture of it." An irregular slab about two feet wide and five feet tall, with its bark intact on the two long edges, had the most intricate markings she'd ever seen on a piece of wood. A reverse bas-relief of a sharp-nosed Indian chief in profile, including headdress, was carved into the slab's surface. The artist's skill utilized the markings in creating the image of the craggy face, the suggestion of eyes, of high cheekbones.

She reached out a tentative hand, the attaché case sliding off her shoulder to land on the plank floor with a soft thunk. "May I touch it?"

At his amused nod, she brushed her fingers around the sinuous curves of the chief's headdress feathers, his flowing hair, his jutting chin.

"How did you make those markings?"

"It's spalted wood. That's the best piece I ever found."

Reluctantly she tore her gaze from the carving to look incredulously at him. Not that the woodworker was hard on her eyes. She just had never seen a more compelling piece of wood. "You mean the wood comes that way?"

"If you're lucky, yes. Basically, spalting is just rotting wood."

"Yeah, right. If this is rot, I drove in on a Nash Rambler."

That amused half-smile again. "No, really. That's maple, by the way. Maple's the best for spalting because it takes the longest to spalt so it keeps its hardness. You find a dead birch, for example, the bark can still be intact, but inside it's all rotted away already."

"But how does it get those intricate markings?"

He rubbed his chin thoughtfully. "Nature makes them. Under the right conditions, the rot will creep between the rings or through cracks. The tree should have grown in a swampy or wet region. When it falls, it should rest on rich, dark earth. Or mossy ground. One way to find it is to look for mushrooms growing on the end of a tree that was previously felled. But if the mushrooms are on the side, it might mean it's too rotten."

"So part of it is luck."

"Yeah. But knowing where to look helps. It also helps to know what you're looking for. Even then, it's luck. It's lucky when you make a vertical cut and find it there. Then you have to let it speak to you. Nakashima's credo was that each piece has an ideal use if only one can find it. That slab sat in my workshop for six or seven months before it told me what it was meant to be."

She cocked her head at him. So much passion. So much talent.

So much man.

"May I see your workshop?"

"No."

Taken aback, she frowned. "I'd like to represent you. Sell your work. I'd like to see where you work, how you work."

"No."

Taking another tack, she asked, "Do you have any more finished pieces I could look at?"

"No."

"How many are you working on?"

He shrugged.

"Look, my clients are well-to-do and discerning. I hadn't heard of you before, but I can tell you this, every art collector in the Philadelphia area will know you before I'm done."

"Is that right?" There was that amused tone to his voice again, as if he didn't quite believe her, as if he was laughing at her. It irked her.

"But I can't take you on as a client if you only have two pieces completed. I want enough to create a buzz. You know, word of mouth excitement." Then it struck her. "Unless you already have an agent?"

"If you hadn't heard of me, how come you're here?"

When you answer a question with a question, that's when the bargaining begins, she thought wryly. She took a deep, fortifying breath. "Jack Peifer bought a one-of-a-kind slab table from you. I heard about it at a reception I recently hosted at my gallery. Where I very successfully launched a previously unknown artist." She bent down to the attaché case at her feet, unzipped an outer pocket and handed him a photocopy of a news article.

She watched his poker face for clues as he read the article by the *Philadelphia Inquirer*'s Roving Art Critic in which he hailed Lyssa Markham's work as "groundbreaking" and "sensual" and "like Georgia O'Keeffe but with twenty-first-century sensibilities". It also mentioned Lyssa was the third unknown artist whose career Kat had launched.

He handed the article back to her. "What makes you think I'm an 'unknown artist'?"

"I didn't know you. No one at my reception knew of you when I asked around."

"And Philadelphia is the art capital of the world?"

Kat bristled at the underlying amusement in his voice, in the slightly offensive question. "No, but their money is green and they rely on my expertise. I can make your name a household word."

"Look, Miss—" he dug into his front jeans pocket and retrieved her slightly crumpled business card "—Miss Donaldson, I don't need to be represented. I don't want to work with you. I'm just a simple wood-carver."

"'Simple' is the last word I'd use to describe your talent. Those pieces are exquisite works of art. With extraordinary workmanship." She reined in the anger starting to build inside her and reminded herself, *it's just a negotiating stance*. "Just answer me, yes or no. Are either of these pieces for sale?"

"Yes."

"How much?"

He folded impressive arms across his even more impressive chest, momentarily distracting Kat by the sheer poetry of his undulating muscles. "Which one? Or both? Who are you buying them for? Yourself? One of your clients?" He frowned. "Or for resale at a hefty commission?"

Hands on her hips, she faced him like an adversary, which she read in his posture and attitude. "Are you saying that you want to screen the person in whose home your work would reside? Sort of like vetting prospective adoptive parents?"

He ran a massive hand through his shaggy blond hair. "Just curious."

"To satisfy your curiosity, I want the Indian chief for myself. For my dining room. The eagle, I think I know someone who would pay a substantial amount for it, and I'll buy it on spec. I'm assuming those pedestals were tailor-made for each sculpture and are part of the package. I'm also assuming you can deliver it. I don't usually handle anything that heavy, it's mostly canvases and acrylic boards, so I don't have muscle on staff."

A corner of his mouth quirked up in a mere ghost of a smile. "No, I don't guess the Indian would fit inside that yuppie-mobile out there."

Kat lifted her chin. "It's a good car. It's three years old and I enjoy driving it. It corners nicely when I downshift on these winding country roads. And I'm not going to apologize if you think I fit the Yuppie image."

"You do. Who in their right mind wears high heels with blue jeans? And a jacket hardly long enough to warm your back? Fur, no less. Aren't you afraid of PETA?"

"I'd show you the label that says '100% acrylic', but you'd probably accuse me of changing labels." Obviously he hadn't been out of his cave in years if he didn't know women thought jeans and heels a perfectly fine fashion match.

Kat put her index finger to her mouth, tapping her lips thoughtfully. "You know, I think you're *afraid* of success. You live out in no-man's-land, your driveway is anything but welcoming, and you're raising too many obstacles for a normal person who's trying to make a living out of his art." She let her gaze wander around the large, loft-like room. Besides the two sculptures, she saw a drafting table by the north-facing window, a large conference table with blueprints unrolled on it. A sofa and chair grouping. Corkboard on the wall near the entrance, with what looked like sketches pinned to it. All the rest of it was visual space. No mementoes, no photos, no plants, nothing personal.

"You're hiding," she said flatly. "Or else you're punishing yourself."

He took a threatening step forward. "If you're finished, Miss Robertson—"

"Donaldson," she corrected.

"Whatever. You'll have to excuse me. I need to finish taking down a tree before it gets too dark, and there's only three or four hours of daylight left."

Her chin jutting out, she met his intimidating stare while she tried to rein in her temper. She'd be damned if she'd blink first.

It was a standoff. He gripped her arm just when she couldn't hold her eyelids open any longer. "I'll see you out," he said, his voice sounding like tires riding on broken glass.

She shook off his hold. "Don't trouble yourself. I remember which door I came in."

Sweeping her attaché case onto her shoulder and pivoting in one smooth move, she strode to the bank of French doors. With her hand on the knob, she turned to him. "Five thousand dollars apiece. Delivered. Including the pedestals. You have my address on the business card I gave you."

Giving him a saccharine smile, she added, "If you don't want to deal with me, my assistant's name is Sandy. She's there from twelve to four every day except Mondays, when we're closed. Sandy is a sweet, grandmotherly type who grew up with four brothers. Maybe she can speak your language better than a Yuppie who wears high-heeled boots with jeans. She'll even tell you when it's *safe* to deliver the sculptures. And she's authorized to write checks on behalf of the Gallery for pieces I've bought, so you'll be paid on delivery without even having to talk to me."

With that dramatic pronouncement, she lifted her head and walked out into the warm sunshine, barely resisting the urge to slam the glass panes out of the French door.

She had snapped herself into the seat belt before she realized it.

She still didn't know the artist's name.

And she'd be damned if she'd go back inside to ask.

* * * * *

"Dammit!"

Whack!

"You stupid shit."

Whack!

"I can't believe you let her just walk away like that."

Magnus had been whacking away at a stack of scrap oak logs for firewood for the better part of an hour, and frustration still fueled his ire. He paused to lift the hem of his T-shirt to wipe the sweat off his forehead. His hair clung in wet strips to his neck. His toe hurt like hell where a bad chop had knocked a big chunk of oak onto it. He should have known better than to tackle wood without his steel-toed boots, but damn, the woman had messed with his mind.

A freaking Valkyrie, that's what she was, a female warrior straight out of Norse mythology. He'd been working at the conference table, facing the doors, when he saw her get out of that sleek foreign car, and he'd been blinded by the fire in her hair under the afternoon sun. Cascading around her face and down her back like ripples on a lake of lava. The sun turning it into a glowing ruby halo. She had the sexiest walk he'd ever seen. Unconscious grace, not like the calculated hip swinging that accosted him every night at Soren's bar. And legs that went all the way up to heaven. In those fuck-me red boots.

"Hell." He lifted the axe again, but stopped with it held at waist height.

A woman just couldn't look that good without makeup. She had to have been wearing some. Every woman he'd ever known wore lots of it. But the roses in her cheeks looked natural, not painted. Those thick dark eyelashes looked natural, not clumped together. Her eyes, the color of the finest teakwood, held all kinds of depth. And when she'd first smiled at him, it was all he could do to keep his knees locked so he didn't kneel at her feet and whimper.

"Shee-it." He lifted the axe high above his head, then brought it smashing down to split off a hefty chunk from the half-round. And another. And another, until it was whacked into manageable pieces of fireplace size.

Breathing heavily, Magnus surveyed the pile he'd accumulated. He'd probably sliced a half cord. And still frustration ate at him. But it was getting too dark—too dangerous—to wield an axe as viciously as he'd been doing. He wiped off the axe blade and set about stacking the logs in the back of the ancient pickup truck he used around the farm. He'd deliver the firewood tomorrow to the farmer down the road who gave him brown eggs all the time.

But meanwhile, he had to exorcize the color of that woman's eyes, her blazing hair.

How the hell was he going to accomplish that?

More importantly, where did he think he had the brass to turn down five grand apiece for his sculptures? If that newspaper article was correct, and he had no reason to think it was a shill piece, that woman did have a knack for finding new talent.

He sure as hell knew he had the talent. Grandda had told him many times that he'd be even better than his teacher. Her first reaction to seeing his eagle had to have been spontaneous. She'd been impressed. And she'd said she wanted the Indian for her own dining room.

So why had he all but kicked her out?

"You know why, Magnus. Face it. You simply flat-out don't trust someone who looks like that."

She had oozed sensuality like an aura. Oh, no, she hadn't made any overt comments. But her body language said, "I'm available and I'm good, and I like what I see." If she thought she could get him to roll over and play dead just because she was a woman with class-A assets, she didn't know Magnus Thorvald. He'd learned a bitter lesson. Two lessons, in fact. He would not go down a third time.

Even if she was a Valkyrie in tight jeans.

Chapter Four

ဢ

"Aaagh! You don't know how frustrated I was!" Kat paced the aisle between her kitchen and family room, a bottle of sparkling water in hand.

"He all but kicked me out! And this after I offered him five grand — each! — for his sculptures." She set down the bottle of water on the kitchen island and spun around to face her friend. "Lyssa, that's the best stuff I've ever seen. Doesn't the man want to be successful? What happened? Where did I go wrong? Should I have offered him five hundred and let him bargain me upward? Or was he insulted by a mere ten thousand smackeroos in one swoop?"

Lyssa Markham sat on a Bentwood stool at the island, elbows on the wood-block surface, chin rested on her stacked hands, her eyes tracking her friend's restless progress around the room. "Better than my stuff, you mean?"

Kat whirled around, stricken. "Of course not. You know what I mean. He uses a different medium."

"I've never seen you so riled up. Not even when I refused to show my work."

"But you eventually saw the wisdom of it."

"And how long did you spend wearing me down?"

A slow smile eased the frown from Kat's face. "You're right, of course. Artists can be so temperamental. He probably wants to be chased. Maybe he even has a bidding war in mind. He'd probably have been glad to rub it my face if he already had an agent."

She resumed her pacing. "Hell, Lyss, I don't even know the man's name! When I got out of his driveway — almost broke the springs on my Beemer, by the way—I stopped by two what could loosely be called neighbors, asking if they knew who lived there, but one guy didn't know and the other didn't answer the doorbell."

"Good thing you have a real estate agent as a friend."

Kat stared at her a moment. "Oh, wow, yeah. Of course. I'll give you Mrs. Peifer's directions and you can look them up at work. Great! Thanks, Lyss."

"Tell me a little bit about him, about his place."

Kat let her eyes go unfocused. "The first thing I thought of when I saw him was, A-plus Platinum Society material. My second thought immediately canceled out the first one—I want him for myself. No sharing."

She took another anxious turn around the floor. "What? You look like a cat that had two canaries for lunch."

"Did you hear what you said?" Lyssa's smile could have lit an underground cave.

"What? What did I say to make you smile like that?"

"Never mind. Just tell me more about him."

"He's pigheaded, that's what he is. As stubborn as a fencepost set in concrete. Arrogant. So cocksure of himself. I wanted to kick him right in that gorgeous ass of his." Kat sighed. "And soooo talented." She flopped into a lounge chair sideways, her long legs, under snug jeans, dangling barefoot over one plump leather armrest.

"He simply has to have more pieces to show. He couldn't have gotten so good on his first two tries."

"You're right. After all, he made that table that got you interested in the first place."

"For sure. I have a half a notion to go to the Peifers' home and see that table for myself."

"Later. Right now I want to hear more about his gorgeous ass."

"What? Who said anything about—"

Lyssa laughed out loud, a happy, pealing sound that made Kat smile. "What? What's so funny?"

"You know, Kat, you'd make one lousy poker player."

"*What?*" Kat all but shouted in frustration.

"You don't even know what you're saying. You said you wanted to kick him right in that gorgeous ass of his. And you, Miss Play-the-Field-and-Leave-'Em-Panting, you also said you didn't want to introduce him to the Platinum Society because you wanted him all to yourself. This from the woman who went as a very naked Lady Godiva to the masquerade party a few months ago. How many dudes did you go down on that night, huh? How many sampled your honeypot?"

Kat waved away her friend's objection and flopped back down on the lounge chair. She could feel her eyes go all gooey and hungry. "Man, that's one prime candidate for *Playgirl* centerfold. And I wish I was the photographer."

"No, you don't," Lyssa said, laughing again. "A photographer has to keep her hands on the lens and the shutter. What you want to be is the assistant who applies the oil that makes their skin glisten."

"Oh God." Kat closed her eyes in ecstasy at the thought. "You're making me want to play with myself. This guy is a Norse god. He's got to be six-five, maybe six-six. His shoulders would fill the space between two goalposts. Those Nikes he wore must have been special-made for him, I swear they don't make them that big in regular sizes. Ice-blue eyes, blond hair a little too shaggy-long but on him it looked absolutely right, like he belonged on a Viking ship with a bearskin across his chest."

She shivered, a delicious tingle that went all the way down to her pussy, just thinking about him. She could make a meal of him, no question. A feast. Lick him from one end to the other, front to back, up and down—and out, and out, about ten inches or so, if his cock was in proportion with the rest of him.

Would the hair around his cock be the same blond as his head, or —

"Kat?"

Lyssa's soft voice barely penetrated her sexual haze.

"What are you going to do about it?"

"Hmm? About what?"

"Your Viking. What are you going to do about him? Besides daydream, I mean."

Kat sat up in the lounge chair, fierce determination on her face. "I'm gonna nail him, Lyss. Whether it's professional or personal, he's going to bow down to me. I'm gonna make him a star. My star."

Chapter Five

ജ

"Dammit, Mags, this isn't like you. You haven't cut two burls a year, and we've already sawed through four of them today. What the hell's gotten into you?"

Rolf knew how highly prized burls were to woodworkers like Magnus. Burls were aberrations growing around a trunk or branch, caused by fungus attacks or injury to the living part of the tree, or dormant buds that never quite grew through the bark. The burls they'd halved so far had some incredibly complex patterns that evoked a kinetic sense of energy.

"I'm looking for a certain design. I'll know it when I see it. It needs more bark inclusions than we've uncovered so far."

"But you're destroying your entire air-dried supply."

"No, I'm not. They were ready to cut." Magnus waved away the objection. "I was sure I'd find it in the walnut—the outside looked perfect. Hell, the gray birch root burl looked right, too. But this is the one. I feel it in my bones. I should have done the cherry first. That's the right shade for what I envision."

"It better be, because I'm plumb sawed out today. It's too damn hot for the first weekend in November." With fifty-degree weather, both had shucked their flannel shirts in favor of T-shirts with their jeans and steel-toed boots. Magnus had tied a red bandanna across his forehead to keep sweat and hair from his eyes.

"Last one, baby brother. I promise."

Rolf gritted his teeth. Magnus had his grouchy moods, but he'd been a bear for the past couple of days. Thank God tomorrow was Monday and he had the excuse of going to work, or Mags would have him out here again, cracking the whip like a stagecoach driver being chased by bloodthirsty Comanche.

Magnus set down the regular chainsaw he had used to make the first freehand cut—or kerf—of the massive cherry burl, chocked at an angle on wood blocks. Rolf tightened his gloved, two-fisted grip on the helper handle of the Homelite Super 1130G gear drive chain saw while Magnus positioned the five-foot blade in the kerf and pulled the cord. The motor roared to life.

From that moment on, words were impossible—too much noise. But Rolf had helped Magnus on the two-man saw for years. Behind his safety glasses, he watched Magnus for body language signals—when to ease up, which way to lean to tilt the angle of cut, when to brace his body. They worked for ten or twelve minutes before Magnus called a halt.

Rolf stood upright, easing the kinks out of his spine, as Magnus hammered in a pair of wedges to keep the saw from binding inside the kerf. Then at a nod, they continued, gradually walking the length of the log as the saw blade bit into wood, until it exited the lower end of the burl under their careful guidance.

Amid much grunting and groaning, they manhandled the cut section to the ground, positioning it to stand upright on the chunk of normal log below the burl. Pulling at his gloves absently, Magnus studied the swirls and striations with intense concentration.

"Wow. It looks like an explosion of frozen marble."

Rolf spun around at the melodic feminine voice. And whistled, low and long. A beauty of a woman, whose wildly curling hair looked on fire from the sun's slanting rays, stood in the opened gateway to their enclosure. The bulky-knit, rust-colored turtleneck sweater over what looked like sprayed-on black tights outlined a body he'd give his left nut to rub naked against. Her high-heeled black boots conjured up images of whips and leather and moans of passion.

Down, boy.

He tossed his gloves and safety glasses onto the chunk still lying on blocks and ran his hands through his dark brown hair to dislodge stray bits of wood and bark. He could feel his T-shirt, wet with the sweat of a long day's exertion, clinging to his chest. Figures he'd meet a horny man's wet dream when he looked and smelled like he did.

"To what do we owe the pleasure of your company, oh Goddess of the Blazing Sun?"

The woman raised a perfectly arched brow at him, giving Rolf an inspection that made him happy his jeans were snug enough to hide his randy — and immediate — reaction.

"Kat Donaldson," she said, lifting her sweater to reveal a small fanny pack around her tiny waist — and a tight, curvy ass that could make a grown man weep. "I'm an art dealer and I'm here to continue my discussion with Mr. Thorvald here."

From the fanny pack she withdrew a business card and handed it to Rolf, then cocking her head turned her attention to Magnus. "Are you really determined not to be a success?"

Magnus gave her a dismissing glance. On his haunches before the split burl, he continued to study the design of the inclusions.

"You've talked to him before? Are you here about his carvings?" Rolf asked, sensing the tension between his brother and the visitor. Had she insulted his work? Or was he just shielding his heart against another beautiful woman?

She turned a warm amber gaze to him. "And you are — ?"

"Rolf." He extended his hand, looked at it, wiped it on his thigh with a sheepish grin.

"That's okay." She offered her hand with a slight smile and grasped his with a solid grip. "A little sweat doesn't turn me off."

Rolf felt his cock twitch. Was she coming on to him? Or was that just his pecker talking?

"What did you want to discuss about Magnus' art?"

"Are you his agent?"

"Let's just say I'm an advisor."

Magnus shot him a withering glare, which Rolf ignored. "Magnus is an artist, not a businessman. What do you think of his art?"

"I've done my homework. It looks like the acorn doesn't fall far from the tree. Magnus Thorvald apprenticed under his grandfather, Knut. The old man worked in veneers. I saw photographs of a Carpathian elm burl veneer table in the Mercer Museum and a hinged marquetry box at the Museum of Modern Art. Beautiful workmanship."

She glanced at Magnus, who still had his nose buried in the rough-cut wood. "I've only found two pieces of the grandson in museums, a burled bowl in myrtlewood and an exquisite spalted birch vase only five inches high. I also saw the freeform table he made for the Peifers. It's a breathtaking piece.

"The man definitely needs more exposure." She plunked long-nailed hands on her hips. "And I'm the one who can do it. I *want* to do it."

Bristling, Magnus stood, his shoulders wide and muscular in his damp T-shirt. He strode to the art dealer and tried to intimidate her, if Rolf read the big man's body language correctly. "And how are you going to *expose* me?" he growled.

She flashed fire at Magnus with her eyes, not intimidated in the least. "I've launched three unknown artists so far, with nothing more than good publicity and word of mouth in collectors' ears. I turn over twenty million dollars of merchandise in a year. I can make you."

Magnus gave her body a slow, insolent once-over. "So you're going to expose me and then...make me?"

Was that a flush Rolf detected in the woman's cheeks? This was getting interesting.

"Look, Miss McDonald, I told —"

"Donaldson," she said through gritted teeth. "I hope the reason you haven't delivered my purchases yet was because you've been too busy creating more pieces for me to sell." She reached back into that fanny pack, making Rolf's cock twitch again when she turned that fine ass to his view while facing Magnus. "Now that I've discovered your name, I made out a certified check for ten thousand dollars for both of those pieces you have displayed in your office. I'd like to have them delivered within the next seven days."

When Magnus just stood there frowning at her outstretched hand, she turned and gave Rolf a smile that melted him from ten paces. "Does Mr. Thorvald's advisor think he can follow up on that delivery?"

"With pleasure." He stepped up, took the check from her hands, folded it, and slipped it—carefully—into his front jeans pocket. "Is there anything else I can do for you?"

She scrutinized his shoulders, his waist, his legs as though she had X-ray vision. Rolf felt the sizzle down to the tightening skin on his balls. "Yes, there is. I teach an art course at my gallery. We need a model for our life class. Do you have any evenings free?"

"Life class?"

"You know, sketching the human body. Our classes are small, about ten students. Although when they see who the new live model is, I'll wager I'll have a full loft."

"So this would be…what? Sitting on a bench like *The Thinker*? Flexing my muscles like The Rock?"

One side of her mouth twitched. "It would entail posing in the nude, with artful lighting sculpting your muscles." She cleared her throat. Her gaze lingered on the bulge of his jeans zipper. "All of them. The model poses at the pleasure of the students."

Rolf sharpened his gaze on her.

"My art patrons as well as my students tend to be liberated in their taste. I sell a lot of work with, shall we say, sexual nuances. Like my latest find, Lyssa Markham." She tossed a quick glance at Marcus, who still pretended to study the burl cut. "You've read the article about her."

Not getting a response, she returned her attention to Rolf. "The *pièce de résistance* in her collection looks, at first glance, like some wild animals lapping at a waterhole. On closer examination, the astute connoisseur discerns a female body within the undulations of the ripples, and a black panther is lapping, not at water, but at her body."

"Christ on a crutch, what a come-on!" Magnus exploded. "You want stud service, I don't want to hear about it." He stalked out of the pen, tossing over his shoulder, "Don't forget to clean the saw before you go. And lock the pen after you get rid of the she-cat."

Rolf watched the woman watching Magnus as he strode down the dirt path, anger radiating from both of them. Something had happened at their first meeting, he decided, something to make them strike sparks like Vulcan hammering a steel sword in a fiery forge. Either that, or they were so attracted to each other, it repelled them.

It would be fun to watch it play out.

"I'll do it. What time do you want me?"

Chapter Six

🙰

Rolf stepped up to a platform about two feet high set against the long wall of the loft. He shrugged out of a white terrycloth robe and draped it over a waist-high railing. Kat's students drew an appreciative breath.

Magnificent. As she'd known he'd be. A scattering of dark hair, not enough to obscure well-defined pecs, traced a line down a true six-pack belly to a darker nest of hair surrounding a G-string that hid a formidable bulge. Kat wondered if having so many women staring at him would thicken the cock that was barely hidden behind the white nylon pouch.

She scanned the room. Her class included an eclectic collection—college students taking a no-credit course that typically offered more freedom than an art school, housewives looking for some vicarious adventure, members of the Platinum Society dabbling in art. To a woman, their expressions conveyed avid interest, if not outright lust. A couple of Society members had that speculative look, no doubt thinking, how would he perform at an event?

"Take your pose, please," she instructed Rolf. Class consisted of three half-hour poses with a fifteen-minute break between for the model to rest. In addition to the class fee, each student paid a ten-dollar cash tip to the model.

"Yes, ma'am." He sat on a stool-height captain's chair, one hairy, muscular leg stretched out in front of him, the other hooked over a rung. He eased back against the curved backrest, elbows on the armrests, and slouched as though leisurely watching his lover get dressed. Kat adjusted the primary gobo lamp at his far left to add more definition to the shadow cast by the impressive ridge of his cock.

Twenty-three chairs massed close to the platform in two semicircular rows, the view magnificent from every angle. Word of mouth of the exceptionally virile subject had raced through her mailing list and every seat was taken. The students set to work in charcoal, pencil, or acrylics. They'd had two evenings of theory and drawing from workbooks. This first "live" class was for quick sketches to capture muscle definition, light and shadow, proportion. And Rolf was perfectly proportioned.

After the soothing, new-age music ended its half-hour run, Rolf casually stepped into his robe and strolled barefoot to the back of the loft and into the small, private room where he had first disrobed. It held a table and upholstered chair where he could rest and have a chilled glass of soda or bottled water.

Kat continued circulating among her students, making a suggestion here, a correction there. This fifteen-minute section of the evening could be used for completing the sketch from memory, filling in more definition or background, or taking a bathroom break. As she overheard their bawdy comments about his superb apparatus, Kat smiled. She'd probably have to hold her next life class in a rented auditorium if Rolf came back for more.

When the music started again—music that was piped into the model's breakroom—Rolf returned without prompting and stepped up to the dais again. This time he turned his back to the class before dropping his robe to the floor.

Kat swallowed hard. Gasps came from the students. Rolf had removed his G-string. Every taut inch of his ass cheeks stood open to view. She felt a tingle in her cunt. When the music stopped, would he turn around and face the students in all his naked splendor? Would his cock be swollen and mouthwatering?

This was one of the parts she liked most about nude models. Their unpredictability.

Some would stand and pose woodenly, and not be invited to return. Others—and Rolf appeared to be one of them—were totally unselfconscious about their nudity, in fact seemed to relish the thought of strutting naked before a group of gawking, enthusiastic women.

He assumed the pose, legs about a yard apart, arms raised to grip an overhead pipe. The hollows in his ass cheeks became more pronounced. His back muscles rippled. Kat adjusted the gobo to highlight the fine hairs covering his ass and disappearing into the recesses of his crack. Her fingers itched to stroke those hairs, to see if they felt as soft as they looked against the firm skin of his butt.

Reluctantly Kat turned her attention to her students, helping, critiquing. As the second half hour passed, her mind wandered to the woodworker. Would Magnus Thorvald look as good naked? Did he have chest hair or was it smooth? She had no doubt it would be every bit as sculpted, as worthy a subject for canvas or sketchbook.

She mentally shook her head. Whatever possessed her to compare the two? That insufferable, pigheaded Neanderthal might never condescend to having her for his agent, but at least Rolf had delivered the two sculptures earlier today. No doubt whatsoever of the magnitude of Thorvald's talent. Or of his conceit.

Maybe she could make a virtue of his being a recluse, give him an air of mystery. She should…

What was that?

Sounded like the outside door opening. A quick glance at her gold watch told her the pose had six minutes to run. She'd just dash downstairs and check. If a last-minute straggler wanted to participate, she'd still charge the entire fee. If she wasn't back when the music stopped, she knew Rolf would automatically take another break.

Noiselessly Kat descended the stairway. The only unlocked entrance was the hallway that accessed the loft. The gallery, her office, the workroom, were off-limits to students. She wasn't worried about a burglar—a state-of-the-art security system protected the entire building.

At the bottom step she stopped. The man himself stood in the small lobby.

He raked her with his gaze, from her unruly auburn mane to the red baby tee that bared her midriff to the low-rise jeans snug against her hips to her favorite red high-heeled boots.

"Are you here to take the class?"

"Class?" Magnus Thorvald echoed as if innocent of the knowledge of Rolf's presence upstairs, as if he hadn't just read the schedule within the glass-enclosed bulletin board on the wall.

She crossed her arms below her breasts. His attention snapped to the cleavage in the scooped neck that her action produced.

"Don't tell me. You just *happened* to be in the area tonight while your advisor is posing for the life class."

"Is he?"

Her expression turned sardonic. "You mean you didn't know? You just stopped by to see the woman who's going to make you famous?"

"I know Rolf brought my sculptures here this afternoon."

"They're my sculptures now."

A muscle jumped in his jaw. "I thought I'd see how you're presenting them. You know, spotlights, placement. If they look better under artificial light than skylights."

"If you're looking to be stroked, I'll give you all the stroking you seem to need. You're a magnificent sculptor, Magnus Thorvald. Those two pieces would look good in any light. But I give you my word, as soon as Lyssa Markham's exhibit ends, your eagle will have pride of place in my gallery, and you'll see how it will dominate the space."

"And the Indian?"

One side of her mouth curved up in a soft smile. "You'd like to see how I'm displaying that one, as well?"

"Sure, I'm curious."

"In my home?"

He looked a little uncomfortable, as if he'd forgotten she bought the Indian for her private collection. "At your convenience."

"Are you inviting yourself into my bedroom?"

His mouth thinned. "I thought you were putting it in your dining room."

"I've changed my mind. I want to see it first thing when I wake up in the morning."

"You're mocking me."

"Not at all. It will remind me of you."

He snorted. "And you want to think of me first thing when you wake up in the morning?"

Kat's eyes raked up the length of him, from his extra-big feet shod in loafers, to his khakis snug at the muscular thighs, to his unzipped brown leather jacket exposing a blue button-down shirt, to his shaggy blond hair curling to his shoulders, to the piercing ice-blue eyes riveted on her face. He was still inches taller with her standing on the bottom step.

"I can think of worse fates than having the image of you in my bed." A smile played about her mouth.

Magnus took an intimidating step forward. "Do you come on to every male you meet?"

Her smile widened. "Only the interesting ones."

She cocked her head, listening. "The music stopped."

"Meaning?"

"Meaning, Rolf is taking his second break. I should be critiquing my students."

"So he *is* here."

"You never had any doubt, did you? Didn't you come here to see your competition in action?" She tossed the comment over her shoulder as she ascended the stairs with a bouncy, featherlight step.

Magnus stared at the magnificent ass inside those tight jeans, the expanse of willowy waistline whose bare skin looked smooth as cream, the flaming hair cascading down her back, until she disappeared around the corner.

"Damn you," he whispered, jiggling his hard cock to a more comfortable position inside his jockey shorts. If she was wearing panties under those jeans, he hadn't seen a line of elastic. He clenched his hands into fists against the urge to strip them off her to see if she went commando style.

I'll give you all the stroking you seem to need, she'd said. *I can think of worse fates than having the image of you in my bed,* she'd said.

Did she always toss around double entendres so casually? What the fuck was the matter with him, that he couldn't control his cock around this woman? She didn't deny that she issued invitations like that to every man she met. Did she try to play one against the other to see if they'd fight over her? Did she expect them to roll over and let her dominate them?

Christ, he didn't want another man's leftovers, didn't want to stand in line. Didn't want to be third or fourth in her thoughts.

Hell, he didn't want her at all. Why was he even thinking like that?

Fighting the impulse to creep upstairs and see exactly what Rolf was doing, he paced the small foyer. What the hell was he doing here? Why couldn't he get that promiscuous redhead out of his mind?

The gallery. He'd wanted to see that artist's work, the one she "launched", see how she displayed them. If she was going to be his agent, he needed to see how professional she was. Yes, that was it. He'd wait until class ended and ask her for a walk-through of her own office. She wanted to see where he worked? Let her show him hers first.

His head jerked up. The music had started again. Did that mean Rolf was posing again?

Shit. He found himself sneaking up the steps. At the top of the stairs he turned left toward an archway leading into the loft. Keeping within the shadows cast by the wall, he peered inside.

Wearing a white robe sashed around his waist, Rolf stood barefoot on a platform facing the crowd. Chairs and easels clustered in ragged semicircles around him. Kat climbed the platform and spoke to the students.

"This is the fun part, class," he heard her say. "You get to pose the model."

"I want to see him like Yul Brynner in *The King and I*," a gray-haired woman said. "You know, where he stands glaring at you with his arms on his hips and his feet spread wide apart like he owns the world."

"No." A thin woman with long, straight brown hair jumped up. "He should be like this," she said, lifting her arms over her head, wrists crossed. "You remember that Dara Joy cover where the hero was handcuffed to the ceiling?"

"Oh yeah," said another young woman, this one with a curly mop of short blonde hair, "like he has to do our bidding—or else."

A murmur of general agreement reached Magnus' ears, with a word here and there jumping out at him, "Dominate him…helpless…in our power."

He gritted his teeth. He'd be damned if he'd let a woman dominate him. *He* would do the dominating in a relationship, or there wouldn't *be* a relationship.

Rolf stood calmly as they debated his next pose, eyes roving the class as though trying to choose which artist he would allow to dominate him. Then his eyes focused on Kat and turned intense, burning. Magnus felt himself go rigid. *No.*

Rolf was too young for Kat, dammit. She was a mature, worldly woman. Would his kid brother let a domineering woman walk all over him just to get laid?

He watched as Kat spoke quietly to Rolf, gesturing with her hands, then stepped down.

Rolf dropped his robe to the floor and grabbed the overhead pipe with both hands, his head lifted up as if in supplication—or pain.

Magnus felt his jaw drop. Rolf was totally naked, and his dick stuck out thick and pointing like a man who enjoyed being humiliated.

He must have gasped, because Kat's eyes darted to where he stood in the shadows. He spun on his heel and took the stairs three at a time, then punched the outside door open. What kind of farce was she pulling? And why didn't he just get the hell out of Dodge instead of standing in the doorway, breathing deeply of the cool night air?

"Magnus, wait!"

Belatedly he moved to take that last step onto the sidewalk, to put distance between him and the woman with the morals of an alley cat that he couldn't get out of his mind.

Kat grabbed his arm and pulled hard. "Wait!"

He spun to face her. "What the hell are you, a pimp? You get your kicks finding young studs to parade in front of your paying customers?"

"He's old enough to make up his own mind."

"The hell he is. Just seeing him there with his cock sticking out like a horny satyr's tells me he doesn't know what he's doing."

"He's reveling in it, Magnus. Most of my male models pose absolutely nude, but their cocks don't all get hard and proud when they're the center of attention. Rolf is of the 'If you've got it, flaunt it' school. Believe me, he's exactly where he wants to be."

"Do you fuck all your models?"

Kat's eyes narrowed. "I beg your pardon?"

"Are all your models young and good-looking and hung like stallions?"

She shrugged. "I don't know until they take their clothes off. What I look for is more of an attitude, not how big their cocks are. Remember, even Michelangelo's *David* doesn't have a big—"

He cut her off by crushing his mouth to hers. His kiss was demanding, almost cruel, in its quest to dominate, to mold her to his will. As easily as a feather, he lifted her by the waist and slammed her against the wall, holding her there by pressing his rage-fueled body against her, fitting his rampant cock between her legs. His tongue stabbed into her warm mouth again and again as both his hands roamed up and down the naked length of her waist, dipping down inside her hip-cut jeans, then up to the curve of her breasts.

A muffled curse escaped him. No bra. The softness of her tits against his work-roughened hands penetrated his unreasoning fury.

Awareness came to him gradually—her fists, rigid balls against his shoulders, contrasting with the slackness of her mouth. Her wide-open eyes staring into his heavy-lidded ones. The dangling movement of her legs.

"Oh God," he mumbled, slowly easing her to the floor. "I'm—"

"Get out, you bastard," she hissed. "Get out and don't come back."

She wriggled away from him and ran up the steps. Away from him and toward safety in numbers.

"God*damm*it!" Magnus punched the steel-clad door, winced at the pain.

Pain he more than deserved. Welcomed.

Fury spent, he staggered into the night. Sleep would be a long time coming.

Chapter Seven

ဆ

"Open the goddamn door. I know you're in there."

The chisel slipped, gouging a groove in the massive cherry burl clamped in the vise on the workbench. Magnus swore under his breath.

"Dammit, I swear I'll kick the door down."

With a weary sigh, he stripped off his protective goggles and tossed them on the table. Rolf was nothing if not stubborn. A family trait. If the barn had a doorbell, he'd lean on it for a half hour if that's what it took to get his way.

Meticulously he set down the chisel and mallet in their accustomed spots and trudged around his workbench to the solid-oak door that was original to the 1850s stone barn. Magnus reached above his head for the key he kept on a nail on the lintel and unlocked the recently installed Yale deadbolt.

"You son of a bitch," Rolf growled by way of greeting, green eyes flashing with anger.

"It's two o'clock," Magnus said. "What's so all-fired important that it couldn't wait until morning?"

"I ought to knock your head into the wall. What the fuck is the matter with you?"

"Settle down, little bro."

"Don't you go pulling that older brother shit on me. What the fuck did you do to her?"

Magnus' shoulders stiffened. Had the redhead cried on Rolf's shoulder? "What are you talking about?"

"Don't play dumb, Magnus. Don't tell me that wasn't your voice I heard right before Kat came shooting into the loft like the devil was after her, her lips all raw and swollen. It was all I could do to keep from breaking pose to go to her, to calm her, comfort her."

A muscle in Rolf's jaw worked. "I'll say this for her, she pulled herself together like a trouper. She is one classy dame. After a few deep breaths at the back of the room, she started circulating among the students as though nothing had happened. None of the students saw the fear, the loathing in her eyes.

"But I did." Rolf advanced until he crowded Magnus' personal space. "I'll ask again. What the fuck did you do to her?"

Magnus lifted his chin, trying to dispel the feeling that the collar of his unbuttoned shirt was too tight around his neck. "I kissed her."

"You *kissed* her." He snorted. "Is that why she looked so wild-eyed and afraid?"

Unable to hold his brother's searing glare, Magnus turned away. "She asked for it."

"You unbelievable prick. You mean she came up to you and said, 'Magnus, honey, why don't you give me a little kissy-kissy right here on my lips?'"

"Christ, Rolf, you saw her yourself. Dressed like a whore, all that skin showing, ogling you in all your splendid naked manliness," he said with a sneer.

"What do you mean, 'all that skin showing'? You talking about those low-rise jeans that even overweight ten-year-old girls wear these days? Man, you are so behind the curve on style, you're flat."

Not knowing if Rolf's observations on style were correct, Magnus plowed on. "Every sentence out of her mouth was loaded with innuendo and double meaning. Of course I took what she was offering." He ran a hand through his shaggy hair. "What I thought she was offering," he corrected. "Hell, I didn't know she didn't share my itch until I opened my eyes and saw her staring at me with fear in her eyes, saw her hands fisting."

Rolf stalked in a tight circle around Magnus. "You know what I think?" He stopped, looked him in the eye. "I think you're jealous."

"Jealous—me? Yeah, that's a good one. Jealous that the woman comes on to every man she meets? Jealous of a woman who acts just like my ex-wife? Right."

The younger man stepped back a few paces, rested his butt on the deep windowsill. He studied his brother a few moments. The silence unnerved Magnus.

"There's a way you can get her out of your system," Rolf said finally.

Magnus sliced a glance to him. He would *not* ask.

"I took her out for coffee afterwards, thought she needed a sympathetic shoulder. She told me about a club she belongs to, invited me to come visit. Ever hear of the Platinum Society?"

Magnus thought a moment. "No."

"Now don't get mad, I'm just transmitting information." Rolf took a deep breath. "It's a kind of a sex club, where anything goes. With anyone. You don't have to do anything, and if someone says 'no', you have to leave them alone. But they have events often, and, well, I'd think she'd be more receptive to your advances there. I mean, it's a given that she'd be going there to have sex. You could boink her and then walk away."

"I don't do things in front of an audience," Magnus bit out. *Unlike my ex-wife.*

"Way I understand it, they have corners and alcoves. Maybe even access to a bedroom upstairs, depending on whose home it is. You wouldn't have to fuck her in public."

"I don't *fuck*. When I'm with a woman, I *make love* to her."

"When was the last time you *made love*?"

Magnus spun away from his brother's knowing smirk. Maybe that was his trouble. He hadn't had any sex in, what, three years? Not since he'd found his wife —

Damn! He wouldn't go down that road again. Hell, a little hand job now and again suited him just fine. If it meant opening his heart to a woman again just to get laid, it wasn't worth the anguish afterwards. And he refused to avail himself of any of the freelancers prowling Soren's bar who threw themselves at him.

Suddenly weary beyond measure, Magnus allowed his shoulders to slump. "Look, I'll apologize. I'll send some flowers or something."

As if satisfied by the suggestion, Rolf turned his attention away from Magnus and wandered around the workshop, picking up a tool here, stroking a finished piece of wood there. "Hey, isn't this the piece we cut the other day? The one with all the inclusions?"

"Yeah. The cherry."

"I thought you had to study the wood for months before you knew what it wanted to be."

"Usually I do. But this time I knew what it wanted to be, I just had to find the right piece of wood."

"That's a switch. What's it going to be?"

In his mind's eye, Magnus saw the wildly curling red hair, the smooth skin, the slender curves of the final product. "You'll see it when it's ready."

Chapter Eight

ജ

Deep in thought, Kat circled the two Thorvald pieces she'd just acquired. They stood on their pedestals in her gallery's spacious workroom. She decided she should exhibit the Indian before taking it to its final home in her bedroom. It was simply too good to be hidden from an aficionado's eye and would, of course, whet a collector's appetite. Totally different they were, the eagle—languid and sinuous, even though full of kinetic energy, the Indian—craggy and twitchy, the raw bark edges merely intensifying the feeling. A study in contradictions.

Like the man himself.

Kat suppressed a sigh. How could a man with such finesse in his art have absolutely no subtlety when dealing with the opposite sex? Some women probably fell for that "Me Tarzan, you Jane" shit, but not her. She would be in control of the relationship, or there'd be no relationship.

And what a relationship it would be, she thought. His masterful possession of her mouth, the take-charge way he sandwiched her body between the wall and his hard length. She had felt his cock twitching and pulsing even through the layers of their clothing.

Was he trying to show her he was more of a man than her model? Rolf was gorgeous, he was hunky, and sweet as they'd talked over late-night coffee.

He was a puppy.

Magnus had a lived-in face, a world-weary attitude more in tune with her thirty-six years of vigorous living. Dammit, if he wanted to fuck her, why wouldn't he take the obvious route of giving her his work to sell? They'd have to spend a lot of time together, wouldn't they? Wouldn't that be the quickest way to get her to spread her legs? And spread for him, oh yeah, she would. God knew, she'd given him enough signals to let him know she wouldn't turn him down. Men didn't like to be turned down, so Kat always made sure they knew when she was interested.

Yeah, sure, she'd had many men in her life. Why not? This was the twenty-first century, where women had as many choices as men. Her mother had Haight-Ashbury as her playground. She had the Platinum Society. Why shouldn't she take a man to her bed whenever she felt like it? Some people just had more sex drive, and she was one of them. As she'd told Rolf in the coffee shop, her philosophy was "Dance like a butterfly" amid all the flowers in the garden, not just daisies.

"Kat? Can you come into the gallery a moment?"

Her assistant's voice through the open doorway interrupted Kat's musings. "Sure."

She walked through the door from the workroom to the rear of the gallery, where her antique rolltop desk and mini-credenza created just enough office ambiance to handle sales and credit card slips. The bulk of her paperwork was done in her own high-tech office, at the far end of the building.

A quick glance around the gallery told Kat that they were alone for the moment, so it hadn't been a client seeking more information. "What's up?"

"This was just delivered." Sandy gestured to the desk. On it stood a charming wicker basket containing two dozen miniature pink rosebuds arranged around a central glass chimney, probably meant to hold a fat candle. Inside the chimney was—something—surrounded by white tissue paper about a foot high. The wrap looked amateurish next to the flower arrangement.

"No card." Sandy Smith, a grandmother twice over, wore her salt-and-pepper hair short and curly. The twenty extra pounds on her short frame made her look warm and cuddly, which she was. The most even-tempered person Kat knew, Sandy always had a soft word or ready laugh.

"So we have an unknown admirer?" Sandy asked.

"Maybe the giver wrote on the tissue paper." Kat studied it a moment. "I guess we'll find out." Gingerly she pulled the package out from the glass. "It's pretty heavy."

Reading its contours with her fingers, she said, "Can't tell."

"Oh, for heaven's sake, Kat, just open it! This is like getting a Christmas present."

Kat unfurled the tissue. Into her waiting palm rolled a small piece of wood sculpture.

"Oh." Her breath caught.

The figure was no more than eight inches from head to toe, its slim, elongated torso hinting at curves in the right places, slender arms blending into the hips, legs only suggested beneath a long, flowing skirt. The face was blank except for a suggestion of closed eyelids. Ripples of wavy hair cascaded down the figure's arched back. Its artistry was unmistakable.

She turned it round and round, stroking the smooth patina of rich cherrywood. Lifting the bottom, she saw—as she knew she would—the letters engraved in a stylized logo she'd seen on two other pieces in her gallery. "MT," the "M" under the sheltering arm of the crosspiece of the larger "T".

Below the logo had been carved "1-03", probably the date of completion.

Disappointment speared through Kat. He hadn't done it of *her*. This had been sculpted before they'd even met.

Still, as apologies went, this one was more than acceptable.

Kat found herself smiling.

"Why are you smiling like that? You know who it's from?" Sandy reached out to take the piece from Kat's still stroking fingers.

"Aha. MT. Magnus Thorvald, right?" Sandy said triumphantly. "Is this his way of saying he wants you to represent him?"

Kat let out a long breath. "Not quite. We had—a disagreement, and he's apparently apologizing."

"Well, if you have a fight every day between now and Christmas, you'll have enough of his work to put on another 'Discovered' show," Sandy said gleefully. She studied the piece. "I'll bet this was commissioned by his subconscious mind."

Kat laughed. "What do you mean?"

"He didn't know what—who—he was looking for, so his subconscious told him what to sculpt. And now he found it. You." She held the sculpture up. "This *is* you."

Kat laughed again, this time much more nervously. "Yeah, right. He's much too Neanderthal for me."

Sandy eyed her speculatively. "I meant as an agent."

"Of course." Turning away so Sandy couldn't read her expression, Kat swallowed hard. "That's what I meant, too. He'd be hard to work with, given that attitude. And this is *my* gallery, *my* reputation."

"As I recall, not all your clients are as amenable to suggestion as your friend Lyssa. Remember what's his name, the guy who did those dark, scary abstracts? Now *there* was a Neanderthal."

A hoot escaped before Kat could stop it. "Jenko."

"Yeah, that's the one. You let him go as soon as his first show ended."

Kat laughed. "He didn't even want to sign a contract unless it was with a man."

"And thank God it was only a handshake, not sealed in blood." Sandy gave a mock shudder. "I could do without guys saying, 'Get me some coffee, one teaspoon of cream and two tablespoons of sugar'. Or 'I'll need my tuxedo picked up for the opening'."

"I forgot about the tux business," Kat said. "If he'd've said something like, 'I won't have time to pick up my tux, what should I wear', I wouldn't have minded picking it up. But ordering me? Oh, no."

They stood in the gallery reminiscing, laughing about artists' foibles, Kat occasionally glancing at the tiny sculpture that she couldn't bear to put down, not knowing she was under scrutiny from across the street.

* * * * *

Magnus frowned in disgust. She kept looking at the sculpture he'd inserted into the candleholder—and laughing.

It had been a crazy whim anyway. Maybe he should have written the words, "I'm sorry." Well hell, he wasn't sorry. "I apologize" would be better. He could have apologized for his boorish behavior without being sorry he'd kissed her, something he'd wanted to do ever since she stepped out of that Yuppie car at the barn and walked into the blazing sunlight that set fire to her hair.

After Rolf had vented his ire and left, he'd spent a fair amount of time rooting through his finished and unfinished pieces, seeking something suitable for an apology. As soon as he'd spied the carving he'd whimsically entitled *Dream*, he'd known it was *her*. Long, lean, willowy, brick-red. Seductive.

Damn. And now she was laughing at him.

He'd been waiting for the appropriate moment to cross the street and walk into the gallery, hoping the peace offering would have allowed them to talk.

Not bloody likely, given the mirth the two women shared.

Hell. He'd finish his coffee and get the hell out of this deli. He'd begun feeling like a goddamn peeping Tom anyway, sitting here for a half hour nursing a mug of regular black.

He was standing to pull his wallet out of his back pocket when he saw Kat Donaldson disappear behind a door. Just as well. He couldn't spend his time like a sick would-be suitor waiting for a glimpse of his obsession. He tossed a tip on the table and strolled to the front to pay the outrageous charge for one cup of Main Line Philadelphia coffee. And stopped.

Her Yuppie car pulled out of the alleyway alongside her gallery and made a right turn. Magnus made his decision. He might as well do it now. At least the other woman wouldn't know him, wouldn't laugh at him.

Stepping off the curb in the center of the block, he jaywalked across the street and strode into A Discerning Eye.

The sight that greeted him stopped him in his tracks. A painting about two feet by three, on an easel and artfully spotlighted, drew his eye. *The Oasis*. The newspaper reviewer had raved about its many levels of meaning.

At first glance, it looked like an ordinary waterhole in the hot plains of Africa, with animals dipping their heads for a drink. On closer inspection, he could make out the shape of a nude woman reclining within the sparkling wavelets, the panther's tongue lapping at her skin as other animals dipped their heads to do the same.

Not wanting to seem a voyeur, he strolled to the next painting. *Unfolding Rose*. Good grief, it looked just like a woman's—

He blinked. It still did. Were thoughts of Kat Donaldson coloring his vision?

At the next offering he fared no better. A trio of pristine white lilies in close-up, the focus on the pistil—stamen?— whatever it was called, it was the reproductive organ, Magnus was sure—each of them showed a drop of milky white fluid that looked like it had just withdrawn from the dewy center of the unfolding rose.

Magnus shook his head. What the hell was he thinking of, a *ménage a trois*?

He had to get out of here. Everywhere he looked reminded him of sex.

"Oh hello, I didn't hear you come in."

He stopped as a rosy-cheeked woman—the woman who had been laughing with Kat—approached him, giving him a warm smile that touched into her eyes. "This is our latest discovery. Lyssa Markham. We have the honor of being the first to show her work in public. Here's a brochure listing her current offerings. We think she'll be a major star in the art world. If you have any questions, please don't hesitate to ask. I'll be right here at the desk."

She sat down and pulled out a pile of what looked like business cards and began to do things with them, unobtrusively at the customer's beck and call.

Trapped, Magnus decided, what the hell. He'd kill a few more minutes then politely leave.

The next painting showed a star-speckled midnight sky, midnight water reflecting the stars, and the suggestion of two bodies entwined within, all luminous and glowing.

This artist really *was* all about sex, he thought. And, dammit, almost all of them sported discreet "sold" signs.

Funny part was, he "caught" every nuance, even before reading the description. After a while he made a game of it, trying to discover the sex within before peeking at the answer.

"Magnus."

He whirled around. Kat Donaldson stood before him, her wild hair severely tamed by a braid hanging halfway down her back. Black slacks, black silky sweater with half-sleeves, black boots. Mouth as dewy and ripe as that rose in the painting.

Idly he wondered why she wasn't wearing those red boots that conjured up all sorts of erotic images in his mind.

Furious with himself, he nodded curtly. He made the first move, he reminded himself, by giving her *Dream*. Now it was her turn.

Smiling, she extended her hand. "Thank you for coming to the gallery."

He stared at it as though it was a snake about to pounce. His heart lurched. He didn't think he should touch her. Didn't dare touch her.

So he backed up a step.

Her smile dipped a tad as she let her arm down. "And thank you for the flowers. And the sculpture. It's beautiful."

Then why were you laughing at it? he wanted to ask.

"The lines are sinuous, sensual, without being blatant."

Magnus raised an eyebrow. "You mean, not like the current exhibit?"

She laughed, a deep, sensual laugh that arrowed a spark right down to his groin.

"It's not for everyone, I admit. But to those who 'get' it...I love to watch their expression as they become aware of the deeper meaning." Her expression turned serious. "Have you seen the entire exhibit?"

"Yes."

"What did you think?"

"You mean, did I 'get' it?"

A smile played at one corner of her mouth. "Well, yes. Did you?"

"I got it."

"As a fellow artist, you couldn't not get it. Speaking of which, I really would like to see more of your work."

"Unfortunately, mine doesn't have any 'getting it' attached to it."

"Your work speaks for itself. Even the tiny piece delivered inside the roses—which, by the way, was very clever—showed exquisite workmanship. Usually in a piece that small, there are finishing flaws inside the crevices. This was perfect in every millimeter of its surface."

Grudgingly Magnus admitted to himself that he was pleased by her observation. That she "got it".

"Magnus, I'm sorry about last night. I overreacted. I think we can have a mutually beneficial relationship built around your immense talent and my far-reaching contacts. I really would like to take a look at your output. Judging from the meager biographical information out there, you've been working with wood since your teens. You've got to have at least a dozen good years of carving behind you. Please. Say yes."

Oh, he was tempted. In more ways than one. This time he wouldn't ravage her mouth, he'd seduce it, slowly, one kiss, one lick at a time.

Christ, how could she turn him into such a blithering idiot?

"Lyssa Markham's exhibit runs through New Year's Eve, then I have a 'Best of Pennsylvania' exhibit ready to hang in January. If we're going to launch you this spring, I have to start planning now. That means I have to know what you've got, how much product and how much space it takes up, how to move it, how best to display it. To say nothing of how to publicize it. Four months isn't a lot of time. And I want to be the one to launch you, Magnus Thorvald."

He did *not* want her to be the one. In any way, shape or form. He gave her an unfathomable look. "Nice speech."

Her eyes narrowed. "You know, I've worked with temperamental artists before. And pricks and idiots. Oh yes, and Neanderthals. When it comes to art, I'm totally professional and totally committed. We'll get along, you and I. If you'll bend thirty percent, I'll bend the other seventy."

She stuck out her hand again. "Do we have a deal?"

Folding his arms across his chest, Magnus countered, "And what do you get out of all this?"

Again her arm retreated to her side. "The house commission is twenty percent of anything I sell. I guarantee you, I can sell your work for at least twenty-five percent more than you would get on eBay, or door-to-door, or any other art dealer in the area. You won't have any cause to regret signing with A Discerning Eye. My contacts range all up and down the East Coast. Do yours?"

"Tell you what," he said slowly. "Why don't you come to the barn tonight and look around. If you like what I've done, we'll talk some more."

Her mouth turned down in a frown. Then, "I've made plans for this evening. Can we do it some time tomorrow? I can make myself available during the day or the evening. But not tonight. I'm very sorry about that."

"So this means tomorrow you'll have to bend eighty percent?"

She blinked. "Like you said, we'll talk some more."

"Deal. I'll call you and let you know what time." And he walked out of the gallery, leaving its owner standing there with her luscious mouth agape.

Chapter Nine

∞

"Hey, Magnus, what brings you here on a Tuesday night?"

Soren automatically drew Magnus a long seltzer water, his drink of choice while working in the bar on weekends. Magnus waved it away. "Give me a Sam Adams."

You damn well better not make a snide comment to go with that raised eyebrow, Magnus thought as his brother silently pulled the lever to fill a frosty mug of draft beer, then slid it across the polished surface of the bar to his customer. Said customer was in a crappy mood. Magnus still hadn't figured out how to camouflage the gouge he'd inadvertently made in the burl sculpture when Rolf interrupted his concentration by pounding on the door last night. He was pissed off at Rolf for reading him the riot act. He was pissed that Rolf had his facts right. He was even more pissed off at himself for letting the she-cat's innuendoes get to him.

"You look like you just ate the chain off your saw and it's trying to come out the other end," Soren commented as he wiped up a drop of foam off the counter.

He gave Soren a glare. "Don't you start on me, too."

Soren cocked his head. "Too?"

Magnus swiveled on his stool to avoid Soren's knowing gaze. "Rolf's on my case."

"Hmph. 'S not what I heard."

He wouldn't be baited, dammit. Magnus stared out at the patrons scattered among the tables and booths. At eleven o'clock on a Tuesday night, it was probably as crowded as it would get. A plaintive country song about a long-ago love wafted over hidden speakers. He sipped his Sam Adams.

Soren plunked his elbows on the bar, leaned close to Magnus, and spoke low. "I heard Rolf offered to take you to a sex club. He seems to think you need to get your rocks off."

Magnus snapped his head around. "I wasn't the one with my dick hanging out in front of a roomful of overeager women."

"Precisely. Rolf gets more pussy than any two guys I know."

His response was a grunt. He didn't need to be reminded of that.

"You should see his latest," Soren continued. "What a knockout."

Magnus took another slug of his Sam Adams. "Kid's got more balls than brains. He'd better be using protection."

"They're shooting pool in the back room right now. Hey, you wouldn't want to take over the bar for ten minutes, would you? I'd like to go back there and get a good, long look. She's a real woman. Mature, not like those kids come in here looking like they're not old enough to vote. I've never seen a woman look so good in tight jeans. You know, the ones cut real low, shows off their hipbones, gotta have Lycra in them because they mold to her ass like a wet handkerchief. I keep imagining what she'd look like bending over the pool table. Mm, hmm. And those man-killer red boots. Three-inch heels. Man, did they make her hips sway when she walked."

Red boots. Kat Donaldson.

So what? Magnus drained his glass and thumped it down on the bar. "I'll have another."

From his peripheral vision Magnus could see Soren's mouth open as if he wanted to make a comment. After a moment, he pulled his professional demeanor around him and reached for Magnus' mug to fill it.

Hell, he was thirty-five years old, Magnus reminded himself. He could have more than one beer without his brother going all preachy on him. Just because he didn't drink every day, or once a week or even once a month, didn't mean he didn't enjoy hoisting a few now and again.

The vision of Kat Donaldson in her fuck-me red boots wouldn't go away. He could see her lying on his king-size bed, her wild fire-hair fanned out across his pillow, legs spread wide open and inviting, wearing nothing but those boots and her gold hoop earrings. Annoyed at himself, Magnus slugged down a hefty portion of his second beer and slid off the barstool.

Ignoring Soren's muffled snicker, he sauntered to the back room carrying his mug. Damn, but Soren was right. He saw Kat bent over the pool table, her perfectly formed ass thrust out into the room. A long expanse of smooth ivory skin showed between the bottom of her short sweater and the top of her low-cut jeans as she reached out over the green felt. Magnus thought he could see a shadow that could be the top of her crack. His fingers tightened on the mug.

Rolf's arm encircled Kat's shoulders as he snuggled close to her body, his cheek next to hers, and sighted down her cue stick.

"A little more to the right," Rolf was telling her. "That's it. Now take a few practice strokes. That's right, slow and easy. Then when you're ready, just kiss it with the stick. You don't want the cue ball to go very far. Just enough to nudge the six into the pocket."

Magnus watched Kat's elbow slide back and forth several times. Then, with Rolf still glued to her side, damn him, she took a deep breath, let it halfway out, and slid the stick through her fingers. He heard the crack of one ball hitting another, then the satisfying clunk-thunk as it rolled down the pocket.

Kat let out a little squeal of delight and stood upright, forcing Rolf to back up a step. Magnus swallowed hard. From a three-quarters view she looked even more delectable, shoulders back, the red sweater molded to a pair of perfectly formed tits he desperately wanted to taste. Excitement had peaked her nipples into hard beads that poked out through the silky texture of the sweater. He'd bet his next commission that she wasn't wearing a bra.

The men at the two other tables paused in their game to look their fill.

Magnus took a long swallow from his mug as an unpleasant thought occurred to him. Maybe the excitement had to do with Rolf's embrace, not with her dropping the ball into the pocket.

Then her gaze collided with his. "Magnus," she said, low and throaty.

Rolf spun around. "Hey, Mags, what are you doing here on a Tuesday night? I thought you had to finish that cherry burl piece."

"Needed some inspiration. Thought I'd get out in the world, nurture my left brain."

"You're just in time to buy us a couple of beers while we finish this game. What do you say, Kat, you ready for a third?"

Kat gave Magnus another one of those looks that made him think she was mentally stripping him naked. Unconsciously he stood a little straighter, tucked his ab muscles tighter beneath his denim shirt. With a slow sway of her perfectly curved hips, she walked the ten feet or so to him, her navel winking at him. "I don't need another mug. Just a sip will do."

She looked Magnus in the eye, throwing down the gauntlet. "May I?"

An unwilling hint of a smile tipped up one corner of his mouth. "Aren't you afraid of germs?"

Her sultry gaze dipped down to his mouth. "Not yours."

Magnus took a slow, deliberate sip from his mug, hoping it would cool the sudden fire that made his cock take a leap inside his jeans. Then he held out the glass. "Be my guest."

"Thanks." Holding his gaze, she lifted the mug to a mouth that looked shiny and pink and much too kissable. Turned the mug around to place her mouth in the exact spot on the rim where his mouth had been. Took a slow, deliberate sip. Slowly licked the foam residue off her upper lip. Then gave the mug back to him with a dazzling smile that sent flares of lust rocketing up through his now-hard cock. "One sip, just like I promised." Then turned her back to him.

Magnus couldn't help it. He watched the sway of her ass as she sashayed back to the pool table. Of its own volition, his mouth opened. "I'll play the winner."

He joined them at the table, one hand in his jeans pocket to hide the bulge at his zipper.

Her throaty laugh reached his ears as her eyes sparkled. "What fun would that be, having to watch two guys play when I was promised a personal lesson?"

"I can teach you." That, too, popped out without his conscious decision.

Rolf insinuated himself between Magnus and the she-cat who was definitely flirting with him. "I hate to put a damper on your evening, Mags, but you're horning in on a date." Rolf put his arm around Kat's shoulder in a proprietary fashion. "If you think you can teach Kat something that I'm better at than you—whether pool or anything else—you'll have to make your own arrangements." His lips grazed Kat's temple as if to make his point.

"Fine." Magnus' gaze snapped to Kat. "If you want to see my sculptures, I'll be available at eight o'clock tomorrow."

He spun on his heel and strode to the door then tossed back over his shoulder, "That's a.m., not p.m."

And hauled his ass out of the bar and into the cold night before he did something *else* stupid.

Chapter Ten

ες

My, my, my, but she was getting through that prickly façade, Kat thought as she negotiated the winding country roads leading to Magnus' barn. If that grouchy hunk of gorgeous man thought she would cut her night short because she had an early appointment the next morning, he didn't know much about her. Kat had long ago discovered that she didn't need more than six or seven hours of sleep a night. Many a day she functioned well on as little as four or five.

How much sleep did *you* get, Magnus? she wondered as a smile twitched her mouth. Did he wonder what she and Rolf had done after Magnus had stormed out of the bar? Would Rolf tell him?

At eight o'clock to the second by her gold watch, she rang the bell on the jamb.

The door opened immediately.

"I guess you didn't expect me to be late, if you were right at the door—"

Instead of inviting her in, Magnus strode out onto the ramp, pulling the French door shut behind him. "We'll take your car." In four long strides he stood next to the passenger door of her Beemer, the collar of his blue and white flannel shirt standing up around his neck, well-worn jeans snug around his long legs.

"What—?"

"Do you want to see my storeroom or not?"

"Of course. I just thought it was inside—"

"Why don't you stop thinking and unlock the passenger door for me? You don't need to lock up every time you jump in and out of the car, you know. You're not in the city now."

Kat pushed the remote button. Both locks clicked open. "Yes, I do know I'm out of the city. Way out, in fact. I'm wearing my backcountry boots. Brown, to cover up the dust. Low-heeled, the better to walk over hillocks and rabbit holes."

She thought she saw his mouth move upward for just a second as Magnus folded his large body into the passenger seat and clapped his palms over his knees.

Kat settled behind the wheel, engaged her seat belt, and turned the ignition. "Where to?"

"Out the driveway, turn left."

She did. Just as she pressed the gas pedal to accelerate at the dirt road, he said abruptly, "Turn in here."

She slammed on the brake. "What?"

"Right in there," he said with exaggerated patience, gesturing beyond the windshield with one big hand. "That's a driveway. Pull up in front of the ramp. You've heard of barn doors, right? That's what those big brown squarish things are. They slide back just like patio doors."

"But it's the same barn! How come we had to drive?"

"If you tried to climb down the rickety ladder inside to get to the lower floor, you'd break your skinny little neck. I wouldn't exactly call those things on your feet 'low heels'. They're almost as high as those red things you wore—" He snapped his teeth shut and turned away to open the car door. "I didn't want you to have to walk over hillocks and rabbit holes to get to the buried treasure."

Her face broke into a slow smile. "It's so sweet of you to be concerned. These are only two-inch heels and they have a solid, thick heel."

"Don't get the idea that I'm concerned. I'm just being careful because I don't have homeowner's insurance." He plunked his big feet onto the frozen weed clumps. "You coming or not?"

Getting out of the car, she deliberately flashed the key ring as she pushed the remote button to lock the car doors again. "Coming," she said, injecting as much throaty sizzle as she could into the word. Let him stew on *that* a while.

By the time she got to the doors, he was rolling them open.

"Hey, that's a padlock! I thought you didn't have to lock your doors out here in the back of beyond." Her temperature shot up a few notches, even though she could see puffs of her breath turning into frosty mist as she spoke.

Magnus turned around, grasped her shoulders through her sedate woolen car-coat, bent his head close to her temple. "Buried treasure," he whispered in her ear. "Gotta protect it."

With a little shiver, Kat felt herself leaning into him, into the heat radiating out of him in this cold, misty morning, with the sun giving off no more heat than a twenty-five-watt bulb. She smelled the rich loam, the crisp dead leaves, the earthy scent of a man in his prime. A sparrow or some other small bird twittered deep within one of the shrubs growing low and thorny against the barn.

She lifted her face to his. He was looking at her with those fathomless blue eyes as though trying to see into her soul. Her mouth softened, opened. Her gaze dropped to his mouth — also softened, also opened. *Kiss me,* she thought.

"Not only that," he said briskly as he let her go and strode inside the cavernous barn, "but there's another lock on my storeroom."

Shaken by the depth of her disappointment that she hadn't taken the initiative to kiss *him,* Kat ordered herself to move. Perhaps she shouldn't have worn even two-inch heels, she thought, realizing how wobbly her legs were as she followed him inside the barn.

Dammit, it was a game, and both of them were playing it. She straightened her spine and looked around. The huge room was divided into roughly four parts, the entrance quarter being a spacious access for large vehicles. Straight ahead sat a bulldozer or tractor or whatever, some piece of yellow farm equipment. To her left, a shiny black truck with the ram logo loomed high off the ground, the epitome of macho wheels that she couldn't see past when parked next to one of them in a lot. The far quadrant was walled off in sheets of white-painted plywood, with a double door cutting off the near corner at a diagonal.

"Open Sesame," Magnus intoned as he withdrew the hasp from the eye and hung it over a handy nail. The doors opened under his nudge. He reached inside and flicked a switch. Lights flared to life.

The sharp prickle of tears pushed against the back of Kat's eyeballs as her mind slowly absorbed the pieces finally revealed to her. She blinked.

Treasure, indeed. She knew she was standing in the presence of greatness. She *had* to bring this man's talent to the public's eye. She would withstand any teasing, any taunt, any torment. She would demean herself, grovel, whatever it took, to become his agent, his mentor, his guide through the tricky shoals of the art world that could chew him up and spit him out like a wood chipper sucking up waste branches.

She was nothing if not serious about her calling. She'd braided her hair this morning in her no-nonsense work style. She wore a business-like black thigh-length coat and loose stovepipe slacks. She'd foregone primping, opting for only a smear of protective lip-gloss. Though she might be on the prowl at a pool table or a Platinum Society affair, she kept her professional vision firmly in sight when dealing with a potential client.

At least, she *usually* did. Magnus Thorvald, the man, kept distracting her from Magnus Thorvald, the artist. It was up to her to keep them separate and distinct inside her brain.

Brackets holding sturdy shelving were nailed onto two-by-fours on the two inner walls. The outer stone walls stood bare, probably something to do with humidity or seepage from the ground, she surmised, since the back of the first floor was completely underground. The center of the room held a number of large, partially carved objects, some hewn from blocks, some from burls such as she'd watched the two brothers cut a few days previously. Several pieces had free-hand designs sketched on all sides as a blueprint.

A small, delicate table caught her eye. Exquisitely matched pieces of wood formed an X on the flat of it, with simple straight legs contributing to its sleek look. She brushed her fingers across the finish. Perfectly smooth. Perfectly lovely. Perfect for a writing desk with its two narrow drawers across the length of it. Perfect for the guestroom in her home.

Several carved vases and urns graced the shelves. Spalted, that's what he called the markings in the wood. She could see the consummate artist's eye in the way pieces were carved to take design advantage of the intricate lines of the spalting. Here a settee, a slab seat with the long back end left in its irregular-bark state contrasting with the smooth slats of the backrest. There a long, low bowl using a burl to perfect advantage on the outside, its interior a smoothly carved hollow—except for a fanciful dolphin leaping up from one irregularly higher side.

"Magnus." Her voice was unsteady, breathless.

Magnus had been standing to one side, watching her as she touched, caressed, smoothed her fingers over one piece or another. Her eyes had a soft glow, her expression tender, as if a lover had been stroking her. He wanted to be the man to bring that soft glow, that tender expression to her face. He wanted to—

"Have any of these been shown before?"

He had been leaning a shoulder against the cold stone wall, his stance casual, as though uncaring of her opinion. But he knew that having his arms folded across his chest was a way to figuratively protect himself from an unfavorable opinion. He pushed off the wall and came to stand before her in the far corner.

"No one outside my family's seen anything in this room."

Eyes shimmering, she turned to face him. "Magnus." She spoke his name almost reverently. "Your work is so good, I'll lower my commission to fifteen percent if it will help convince you to sign with me. I want to be the one to announce you to the world. Please. Let me represent you."

He wanted to jump up and flail his fist in the air in a victory flourish. Instead, he folded his arms across his chest again. "Is that your final offer?"

Her chin lifted. "You tell me. What would it take to be your exclusive agent?"

A surge of blood into his cock at the implied invitation propelled him even closer. Without sorting through the consequences, he cradled her perfect oval face in his big hands and lowered his head. His mouth grazed hers, moving slowly from side to side, not landing, just nibbling, stroking, tasting.

She moaned, leaned into him. He saw her eyelashes flutter closed as she fitted her body into him, snaked her arms around his waist. In an instant the fire in him leaped out of control.

He dipped his tongue into her soft, yielding mouth, explored that warm cavern with it, ran it along the sharp edges of her teeth. His hands moved to lift the bottom of her coat, then the shirt that she had tucked inside her pants. He pulled, tugged, until the hem came free from her waistband.

Impatiently his hands searched for warm, bare skin. He pulled her closer, deepened the thrusts of his tongue as he sought her breasts.

A bra? His muzzy brain wondered at the unexpected barrier as his cock grew harder and his kisses more demanding. She hadn't worn a bra at the bar. Or at the art class. Why now? He fumbled for the clasp. He wanted to just rip it off, to hold those ripe tits in his hands, or better yet, in his mouth. The feel of her, the smell of her musky perfume, was driving him to a frenzy.

"Magnus," she murmured against his mouth, putting a millimeter of space between their bodies until he felt the loss of her warmth, her softness. "Is this what it will take?"

"Hush up." His mouth closed on hers again, cutting off speech. He sucked her tongue into his mouth, wanting to share with her how a man felt when a warm and wet pussy clung to his cock like a vacuum cleaner. Forsaking the bra he couldn't unfasten, he grabbed her ass cheeks in his big hands, lifted her up and settled the vee of her legs right on his rampant cock, all the while alternately thrusting his tongue and sucking on hers. Coherent thought fled. All he could think of was putting that rhythm to better use with his cock slick and throbbing inside her, banging into her until she cried out in ecstasy.

"Magnus," she gasped. "Are you trying to tell me that sex with me is your price?"

Finally her words penetrated the fog of his lust. What the hell was he doing? How could he treat a woman this callously? He set her down roughly on the oak planks of the floor, as though he'd just realized he held a cougar in his grasp. Long, angry strides propelled him through the storeroom door and out the barn door. She caught up with him halfway down the dirt ramp, grabbed hold of his arm. The feel of her palm through the flannel shirt seared his skin.

"Magnus, wait! Please." Her voice was breathy, as if she'd run a mile.

He kept walking. Her hold on his arm didn't loosen as she trotted down the dirt road to keep up with him. "Magnus, please. Let's talk about this."

Magnus stopped abruptly, sloughed off her hand. He didn't know who he was angrier at, her for tempting him, or himself for succumbing to that temptation. A muscle worked in his jaw as he stared at the trees growing in ragged rows on the opposite side of the creek. His hands clenched into fists. With conscious effort he loosened them. How could this she-cat make him forget everything he knew about how a conniving woman used her body to get what she wanted? He took a deep, calming breath. It only marginally helped. "Okay, talk."

"I don't know how to read you, Magnus. One minute you grab me and kiss me like I'm the only woman you'll ever want, and the next minute you act like I'm leading you on the road to hell and damnation. Let's not let personal animosity get in the way of your genius. I want to represent you. You deserve the best, and that's me. My offer stands. I'll lower my commission to fifteen percent to handle your work. If you want more from me, please, let's discuss it."

Magnus thrust his hands into his jeans, more to ease the strain of his cock against his zipper than to warm his fingers in the winter wind. Or maybe to keep from wrapping them around her neck and squeezing. "'If you want more from me'," he repeated. "See, there you go again. Everything you say has a double meaning." He squinted up into the wan winter sun. "Do I want more? Hell, yes. I want to fuck you until you don't know which way is up. I want to hear you scream my name when you come. I want to—"

"That can happen, Magnus. I can't deny I'm physically attracted to you. Good Lord, it would be no hardship to sleep with you. But you'll have to make your desire clear, because every time you kiss me, you wind up backing off just when my engine has been revved up like a NASCAR entry. I'm not a yoyo you toss on a string."

He spun to face her. "You mean my little speech wasn't clear enough? I said I want to fuck you until—"

"I heard you. But we should set some ground rules."

Dumbfounded, he stared at her a moment, trying to get himself under control. "Yeah, like I'm a handy stud at your beck and call? You're a piece of work, you know that? What kind of ground rules does it take to fuck? Number one, take off your clothes. Number two, spread your legs. Number three—forget it. Prostituting yourself just to get my business leaves a bad taste in my mouth. Just take your twitching ass somewhere else—"

"You're jumping to conclusions. I certainly wasn't soliciting. You expressed an interest in making love with me. I informed you of my interest in the same occurrence."

"No way, lady. First, you sure as hell were soliciting. Second, 'no hardship' isn't exactly a ringing declaration of desire. Third, I didn't say I wanted to make love. I said I wanted to fuck you."

Daggers shot from her eyes. "Magnus, read my lips. I'm a big girl. I can fuck with the best of them."

"Yeah, I'll bet. How many men from that Platinum Society have you fucked? Ten? Twenty? A hundred?"

"What do you know about the Society?"

"Don't go all innocent on me. You invited Rolf to a gangbang because he showed off his big schlong and you found him acceptable. If you brought a super-stud like him to the party, your standing would go way up in the eyes of your dirty friends."

"My friends are not dirty. *Sex* is not dirty."

"Sure looks that way to me when a guy struts around with a cock sticking out a foot and a dozen women can barely restrain themselves from grabbing hold of it."

Her voice suddenly turned quiet. "Magnus, who made sex dirty for you? Who hurt you?"

All the fight seeped out of him. He felt his shoulders slump. "I'll make it easy for you. I'll arrange for Rolf to bring you to the storeroom tomorrow, when I'll be at the sawmill. You log every piece you want to exhibit, give him a list, tell him your estimated selling price. We'll work from that as a basis for negotiation."

He ran his fingers through shaggy hair that still hadn't seen a barber and looked up at the bleak sky, then the dead weeds lining the driveway. "You'll deal exclusively with him as my representative. I don't want anything to do with you. I don't want to be in the same room with you. I don't want to talk to you. I don't want to want a whore."

With that last barb, he turned from the stunned look on her face, leaving her to stare at him from down the dirt road as he jogged back to the barn and slammed the big doors closed.

* * * * *

Magnus slugged back two fingers of single malt Scotch from a jelly glass and let the burn set fire to his gut all the way down to his dyspeptic stomach. Damn the woman. To hear Rolf tell it, Kat Donaldson gloried in relating, in juicy and intimate detail, all her sexual escapades at the Platinum Society. How the hell could he want to fuck a woman who was so indiscriminate? Hadn't he learned his lesson?

He grabbed the elegant decanter of Scotch that had been given to him by a customer enthralled with his acquisition of Magnus' unique table, and poured another shot. Sipping this one slowly, he looked out the window of his studio apartment adjacent to his office. He didn't see the trees, with their winter skeletons reaching bare arms toward the cloudy sky. He didn't see the monk-like severity of his surroundings—a standalone sink rescued from someone's junk pile, a two-burner propane stove on a table also used for eating TV dinners, the hand-carved four-panel screen separating the kitchen area from his only concession to comfort, the massive sleigh bed his grandfather had bequeathed him.

Instead, he saw three years into the past, when he'd come back home early from a day at the sawmill directing how a prime cherry log should be cut. At the time they'd been living with his grandfather in Knut's big house at the other end of the wooded acreage. They moved in shortly after they were married, and Lydia complained about their primitive kitchen, primitive bath, primitive everything. After Knut died, Magnus began remodeling, and the day his life turned upside down, he thought he'd surprise Lydia by installing the countertop on the cabinet he'd been constructing between the stove and the sink. Lydia worked as a dance instructor, and he knew she wouldn't be home that day until dark.

By a quirk of fate, Magnus had taken a different route home, swinging into the seldom-used back entrance to the property, past the barn and up to the back entrance of the house. He didn't see the cars out front.

But he heard the raucous music she loved—Eminem, he thought. Magnus grinned. Maybe they'd have a quickie first. Lydia was insatiable—and inventive. It had never occurred to him to question where she'd learned all those tricks.

He followed the sound of the music upstairs and into their bedroom, a large, airy room with late afternoon sunlight pouring through windows on two sides.

And turned stone-cold with rage.

His beautiful wife of the luscious body and long blonde hair was naked on her hands and knees atop their wildly mussed bed, sucking one man's cock while another stud was pumping her from behind and a third captured the ugly scene with a video camera.

The sound of glass shattering brought Magnus back to reality. He'd thrown the jelly glass against the stone wall. The memory shouldn't still have such power over him, he thought with silent rage. He'd kicked her ass out the same day and filed for divorce the next. But something inside him died that day. His trust of women. His desire for sex. His zest for life, for anything other than his work.

So Kat Donaldson wondered who made sex dirty for him?

As if he'd ever tell her.

And he was thinking of having sex with *her*? A devotee of mix-and-match? A worshiper of the more the merrier?

No way. No fucking way.

* * * * *

"But what does he *want*?" If she was a smoker, Kat would have burned through half a pack by now. Instead, she was sipping her second glass of white wine while wearing a path through her artist friend's living room rug. Lyssa was no help at all in the advice department. She'd just recently discovered her own sexuality, courtesy of Robert Savidge, and had no clue of the real world, even though the Platinum Society had brought the two of them together.

"Lyss, he all but spelled it out one letter at a time. He wanted to fuck me. He said so. His exact words were, 'I want to fuck you until you don't know which way is up'. Then he walks away. Correction. Runs. He actually ran back to the barn. This is the first time in my life that a man hasn't said 'Yes'. I just don't get it. What's wrong with me?"

"Maybe he wants to be the aggressor," Lyssa ventured.

"But he *was* aggressive. He hoisted me up for a wallbanger, kissing me full-throttle, all hands and mouth and cock. I could *feel* how much he wanted me. God, his cock felt as hard as that oak he works with."

She upended the glass and drained the wine. "I asked him who made sex so dirty for him that even thinking of making love with me left a bad taste in his mouth."

"What did he say?" Lyssa asked carefully.

The sound of a door closing made Kat clamp down on her response. One look at her friend's face and she knew that Savidge had come home. A look of…belonging. Of deep-down knowledge that she was loved above all others.

They might be one soul in two bodies, but Kat would not reveal her problem to Savidge the way she confided in Lyssa.

The very man appeared in the archway between the hall and the living room. A lump formed in Kat's throat. He had the same look for Lyssa. It was so…private. Kat felt like a voyeur. She had a fleeting vision of Lyssa as a top-top-secret document stamped "eyes only". And Savidge was the only person who had clearance to view it.

Hell, she deserved Savidge, Kat argued with herself. Lyssa had been in an abusive marriage for so long she had no inkling of her desirability, her innate sensuality, until Kat had all but dragged her to the Society's masquerade last summer.

The space between the pair of them simmered with sexuality, desire. And more. Was this the love that poets sang about? She'd been so hell-bent on following her mother's free-love footsteps that she found herself clueless as to the answer.

Kat felt a pang of envy.

"Is this a private party?"

"Um, yes," Lyssa said, rising off the sofa, "but you can come here and kiss me hello before you start dinner."

They met in the middle. Kat averted her eyes. This wasn't the kind of passionate but soulless kiss she'd given and received by the hundreds at an orgy. This was a one-man-one-woman-forever kiss, and not the first one Kat had witnessed between this couple.

Why hadn't her mother ever wanted such a relationship? Why had she bequeathed her only child a blueprint for flitting like a butterfly from man to man without ever finding an anchor? Why did Kat ache inside to become part of a union of such depth that the very world receded from view when *he* arrived?

"Have you signed your new discovery yet?" Savidge asked as he bent down to pour himself a glass of wine.

Ever the entrepreneur known in five states as a keen eye for new talent, Kat rallied. "As a matter of fact, tomorrow I'll be choosing which pieces I want to exhibit." She sighed theatrically. "Although we still haven't signed a deal. He's the most temperamental artist I've ever met."

Flashing his demonic smile, Savidge took a sip of wine. "I wouldn't worry too much. You've tamed a tiger or two that I remember. Lady Godiva knows how to handle temperamental. It's always a pleasure to watch you in action at the Society."

After another kiss to his fiancée, this one chaste but his eyes said differently, Savidge left for the kitchen.

His comment jolted Kat down to her Manolo Blahniks. For the first time in her life, she realized she didn't like the fact that so many people knew of her promiscuity, had seen her "in action".

Was that what had bothered Magnus so much?

Chapter Eleven

෩

"Are you ready for this adventure?" Rolf asked Kat as he unlocked the double doors to the storage room.

"Yes, let's get it over with."

He pulled the heavy doors open. "I'm so glad someone finally talked that thick-headed Norseman into exhibiting his work." When their grandfather died, Rolf had seen how the heart went out of Magnus' sculpting for a while. Then after the divorce, he'd moved out of the big house, fixed an apartment of sorts in the barn, and took up his tools with a vengeance.

"I'm sorry Mags isn't here to help me load the big pieces into the truck." At Kat's request Rolf had backed A Discerning Eye's white van up the dirt ramp and into the barn's garage, then rolled the big doors shut to keep out the twenty-degree weather. "He's supposed to be spending the day at the sawmill with that prize log of claro walnut."

"Yes, I know."

Talk about a curt response. Man, he itched to ask Kat what had happened between them. At the pool table at Thor's Hammer the other evening they looked ready to jump each other's bones, and Mags had pulled a cagey one by inviting Kat to the barn at eight o'clock the next morning, thinking her a lightweight.

He'd also specifically ordered Rolf to "require her presence" at exactly eight o'clock today, two days after her first look at his work, apparently to be sure she'd be long gone by the time he returned with his new slabs.

What the devil had happened between those two times? He'd been pricklier than a cocklebur stuck to the inside of your socks when he barked out his instructions regarding this excursion.

She had come dressed for work, Rolf noted. Gone, regrettably, were the red stiletto boots. Her feet were now encased in fur-lined Uggs with a low, thick heel. A long, down-filled parka covered that splendid ass of hers, and lined leather gloves protected her delicate hands from the pervasive cold that unheated stone barns gathered and retained.

"Here." She handed him a clipboard with a bunch of preprinted forms and a ballpoint pen. "If you fill this in as I call out specs, it will go faster."

Methodically she worked one section of shelves at a time, bottom to top, inspecting, pondering. If the piece passed muster, she affixed a numbered sticker to its underside, called out its height and footprint after measuring with a retracting ruler. She photographed it with a digital camera hung by a strap around her neck and set it down in a clear area near the double doors for wrapping and packing into the van. If the piece was marked with a date, initials, or a title, she noted that as well. If it had no identifying marks, she assigned it a title, like "Woman with upraised arms" or "Pitcher with inclusions".

Rolf found himself wishing she'd be more fanciful with her identifications. Hell, wouldn't someone be more likely to buy "Thor's Chalice" than "spalted drinking cup"?

Occasionally she would strip off one glove and blow warm breath on her fingers, yet she never paused to stop and never complained about what was probably a forty-degree interior temperature. The same as the inside of a refrigerator, he reflected wryly. A secret smile widened his mouth as he wondered if long johns cradled that luscious body under her jeans.

In between recording her notes, Rolf found himself shoving his bare hands inside the pockets of his shearling jacket. He resisted the urge to jump up and down to get his blood circulating. If she could stand the cold, he could too. She was one determined lady.

"Oh, no," she cried.

"What happened? Did you hurt yourself?"

She spun around, startled, as though unaware of having been in his company. Her face had a tragic cast to it.

"Look." She held out a piece of a carving that had been hacked off of something else with a sharp axe.

Rolf tried not to react.

"Who would have done something like this? Look at that exquisite face, like a Madonna. So much anger." She turned it around and around in her gloved hands. "I wonder if this can be rescued. You know, smooth out the edges. That face is haunting yet erotic."

She set it back down and began rooting through the shelves. "I wonder where the rest of the piece is. Have you ever seen it before? What should I be looking for?"

He wasn't about to tell Kat that this Madonna face had been carved in homage to Magnus' ex-wife, that he had gone into a rage one day and chopped the living shit out of it. Then he surprised everyone by announcing he and Lydia were divorcing "by mutual agreement". And he'd never told anyone why.

He wondered why Magnus kept this piece. Or maybe someone else in the family had found it in the woodpile and shoved it willy-nilly onto a shelf.

"Kat," he said mildly. "There's only one grid of shelving left. If it's there, you'll find it. Why don't you just keep going in the same thorough, precise way you've been examining his work. Then before we pack the van, we'll break for some hot tea."

That brought a smile to her face. "That sounds lovely. I don't even know if I have toes anymore. I've been wondering why I hadn't thought to bring a Thermos of hot coffee with me."

Much to Rolf's relief, they finished the last grid without finding the other half of the carving. He wouldn't want to have to explain it to this fire-haired woman.

"Come on," he said, grabbing her gloved hand. "We'll go upstairs and boil some water."

When he came to the door in the interior stone wall between the storeroom and Magnus' workshop, he stopped. She kept going.

"Whoa. We're not going outside."

"We're not?" Her eyes widened in surprise as Rolf turned the knob and swung the door open. "Are you sure that ladder isn't too rickety for me? Magnus said—"

A hearty guffaw escaped Rolf. "You're kidding, right? Magnus said you couldn't get from here to there except by a rickety ladder? That sneaky dog. He was pulling your leg. And what a leg it is, too." He gave her a Groucho Marx leer, waggling his eyebrows like the late comedian. "Ladies first."

* * * * *

Kat stepped over the threshold into a room maybe eighteen by thirty feet and stopped, her gaze jumping from the piece of richly shaded wood clamped in an industrial-sized vise to a well-organized stash of hand saws, chisels, hammers and other tools arrayed on a pegboard to a worktable with hand planes aligned at one edge, to the washbasin in one corner.

"Wow. Look how clean it is."

"Yeah. Magnus is fanatical about his workroom. When he's sanding, he wears a real gas mask, not one of those paper things, and runs the air cleaner. Any time he uses a power tool, he locks both doors." Rolf walked to the worktable and stroked one of the antique planes like it was a lover's hand. "When I was a kid, I used to watch Grandpa work. The thing I loved most was watching the curls fall to the ground when he was planing. My dad died when I was just a kid, and we had to move in with Grandpa and Grandma, because Mom had her hands full with the three of us rambunctious boys, especially since she had to work."

Kat noticed his eyes soften as he continued, "All I have to do is smell sawdust and I remember Grandpa Knut. But I think his death hit Magnus the hardest. I remember being jealous at how close the two of them were when I was growing up." He gave a self-conscious laugh. "But every time I tried to carve something, it was usually my thumbnail. So I gave it up."

A lump formed in Kat's throat. She would have liked to have known Knut Thorvald. Would she have seen how Magnus would look in thirty or forty years?

The thought sent shivers down her spine—Magnus and herself growing old together, here in the richly varied forest and the solid stone barn.

For crying out loud, she rebuked herself, shaking cobwebs from her brain. He was her client, not her lover. He didn't want anything to do with her. He'd sent Rolf as his buffer, his spokesman. Fanciful notions weren't what Kat Donaldson was all about. She was here as an art connoisseur and nothing else.

"The stairs are here."

Rolf walked to the far end of the room and opened a door to what Kat had assumed was a closet. "He thought of everything," he continued as he opened a second door before reaching the stairway. "Two doors to minimize dust to the apartment."

He stepped back. "After you."

Feeling somewhat like a voyeur, Kat slowly ascended the long stairway—sixteen steps, she counted—and into Magnus' apartment. At the top of the steps she stopped. *Primitive* was the only word that came to mind. An old-fashioned porcelain sink on a base stood before a deep-silled window, an avocado refrigerator way past its heyday occupied the corner. Between them, an unpainted bookcase held a meager supply of pots and dishes. About five feet separated the "kitchen" from a small table backed up against an exquisitely carved four-panel screen of flowers and birds set at a diagonal. Beyond the four-foot opening between screen and stairs she could see a bed. A huge bed.

Hurriedly she turned away from the sight of it, from the unbidden thought of a naked Magnus warm and sleepy under the down quilt, and cast a glance at Rolf. She cleared her throat. "He…lives here? Is he, um, land poor that he can't afford anything better?"

"Magnus is a masochist."

"Oh." Kat worried the inside of her cheek. She would *not* ask about his personal life or why he would be punishing himself, why he lived such a spartan existence. It was as though he lived only through his carvings.

Yet he'd felt so alive in her arms, his tongue thrusting deeply into her willing mouth, the massive bulge of his cock pressing between her legs, the heat of him almost melting her bones.

The sound of running water brought her to her senses. She turned to watch as Rolf filled a dented copper kettle, placed it on the two-burner camp stove sitting atop the scarred kitchen table, and turned the propane flame on. He rummaged through the shelves until he found a battered tin. Withdrawing two teabags, he lowered them into mismatched mugs. "Hope you like regular."

"Fine. I'd even take boiling water right about now."

"It's not always this cold upstairs. Mags turns down the thermostat when he's planning to be gone for a while."

Obviously Magnus hadn't expected his brother to invite anyone upstairs today. It was as cold as a witch's tit in a brass bra, as her mother used to say. Rubbing her hands together for warmth, Kat noticed the door in the stone wall. "Don't tell me. This leads to the office, right?"

"Okay, I won't tell you."

She flicked him a cool look.

"Be my guest. He doesn't keep this door locked."

Hesitant for only a moment, Kat turned the knob and entered the cavernous room where she'd first met Magnus and seen the two magnificent sculptures standing proudly under the two skylights. "That dirty rat. He made me go out of his office and around the outside of the barn to get to the storeroom. Rickety ladder, he said."

"Methinks he just didn't want you in his private quarters. You two didn't exactly hit it off the first time you were here."

"An understatement." And she wouldn't elaborate, not to Rolf.

As if sensing that she wouldn't explain, Rolf changed the subject. "You like sugar in your tea?"

"Anything low-cal would be great."

Pouring water into the mugs, Rolf snorted. "Not in this life. Mags does so much physical labor that he needs all the calories he can shovel down that big mouth of his."

Kat closed the door behind her as she returned to the kitchen and accepted the tea plain. She tried not to visualize how finely honed Magnus' body must be with all that physical labor. Wrapping her hands around the mug, she lowered her face so the steam could warm her. She sipped cautiously. "Oh, that feels so good going down. Thank you."

For a moment Kat concentrated on the warm brew, her body thawing out as she sipped. Unbidden, her gaze returned to the sleigh bed half hidden behind the screen. "Did Magnus carve the bed?"

"No, that was done by the old man himself, Knut's father. Haaken was the first Thorvald to arrive in this country, bringing his trade with him. He'd been here twelve years when he bought this land in 1926. Paid cash, as Grandpa Knut liked to remind us." Rolf chuckled. "No such thing as credit in the old days, we heard him say a thousand times. It's been home to woodworkers ever since."

Shyly, because it was Magnus' bed, but eagerly, because it looked like another work of art, she asked, "May I take a closer look?"

In response, Rolf flicked a switch that lit a lamp on a small bedside table, the only other piece of furniture in the room. Kat left her mug on the kitchen table and walked beyond the screen into Magnus' private lair. The bed's tall headboard and shorter footboard swooped upward gracefully, ending with nicely carved scrolls at the corners. Its king-size mattress sat high off the floor, as befitted a race of Vikings, she thought.

"Gosh, a normal-size person would have to jump up to get on here, wouldn't they?" she mused.

"Haaken made a step-stair for his bride." Rolf stooped down and looked underneath. "Yep, here it is." He pulled it out and nudged it to where Kat stood.

"Go ahead, try it."

Kat climbed the two steps and sat gingerly on the bed. She looked down from her perch. "I wonder if Richard Wagner's gods of the Niebelungen had such a royal bed." On impulse she flopped backwards, landing crossways on the puffy duvet, arms flung above her head, and thought about making angels in the down. She let her eyes drift closed. *Magnus.* She could smell his unique scent on the bedding— sawdust, pine trees and virile male.

Rolf leaned a shoulder against the headboard and gazed down at her with soft eyes. "You look absolutely right on that bed," he murmured.

"What the hell's going on here?"

Chapter Twelve

❧

Kat's eyes popped open. *Magnus*. Looking thunderous. Like the God of War himself, his long blond hair in windblown disarray, sprinkles of sawdust on his thighs and denim jacket.

Glaring at Rolf, he roared, "Where do you get the nerve to put the moves on this she-cat in the only private place I have?"

"Magnus, we were just—"

"Get out. Get the hell out. Both of you."

Kat struggled to rise from the expanse of mattress and slid off the bed. "You Neanderthal, he was just showing me Haaken's handiwork."

"Right. That's why you were lying down damn near spread-eagled, your eyes closed in ecstasy. Dammit, woman, what do you expect me to think? If you came here at eight o'clock, as agreed, you should have been out of here long ago. I figured four hours tops, but I added two more just to make sure I wouldn't have to run into you."

Kat's eyes flashed fire. "It's heartening to know you're purposely avoiding me."

"Magnus," Rolf interceded, "be reasonable."

He snapped his head around and redirected his wrath to his brother. "Reasonable? It isn't reasonable to think my bedroom is private? Why don't you post a goddamn sign at the road that says 'Rooms by the Hour'?"

"I was just—"

"Out, or I'll throw you down the goddamn steps. You may be younger than me, but I'm bigger and stronger. And mad enough to do it."

Cris Anson

"Get a life, Magnus." Rolf turned to Kat. "Let's go. I'll help you pack the van."

"You're not even done yet?"

Kat straightened the steel in her spine. "I'm very thorough, Mr. Thorvald. I spent every one of those six freezing hours cataloguing your wares. Your agent Rolf here can show you the level of detail in my listing of the artworks he's handing over to me on consignment. As soon as he and I sign each page, he'll give you a copy."

"Come on, angel. Let's get that stuff loaded."

Magnus went visibly rigid at Rolf's casually spoken term of endearment.

Trying to defuse things before the brothers came to blows, Kat placed a hand on Rolf's arm. "Go, Rolf. The demon he's fighting is me, not you. You were going to use the truck for the biggest pieces, anyway. Go on. He's my client. I can deal with it."

Rolf's searching gaze locked onto hers. "Are you sure?"

"Dammit," Magnus roared. "Just get the hell out of here!"

Obviously reluctant, Rolf nevertheless took a step toward the stairs then shrugged. "I've never been able to talk to him when he's got a broomstick up his ass, anyway. Call me on your cell phone if you need anything, hear?"

Kat didn't speak to Magnus until she heard the outside door of the workshop slam shut behind Rolf. She lifted her chin and turned to him, her professional façade firmly in place. Yet she couldn't look him straight in the eye. She couldn't let him see how having actually lain on his bed affected her.

"You have my sincerest apologies for intruding on your private life," she said, her back rigid. "I profoundly regret having been so brash as to flop down on your bed. My only defense is that I was so lost in the exquisite workmanship of your sculptures, I didn't realize I'd been standing on a stone floor in an unheated room for six hours. It wasn't until we stopped that I felt cold and tired. Then, when I came face to face with a piece of history like Haaken's bed, it was simply too irresistible."

"What a bunch of bullshit."

"Okay, maybe that was a bit of hyperbole, but the sentiment is still the same. I was tired. I *am* tired. But not too tired to pack the van before I go. I'll bring up the consignment list first, so you can look it over before you sign it. Unless, of course," she added over her shoulder as she headed into the kitchen before he heard the rumbling in her empty stomach, "you don't trust that your agent recorded everything I'm taking."

She took his silence for consent and hurried down the stairs and through the workroom to retrieve the clipboard on the floor of the van's cargo area. After one last quick review of the six pages of minute detail, she opened the door to the workroom to obtain Magnus' signature.

And almost bumped into him.

"I'll help," he said gruffly.

"You don't have to. I don't want to impose—"

"You're already imposing. If I help pack the damn things, I'll get rid of you that much faster."

Kat gritted her teeth. "There is that."

He went around the back of the van and stopped short. "You're taking all that?"

"Yes, if it's okay with you."

"Hell, some of this stuff was just practice."

"It must have had significance for you to keep it."

"Maybe I just wanted to remind myself what I've learned."

"See? We do have something in common." She gave him the sunniest smile she could muster. "My thought was to show the maturation of an uncommon talent."

Kat searched his expression. She could tell he was trying not to show any pleasure any time she complimented his talent. Reaching into the cargo area, she pulled out a neatly folded stack of small movers' quilts and tossed the pile onto the floor. "We'll start with the big things. I want to wrap each piece to prevent damage in transit." *Especially when I hit the potholes going up your driveway,* she said to herself.

Side-by-side, they worked silently, swiftly, competently. Smaller pieces were slipped into bubble-cushioned pouches and set on top of the quilted bundles. Soon the van was crammed with A Discerning Eye's next exhibit and Kat's head was crammed with ideas for marketing it.

She was pulling the van's back door closed when Magnus cleared his throat. "I'm sorry."

"What?" Kat blinked up at him.

"I overreacted. I shouldn't have jumped to conclusions. You want a sandwich?"

The abrupt change of subject made Kat decide this man wasn't accustomed to apologizing. Especially since he wouldn't meet her gaze. She debated her response.

"Your stomach's been rumbling for the past hour," he continued. "Made me hungry just listening to it."

Kat could feel the blush creeping up from her neck to her ears, her cheeks. Primly she said, "I'm sure you as an artist have experienced a fugue state where you simply had to complete your vision, that your art was more important than tending to bodily functions."

She could have kicked herself. Usually she didn't have foot-in-mouth disease. But standing so close to him, working so comfortably with him, made Kat think of a bodily function that put out a hell of a lot more heat than eating would.

And she wanted to feel his heat.

"Come on, let's see what we can rustle up for lunch. I haven't eaten since early morning, either." He disappeared through the door to the workshop, obviously expecting her to follow.

After a heartbeat, she did.

By the time Kat reached the top step and walked into his kitchen, a round loaf of pumpernickel bread sat on a small cutting board on the table and Magnus had his head stuck inside the small refrigerator. She took a moment to appreciate his firm ass cheeks so nicely outlined by his jeans, until he stood and turned around, his hands full.

"Stone ground mustard," he announced. "Here's Black Forest ham and here's provolone and here's smoked turkey." He plopped them on a dish, then took a lethal-looking knife from a shelf and began slicing the bread.

The delicious aroma wafting from the thick brown slices made Kat's stomach rumble again. "Smells heavenly. It's making me even hungrier."

"I can tell." He looked up and gifted her with a half-smile. "I bet I could hear it from the other side of that stone wall."

Relieved that he seemed to be in a mood for détente, Kat offered, "What can I do to help? Plates? Napkins?"

"I hope you aren't one of those snooty diners who insists on white-glove service." Magnus picked up a roll of paper towels and ripped off two pieces, handing her one. "Here's your plate. Help yourself. Buffet-style." He gestured with a sweep of his arm and a bow that would have done a maitre d' proud.

As an afterthought, he set a fork near the piles of sliced deli meats, probably a pound of each, still cocooned in their butcher paper. Kat speculated that she was looking at his entire week's worth of meals.

"Thank you." She built a sandwich and spread the mustard on a top slice. Just as she was wondering if she should sit on the lone chair at table, Magnus went into his office next door and returned, carrying one of the side chairs she remembered seeing near the sofa.

"Why don't you sit here?" He slid the new chair to the short side of the table then gestured to the original chair on the long edge. "I need the legroom. You want a beer?"

Kat was ready to refuse. Right about now, she'd kill for a good cup of hot coffee. Then she remembered his "snooty diner" comment, remembered how she'd taken the mug of beer from his hands at the poolroom, and decided to show him that she wasn't averse to drinking like the hoi polloi.

"Sure. Bottle is fine." Besides, she noticed it was getting warm enough to remove her jacket. He must have turned up the thermostat. Or maybe it was his nearness.

She heard the fizz when he popped the tops and realized how quiet it was. No TV, no radio, just the occasional rattle of the windows in their panes as the wind sought entrance. How did he stand the silence? Was he really a masochist, as Rolf had accused? Why was he punishing himself, living like a monk in such cold austerity?

"Thanks," she said when he set the frosty bottle of Sam Adams at the edge of her paper towel.

He held up his bottle. "Truce."

With a smile, she touched her bottle to his. "To the successful launching of an artist of rare talent."

Magnus lifted his bottle to his mouth and took a long pull. Settling himself in his accustomed chair, he marveled at the fact that he had actually invited the she-cat into his apartment. And was *feeding* her, no less. Suddenly uncomfortable at his spartan surroundings, he wondered what she really thought about his present lifestyle. She didn't belong in a cold stone barn with only the barest amenities. She was a champagne-and-satin-sheets sort of woman.

He quashed that turn of thought—it would lead nowhere fast. He picked up his fat sandwich and dug in. For a while they munched, with Kat occasionally commenting on one piece or another of his that she'd thought particularly memorable.

"Kat—"

"Magnus—"

They had spoken simultaneously. "Ladies first," he said gallantly.

Her eyes were downcast. She ran her fingers up and down the bottle, drawing the condensation into droplets. "I, um, I want you to understand where I came from," she said, the words coming out in a halting stream.

Magnus sat up, suddenly more alert.

"Have you ever heard of 'The Summer of Love'?" she asked. "The Monterey Pop Festival, 1967? Where thousands of people gathered to hear Janis Joplin, The Who, The Animals, Otis Redding? This was before Woodstock, before the Establishment realized how much money they could make with rock 'n roll. I can probably recite the entire roster — Hugh Masekela, Jefferson Airplane, Ravi Shankar, dozens of others." She lifted her lids and looked searchingly into his eyes.

Oh God, he could get lost in those dark, mysterious eyes of hers. He blinked. "Was that the place where the women tucked flowers into the muzzles of the cops' guns?"

"Yes. The place where it all started." Her eyes focused on some place far away. "My mother was there. She was living in San Francisco at the time. In a commune. A real hippie-flower child with long hair, no bra, bare feet. No one living there thought anything bad about going from partner to partner. It was just the way it was."

She took a sip of beer. Magnus watched her throat work as she swallowed.

"That weekend, they all piled into a Volkswagen van, with the typical Day-Glo flowers, and drove up the Pacific Coast Highway a hundred miles to Monterey. I—" she cleared her throat. "She never told me, but I calculate that I was conceived that weekend." Her fingers fussed with a corner of the paper towel.

"All the stories she told me when I was a kid. They weren't Cinderella or Snow White. They were about that era." Her eyes focused on him again. "Magnus, I learned at my momma's knee that it was the way of men and women to share their bodies, to change partners. She never told me who my father was. Whenever I asked, she always laughed breezily and said it could be any one of the dozens of men who lived in the commune."

Magnus clenched his teeth and let her talk.

"She was a very strong woman," Kat continued. "We never needed a man around the house. Oh, she would live with someone for a few months at a time, but she never let any one man stay around long enough to allow us to get dependent on him. She said she could take care of her daughter better alone than with some man she'd have to train."

When he didn't say anything, her gaze dropped to her clenched hands. "I—I never knew any other way." She stood abruptly, crumpled her paper towel into a ball and picked up her empty beer bottle. "Where's the trash can? I'd best get back before dark. I still have a lot of work to—"

"Kat." Magnus didn't remember making a conscious decision to do so, but suddenly he stood next to her. Gently he cradled her face in his callused hands and dropped soft kisses on her pert nose, her arched brows. "It's okay. Really. I don't agree with your lifestyle, but I understand you a little better now." He grazed his lips against hers.

She whispered his name.

On a moan, she opened her mouth in dizzying welcome, pressed her lithe body to his. The spark that had constantly hovered between them combusted into flame. He dove in, hands and mouth seeking, grasping, devouring. The elusive scent of vanilla from her perfume tantalized him. He wanted to lick it off of every inch of her skin. He wanted to hear his name on her lips when she came. To be buried so deep inside her, she'd be nailed to the bed. Or the floor, or the desk, or—

"Umph." Dimly he realized she still held the empty beer bottle in her hand when it clunked him on the skull. Abashed at his lack of control whenever Kat Donaldson got near him, Magnus took a step back. "Here. Let me get rid of this stuff."

A giggle escaped her as he took the trash from her hands and bent down to dispose of it in a bag. "Sorry," she said, not sounding sorry at all. "I was so keen to wrap my arms around your neck, I forgot I was holding it. Did I hurt you?"

Magnus straightened and loomed over her. "Hurt me? You bet. You want to know where I hurt? I'll show you." He grasped her hand and placed it over his humongous hard-on. "Here's where I hurt. My cock is throbbing. My balls are so tight they ache. You did that to me, wench. And it's not the first time, either."

She cupped her hand around the hard, hot bulge inside his jeans. "Oh, poor baby. Let me see where it hurts."

Dropping to her knees, she worked the zipper with great care.

He should protest, he knew he should. In his family the man was the aggressor, it was embedded in his Viking DNA. He wanted to show her that he wasn't going to be just another notch on her bedpost, that he could—would—dominate her in bed. But damn, it had been so long, too long, since he'd wanted—needed—a woman. And this woman could damn near blow the top of his head off just with a look, a touch.

And how she was touching him! He felt his belt loosen, felt cool air caress his bare ass as Kat slid the jeans down his thighs. His cock sprang free and proud and huge. He looked down at the length of it, the thick head only inches from that mouth that gave him wet dreams. He couldn't help himself. He tilted forward, touched her chin with the moist tip of it.

Need exploded inside him. He grabbed the back of her head in one hand. With the other, he guided his cock like a heat-seeking missile to her mouth.

Like a prayer answered, her mouth opened and engulfed him. "Oh Jesus," he moaned, fighting to keep his knees from buckling. He released his hold on his cock and put his other hand on her skull as well, holding her head in place. She was heaven and hell, ecstasy and torment, all in one hot cavity that sucked and licked like a greedy fire that consumed everything in its way. She gripped his ass cheeks to pull him closer. The sight of his shaft disappearing between her swollen lips threatened his already tenuous control.

Enough. If she didn't stop sucking him, if he didn't pull out *right now*, he'd shoot his wad like a high-school sophomore with his first girl.

He tried. He really tried to pull out, to make sure he'd satisfy her first before letting himself come. But she clutched him like a pit bull, rode his cock mercilessly in her mouth, her suction and her determination greater than his will to stop, and he felt himself surrendering to the incomparable feel of him fucking her mouth. Finally, finally, three years of pent-up need exploded from the deepest part of him and he felt himself shooting into her in spasm after spasm until he emptied himself of every last drop.

And then his knees buckled.

Chapter Thirteen

ഇ

Kat worried her bottom lip with her teeth as she unwrapped the carvings that she and Sandy had unloaded from the van into the workroom of A Discerning Eye. The heavy stuff was still in the vehicle, waiting for Rolf to move them when he brought the last big piece in the truck.

Dammit, how could she change Magnus' opinion of her if she kept playing the role he saw her in? It didn't matter how much he was hurting, how much he needed what she willingly offered, he still thought she was a whore. She could see it in his eyes when he came down to earth after what she was willing to bet was the best orgasm of his life—the guilty relief that he'd finally ended his drought. The shame that he'd been so rough with her mouth. The realization that she'd breached his defenses and made him come in no more than an eyeblink.

She thought he'd be swayed by hearing about her background. She didn't think there was anything wrong with following in her mother's footsteps. She liked men, the look of them, the feel of them. Liked how they made her feel.

At least she had in the past. Since she'd met Magnus, she didn't find the offerings at the Platinum Society all that appealing. She'd turned down Jules several times when he called, pleading a heavy workload.

That much, at least, was true. She was up to her eyeballs in planning her next show.

"Don't change the subject, Kathryn."

Geez. Magnus Thorvald had her talking to herself.

Maybe she should have let him make love to her. Maybe she shouldn't have bruised his ego by slipping away after he shot his wad into her mouth. Maybe she should have admitted to him that her tender feelings for him scared her and she didn't know how to handle it.

But, dammit, going down on him was something she needed to do. It wasn't about her. It was about him, about giving him some relief. To hear Rolf tell it, Magnus had been celibate ever since he got divorced. Three years.

Kat shuddered. How could a virile, red-blooded man like Magnus be without a woman for three years? She'd about creamed her panties when that awesome cock first popped out of his jeans. Oh, to have that finely honed piece of machinery pumping into her!

She'd wanted to fuck him since the day they met, yet this afternoon she'd put his needs above hers. That disturbed her.

A thought left her thunderstruck. She sat down, hard, on the floor of the workroom to consider it.

Was this how Lyssa felt about Savidge? Did she put his needs above her own?

To take the comparison further, was she…falling in love with Magnus?

Kat shook her head. No. N-O. No. She didn't want a man complicating her life, someone who would need tending or cleaning up after. It was obvious that Magnus had a monkey on his back. She didn't know what it was, but just seeing where he lived should be enough to scare her off. The guy was wallowing in self-pity, for heaven's sake. She'd promised to launch his career. She didn't promise to play psychiatrist.

"Get your head on straight," she admonished as she scrambled to her feet and headed to her private office.

Pushing number three, she speed-dialed Jules' number.

"Kat, sweetheart," he answered on the first ring. "I was just thinking about you."

Kat was taken aback at his prescience until she remembered he had caller ID. Still, she didn't want him to think she was eager for another Dom session with him.

"When's the next Society event?" she asked.

"Tomorrow night," he replied. "If you're coming, I'll bring my cat-o'-nine-tails."

"I don't know, Jules. Maybe I'll just watch."

A long pause. Then, "Are you feeling okay?"

"Yes, of course. Why do you ask?"

"You sound...melancholy. Out of sorts."

"I'm just tired. I hauled a van full of sculptures into the shop tonight and — "

"You should have called me. You know I'd do anything for you. Suppose you hurt your back? Suppose you dropped something heavy on your foot?"

Kat smiled. Jules really was sweet to worry about her.

"You need someone to take care of you. Let me be that someone. My offer of marriage still stands. I think we suit extremely well."

"We've been over this before, Jules. I'm not the marrying kind. You know that."

A soul-deep sigh issued from the phone. "A man can dream."

Her words echoed in Kat's mind long after they had hung up. *Not the marrying kind.* Why did that thought leave her edgy?

* * * * *

He hoped this would work. He'd either win her over or get her out of his system.

Taking a deep breath, Magnus entered the house when Robert Savidge opened the front door at his knock. He had to give his little brother credit. Rolf had moved swiftly when he'd enlisted his help. How he did it, Magnus didn't care. Only that he'd been invited as a guest of a member. And that Savidge had assured him Lyssa would make sure her friend Kat attended tonight's affair.

Scanning a large, luxuriously appointed living room, Magnus was relieved to see it looked like an ordinary cocktail party. Well-dressed men in suits or sport jackets and women in sexy dresses with low décolletage stood chatting in small groups. Female heads turned to give him a once-over as he entered the room, making him feel like a slab of beef in a butcher's case. He resisted the urge to loosen his tie, a piece of apparel he seldom wore.

A passing waiter offered him a glass of wine. He declined the Dutch courage. His head would be perfectly clear tonight. As would his intent.

There she was. Wearing a bright-red top with spaghetti straps tied in two dainty bows on her bare shoulders and a matching swirly skirt that barely touched her knees. Talking to a good-looking younger man who stood much too close to her.

He strode up to Kat Donaldson. "Excuse me. I believe we have some unfinished business."

Kat spun around. Her eyes lit up when she saw him. "Magnus."

The sound of his name on her lips made his stomach do a little flip. The flare of hunger in her eyes made his cock flip as well. He ignored both.

The man with Kat thrust out his hand. "Hi, I don't believe we've met. Jules Rubin."

Magnus ignored the man and took hold of Kat's upper arm with a solid grip. "Come with me, please."

"Hey, wait—"

"It's all right, Jules, I know him."

"But he can't just—"

The man's voice shriveled to nothing at the look Magnus gave him over his shoulder as he half-dragged Kat to the other side of the room.

"Magnus, you're squeezing too hard."

He swirled her around to face him. "Everything's going to be hard before we're done. Get used to it."

Spying the requested object almost hidden beneath a damask napkin on the sideboard, he leaned behind Kat to retrieve it. In seconds, he clicked one cuff on her right hand and yanked it up by its chain, which he threaded through a hook in the ceiling. Quickly lifting her left hand to the dangling cuff, he snapped it on her other wrist, then stepped back. Her breasts thrust out and upward, making his mouth water.

"Magnus, what the hell are you doing?"

"Just trying to make sure you stay put."

"Turn me loose," she hissed. "You're making a spectacle of yourself."

He lifted an eyebrow. "*You* can accuse me of that? Lady Godiva? The original twosie-threesie girl? Platinum Club board member? Look around you, Kat. You're among people who make spectacles of themselves every other weekend. Or have you been too busy making sure every man got a taste of you to notice what anybody else did?"

"This isn't like that." Angry sparks shot from her eyes. "This is a normal, run-of-the-mill cocktail party. There are non-Club members here."

"So?"

"Unlock the cuffs, Magnus."

"I didn't appreciate your running away. You didn't let me reciprocate." He cupped her face in his big hands. "I plan to make up for it tonight." His tongue licked at the tight seam of her mouth. She tried to turn her head. His hold on her face firmed. "Nuh-uh. That mouth of yours is irresistible."

Tilting her face, he rained an army of delicate kisses on her eyebrows, temple, nose. He licked her mouth again, sucked at her lower lip then scraped it with his teeth. Her mouth softened, and he pressed his lips to hers, fitting them together at a better angle. He deepened the kiss, thrusting, tasting, teasing.

On a soft moan, she parried with her own tongue, invading his mouth, straining against her bonds to reach more of him.

With a soft chuckle, Magnus took a step back. "Not yet, sweet."

"Come here, Magnus, I want to kiss you." Her voice sounded unsteady to him.

Ignoring her, he skimmed a knuckle down her cheek to her throat, lodging a finger in the crease her shoulder made in its upraised mode. "Your skin is so smooth."

He toyed with one of the bows on her shoulder. "This looks promising."

"Don't you dare," she whispered, as her eyes darted around to the men and women standing in small groups around the room. "Not here. Not now."

"You like to be in charge, don't you."

"Magnus, this isn't funny. Uncuff me."

"Oooh, a take-charge woman. You call the shots or else you take your baseball and go home. Is that how it works?"

"You don't belong in this group. You haven't been approved by the board. You don't know the rules. The rules say if someone says 'no', you have to let them go."

"I haven't heard anyone say no." He nuzzled her vulnerable underarm.

"Then listen carefully, Magnus. No. N-O. No. Let me go."

He moved his head until his mouth came in contact one of the bows holding her top tied. Then tugged one end with his teeth.

She gasped. "Magnus, don't do this."

"Do what? I'm just kissing your throat." He pulled back slightly, the spaghetti strap tautening in his teeth until the red silk lifted from the upper slope of her breast.

He opened his mouth. The strap dropped. The shimmering red silk dangled at the edge of her breast, the slight weight of the strap sliding, sliding the fabric down until it snagged on the hard peak of her nipple.

Magnus made a rough sound. "Damn. Who would have thought a nipple would get hard so fast that it stopped gravity?" He tongued the nipple in question, leaving a wet mark on the silk. When he heard her moan, he encircled the hard bud in his mouth.

She jerked her body forward, thrusting her breast closer to him.

"I know you're waiting for the other shoe to drop, so to speak," he murmured. "So I won't torture you any longer."

"Yes," she moaned. "Unhook me."

"Gladly." He pulled open the other bow and let the strap drop. The red silk top slithered down her chest, her breasts, and pooled in a soft puddle at her hips. As had already been obvious, she wasn't wearing a bra.

"Magnus, I meant the cuffs! Unhook them. Let me go."

The level of conversation around them had quieted. Her eyes jerked around the room. From his peripheral vision, Magnus saw a number of guests watching them. He was no exhibitionist, but he had to do this. Closing his mind to everything but the tantalizing woman before him, he lifted her full, heavy tits in his hands, molding, kneading them, bringing the tips closer together. "You bet I'll let you go. You'll go on and on and..." He pulled both nipples into his mouth at the same time, sucked hard. She jerked again.

"Please..."

"Are you getting horny? You want to get fucked? Is that what you're asking?"

"No, I don't want to get fucked. I want to make love with you."

"Mmmm. Semantics. You want a cock inside you."

"Yours! I want *your* cock inside me."

Magnus straightened to look her in the eye. "Like this?" He thrust his tongue into her mouth, all the while stroking the exposed skin of her back, her waist, the undersides of her breasts.

"Please, Magnus, don't tease me like this. I want to touch you, I want you inside me."

"All in due time." He tugged at the red silk puddle at her hips. "Let's get rid of this, shall we?" Kneeling at her feet, he pulled, and the skirt came down along with the wrinkled top.

"Ah, you didn't disappoint." He stroked the silky thigh-high stockings, then reached higher, to the expanse of skin between garters and a little red triangle of panties. "A thong. Of course. Sexy to the skin, our Kat is."

He reached behind him to drop featherlight strokes across her bare ass cheeks as his breath caressed her belly. He could feel her shiver under his light touch. Bringing more pressure to bear, he stroked underneath the red lace, finding her engorged clitoris and dallying there. "You're wet, baby. Is that for me? Or because you know every male in this room is wishing he'd thought of this first? Look around you. Look at the guys rubbing their cocks because this turns them on. Look at the expressions on the women's faces, wishing a man would do this to them."

"Magnus." Her breath was no more than a gasp. Her hips moved involuntarily.

"That's it, baby. Tremble for me." He stroked harder. Her breath was coming in shorter pants, her chest heaving. A light film of perspiration covered her skin.

"Please, Magnus. I want you." Her breathy voice was barely a whisper.

"I'm running this show. I'll tell you when to come." Stroking, caressing her clit, sliding two fingers in and out of her cunt. Slowly, slowly, wanting to make her beg. Wanting to suck her cunt dry until she shattered glass with her screams of ecstasy.

"Magnus, *please!*"

Stopping short of bringing her to an orgasm, he kissed his way back up her bare skin until he stood straight and tall before her. He tucked his fingers, slick with her cunt juices, into her mouth. "Taste yourself. Do I do that to you? Or is it letting everyone watch you that turns you on?"

"Fuck everyone else!" Gasping, chest heaving, Kat closed her mouth around his fingers and sucked hard, wanting to show him she needed him *right now*. She tried to lean forward to at least rub her body against his, but the cuffs held her securely. Then she squeezed her thighs together. Maybe she could get enough friction to make herself come. Oh god, he had her so hot she'd do anything, *anything*, to get his cock inside her. Especially now that she knew how big, how hard it was. How good he tasted.

She bit down on his fingers just hard enough to make him withdraw them. "Magnus, I'm begging you." Her voice sounded ragged. "Don't leave me high and dry. Please. I don't care if it's here, my place, the barn, anywhere. Just…please, I want you."

He pulled her roughly to him, ravishing her mouth with his, taking from her like a starving man. She rubbed herself up and down against him, the rough fabric of his linen blazer scraping against her supersensitive bare skin, trying to get his big cock to press harder into her weeping slit. She latched onto his tongue when he thrust it inside her mouth, and sucked it the way she wanted to suck his cock. Greedy. Needy beyond all reason.

Damn, she was ready to come right now. Two more seconds, and she'd —

"Hold that thought," he said, stepping back from her. "I'll call you."

He spun around on his heel.

117

Dazed from his sensual assault, she blinked. She felt the lack of his heat immediately and struggled to make sense of what had just happened. "Magnus, where are you going? Magnus!"

"I primed the pump for your Platinum Society friends. Have at it, ladies and gentlemen."

He stalked out of the room. A moment later, the outside door slammed.

"Magnus! Damn you, get back here and take me down! Magnus! *Magnus!*"

It took a moment to sink in. He'd left her. *He left her!* It had to be his way of showing her what he thought of the Platinum Society.

"You son of a bitch!"

She closed her eyes, trying to control the sting of tears that threatened. The humiliation, the *need*.

Bare skin grazed against her breasts.

Her eyes popped open. "Savidge," she breathed. "What are you doing?"

"Remember how, when I first joined the Club, you tried every trick you knew to get me naked in a corner?" Savidge stroked her nipples, tugged on them.

"Go on," said a soft feminine voice behind her. *Lyssa!* What was she doing? She didn't have the guts to initiate anything in public—with another woman, no less! How could Lyssa stand watching her man's hands roaming all over her? "I want to see what it's like to watch Savidge, um, mating with another woman."

Kat turned her head as much as she could, to glare at her best friend. "Lyss, you're crazy. You don't want to share him."

"But she wants to please me," Savidge said smoothly. "Come on, Kat, if you want to go into a corner with me and let me finish what that bastard started, I'll unlock the cuffs."

"No! I can't do that! I mean—Lyss, you don't want me to do that." She struggled against the cuffs, dismissing the pain in her wrists. "Savidge, read my lips. Go. Away."

"Kat, Kat. All this time, you've been spouting bullshit about how hot I was? About how you wanted to jump my bones?"

Her chin lifted. He'd laid down the gauntlet.

"Savidge, I'd love to, but I won't do that to my best friend."

"It's all right, Kat. Go ahead."

Kat's eyes narrowed as she turned her head as far as she could and studied her friend spooned behind her. "What did he do, hypnotize you? I won't do it. I can't do that to you."

"It's really sweet of you to make such a sacrifice, seeing how revved-up you are. I'll hitch a ride with someone. That way, Savidge can do what he wants with you and you won't have to feel guilty about me watching."

"No, Lyssa. That's not the way it works. Take your man home with you."

Lyssa strolled past Kat and out the archway into the hall. In a moment, the outside door clicked shut. Kat felt her mouth drop open. She snapped it shut when Savidge began skimming his fingers up and down her sides again.

She squirmed. "Savidge, really. I can't."

"You mean you aren't horny after all that? Hell, everyone here is horny, just looking at you and Magnus burning up all the oxygen in the room. You looked ready to pop."

"Dammit, I still am." Kat let her head droop. "But I can't do that to Lyssa."

Savidge tucked a finger under her chin and lifted her head. The smile he gave her dazzled. He smiled a lot more now that he and Lyssa were planning a wedding, she thought muzzily. But the look on his face puzzled her. It was almost as though he knew something she didn't. Something about Kat herself. He gave her a tender, lingering kiss on the lips.

It did absolutely nothing for her.

"Let me, darling." Jules nudged Savidge aside. "We suit each other. Neither of us has any ties to hold us back. I'll unlock the cuffs and take you upstairs. You can use the cat-o'-nine tails on me."

"Just get these damned cuffs off."

"First I want to kiss you."

No, she started to say, but his mouth cut off her words. The fervor in his eyes just before he kissed her registered. He wanted to disobey her so she could discipline him even more. Kat's frustration turned to impatience. He irked her with his need to be dominated. She wanted a man strong enough to stand up to her. A man like Magnus.

No, not a man *like* Magnus. She wanted the real thing. Magnus.

Jules thrust his tongue into her mouth. She bit it.

He jerked his head back, but kept her tightly enclosed in his arms. "Yes, darling."

"No, Jules. Dammit, will somebody get me down from here? What the hell happened to the first rule of the Club? 'When a guest or member says no, the other participant or participants will promptly comply.' Doesn't anyone know the meaning of the word 'promptly'?"

Her angry glare bounced from one member to another. They studiously avoided her gaze.

"What's the matter with all of you? What are you, extras on a movie set? Cardboard cutouts? I'm on the damn board of directors! I can blackball everybody here. Get me down!"

Savidge stepped into her line of vision. "As the host's representative, I'm obliged to look out for the best interests of everyone in the room. Are you saying that you'd rather go home hurting and unfulfilled than to have sex with anyone in this room?"

Kat thrust out her chin. "Yes. I suddenly find the company tedious."

Slipping a hand into his pants pocket, he withdrew a key and reached up to unlock the handcuffs. "I'm at your service."

* * * * *

"That went well, didn't it?" Lyssa said several hours later as she snuggled deeper into the warm haven of Savidge's arms.

"It certainly did. She doesn't know what hit her."

"It's about time."

Chapter Fourteen

ജ

Magnus picked up the back-bent gouge again and carefully smoothed its convex cutting edge around another inclusion, shaving away a millimeter of waste wood. Slowly, very slowly, he was coaxing the riotous curls of her hair from this prime piece of cherry burl, just as he had envisioned when he and Rolf had sawed through it. It was probably the most complex piece he'd attempted.

Although the temperature in the workroom hovered around sixty degrees, sweat soaked into the red bandanna around his forehead. The muscles in his arms ached from the need to hold the tool at the proper angle, to keep the pressure at a light touch. His stomach rumbled. He hadn't eaten since an early breakfast, and the sun had long since dipped down below the horizon. He ignored his thirst, even though the wash-up sink was only a dozen steps away.

Nothing mattered but the act of creation. The fire in her hair had haunted him since she'd first stepped out of her car into the sunlight at his farm. Now he was close to capturing it. Or, rather, the wood was slowly revealing its ideal use under his guidance.

He set the gouge back in its proper place on the worktable then picked up a fishtail gouge to undercut the edge of the curl. Blowing gently, he dislodged the shavings and eyed the piece critically. Gave a brief nod of satisfaction.

Vaguely he heard the phone ringing upstairs in his office. He refused to have an extension here. This room had only one purpose, and it wasn't for talking.

His mind's eye conjured up the vision of her eyes. Teak-shaded irises, long brown lashes, thick arching brows.

Eyelashes were beyond the scope of woodcarving, but tomorrow, after he'd rested, he'd begin carving those big doe-eyes. He'd already roughed out the face, her long, thin nose, the full pouty mouth.

Damn. Just the thought of that mouth made too much blood rush to his cock. He tried to block out how deliciously that mouth had sucked him, milked him until his personal dam burst and he shot his cum all the way down her throat.

Magnus tossed down the tool. He knew better than to let his mind wander when he had a chisel or gouge in his hand. The slightest inattention could ruin an entire month's work. He glanced out the window. Full dark. Hell, he might as well pack it in for the night. A cold shower and a cold beer sounded mighty good right now.

Twin beams of light flashed around the curve and into the driveway. Magnus swore. He didn't need, didn't want any company tonight. He reached for the tarp on a shelf, unfolded it and covered his work-in-progress, then looped a few strands of twine around it and the vise to hold it in place.

Why didn't I shutter the windows, he thought. Then no one could have seen that the workroom was lit. He grabbed the push broom and began sweeping up the curls.

"Hey, Mags, open up. My hands are full."

Rolf. Hell, he'd probably come by to hear a blow-by-blow of last night. He toyed briefly with the idea of not responding. But Rolf's cheshire grin appeared at the windowpane. He sighed. Too late.

"Christ, I left you three messages this evening," Rolf complained as Magnus reluctantly unlocked the outside door to the workroom.

"Pizza." Magnus stared at the large box in Rolf's hands. His stomach growled.

"Yup. Figured you were down here in the dungeon, and I know you forget to eat when that happens. So...Papa John's to the rescue."

"Thanks. Go on up. I'll be done sweeping up in a few minutes."

"What's on the vise?"

Ignoring the question, Magnus pushed the broom until the cherry curls stood in a pile.

"Hey, that looks like cherry. Am I right?"

"The kid goes to the head of the class," Magnus muttered as he reached for a dustpan. He carefully dumped the shavings into a big trash bin and replaced the cover. "Get your ass upstairs." It annoyed him that Rolf stood at the worktable eyeing the tarp. "You ought to know better. No sneak previews."

"I just wondered. Cherry, huh? Conjures up certain... visions." Rolf went to the stairway. "You first, Mags. I can't open the doors with my hands full."

Pointedly, Magnus opened both stairway doors then stepped back. Rolf raised a questioning eyebrow, but took the hint—Magnus would *not* show him his current work. Especially not this one.

Magnus dusted off bits of detritus from his flannel shirt and jeans and followed Rolf upstairs. He grunted when he saw the kitchen clock. Almost eleven p.m. No wonder he was hungry.

Rolf had brought napkins from the pizzeria and was flopping slices onto paper plates. Magnus retrieved a chair from the office for Rolf, then took two longnecks from the fridge and opened them. For a few moments the only sound was of chewing or swallowing. Until after each had taken a second piece.

Casually, Rolf asked, "So, what's it like at the Platinum Society?"

"Bunch of people standing around with cocktails in their hands. No horns, no forked tails."

"But how'd it go?"

Magnus shrugged. "I did what I set out to do."

"Which is…?"

"Got her riled up."

"Riled up? As in hot and bothered? Or as in mad at you?"

Magnus took a long swallow of Sam Adams. "I'm sure you've already heard."

"Yeah, but I gotta get it from the horse's mouth." Rolf grinned.

"Didn't you ever hear that a gentleman doesn't kiss and tell?"

"Hmph. You calling yourself a gentleman?"

"I've been known to masquerade as one on occasion."

"Is that why you left without diddling her?"

Magnus clenched his hand around the beer bottle. He had a sudden urge to knock that smirk off Rolf's face. He schooled himself to lift the bottle to his mouth and take a slow sip. "The lady needed to learn a lesson."

"Oh yeah. And what did she learn?"

Magnus realized he was stroking his mouth with the lip of the bottle. He set it down. "I believe the Rolling Stones said it best. 'You can't always get what you want.'"

"And the lady wanted you?"

"Said she did."

"And you don't want her?" Rolf's grin turned into a wolfish smile from ear to ear. "Does that mean I have a clear shot at her?"

"The hell you say. You're too immature for her. Why would she want a punk still wet behind the ears?"

Rolf's smile turned smug. "Way I see it, I won't find out unless I ask her."

"I suggest if you don't want to find your asshole rearranged, you don't ask her."

Rolf leaned his elbows on the rickety table. "No shit, you're warning me off?"

"Just trying to talk some sense into a kid."

"Did you hear what happened after you left?"

"Now how could I do that?" Magnus said, nonchalantly taking another slice, trying not to admit to himself that he sadistically did want to know.

"Someone might have called to inform you of the climax of the evening."

Magnus' mouth thinned. Rolf was baiting him. Had to be, with that particular choice of words. "Okay, I'll bite. What happened after I left?"

"Well, they kept her cuffed." He gave Magnus a sly gaze. "I guess you'd know something about that. Anyway, seems like two guys had at her. The guy I met, Savidge, was one. He's the main squeeze of that artist Kat's exhibiting right now. Has lots of black hair on his chest. The other apparently has a penchant for a cat-o'-nine tails."

Every muscle in Magnus' body went rigid. "You mean a man...flogged her?"

"Nah. Other way around. He invited Kat to use it on him. He could see how furious she was, how horny."

Magnus jumped off the chair, his hands balling into fists, legs spread apart in a want-to-fight? stance. "Okay, chum. Gossip's over. Thanks for the pizza. Now get out of here."

"Hey, don't you want to hear how it ends?"

He lifted Rolf off the chair by the collar of his jacket. "Don't call us. We'll call you. Out."

"But it's a beaut of an ending!"

By now Magnus had dragged Rolf to the top of the stairs. "Don't make me push you down."

"Okay, okay, I'm going. But you'll be sorry you didn't let me finish the story."

"Out!" He gave Rolf a shove, followed him downstairs. And locked the door behind him.

* * * * *

Damn, damn, damn!

Magnus lay in the dark, staring at the ceiling, head pillowed on his stacked hands. He'd crawled into the antique sleigh bed hours ago, but sleep eluded him. He fought the impulse to go downstairs and hack the cherry sculpture into pieces. He'd done that once before, but it hadn't helped.

Women. He'd done a fairly good job of living without them for the past three years. But this one had gotten under his skin in a major way. It was more than just a spectacular blowjob. She was funny, tender, kind, savvy, intelligent, and hell, there'd been a spark between them from the day she stepped into his life.

Plus he'd agreed to be her client.

How the hell could he work with her now, knowing that he was just the latest in a long string of men who were probably, in her mind, interchangeable.

He was an old-fashioned man. One man, one woman. Okay, so she'd had an unusual upbringing, he'd grant that. She'd learned her ways from her mother — that wasn't her fault. But where did he get off thinking he'd be the man to change her?

One thing he'd vowed never to be again — second fiddle to the woman in his life.

Magnus punched his pillow into a ball. Hell, she probably didn't even want to *be* the woman in his life.

Face it, he thought sourly, he was just another meal ticket to her. She probably looked at him and saw how much money she'd make selling his sculptures. Did he want to sabotage all he'd worked for over the years just because his male pride had taken a hit?

On the other hand, he *had* been pretty domineering, using his greater strength to intimidate her. Then he'd humiliated her by stripping her damn-near naked in front of an audience and kissing and teasing her until her cunt juices flowed all over his hands.

And then he'd walked out, left her with the female equivalent of blue balls. Hell, no wonder she took the next offer. They probably all thought he was a masochist to walk out on a beautiful, stacked woman all aquiver with lust.

Why the fuck had he ever thought it would work?

How could he expect someone with her background to want him exclusively?

Chapter Fifteen

฿

"Ohmigod."

Kat swallowed hard. Through a window of A Discerning Eye, she saw that Magnus had just pulled the truck into a parking spot on the street. How could she face him in public so soon? After she'd begged and pleaded like a nymphomaniac for him to take her, and him spurning her like she was a hooker? Her heart felt as though he'd gouged it with one of his chisels. Or sliced it with a chain saw.

She had hoped she would have more time to adjust to the fact that he had jerked her around, that he'd shown her she wasn't good enough for him because she'd slept around so much.

It had never bothered her before. It was the way she'd been brought up.

But somehow Magnus made her feel ashamed of her past. She worked up some righteous anger. How dare he! She was what she was, and if he didn't like it, why the hell didn't he just keep her at arm's length instead of making her want and want and want some more?

Making her want only him?

"Magnus." As he entered the gallery, she inclined her head slightly in greeting, pleased that her voice held a knife-edge of ice. Still, the sight of him in snug, worn jeans and black T-shirt under a leather jacket caused a momentary weakness in her knees. His blond hair was windblown, his blue eyes intense, his mouth a grim slash in that strong, square jaw of his.

He glanced around. "Can we talk in private?"

Should she tell him no one else was here at the moment? Yeah, right, and make him think she was issuing an invitation to depravity? Hell, no.

"This is fine. It's a slow day."

Instead of speaking, he turned from her and perused the nearest artworks. After a moment he said to the wall, "If you want to rescind the contract, that's fine with me."

Kat fought to keep her voice crisp. "Are you saying you want to withdraw your works?"

"No. I just—thought you might want that option."

"I believe I told you once before, I've represented difficult artists in the past, and I'm sure I'll have more in the future. Something about artistic temperament. It goes with the territory. I try not to allow my personal feelings to color my professional judgment."

He cleared his throat. He still hadn't turned to face her. "Look, about the other night—"

"Don't worry about it, Mr. Thorvald. It's a non-issue. We're both adults."

"Right." He turned slowly. "If you have any questions about my sculptures—"

"I have Rolf's number. I'll be in touch."

"Right," he said again.

A long, silent moment passed. *Go,* she pleaded silently. *I can't stand to see you so distant, so cold.* She didn't dare stare at him. Her gaze flitted around the gallery and darted back to him a couple of times against her will. It looked to Kat as though he did the same.

Finally, he spun on his heel and, without another word, walked out the door.

Kat's knees felt weak. She barely made it back to the antique desk where she kept the receipts and credit card equipment, and fell into the antique chair. *You will not cry. No man is worth your tears.*

The door opened again. Kat's heart skipped a beat. *Magnus?*

"Was that your wood sculptor I saw pulling away in that truck like a bat out of hell?"

"Oh. Hi, Lyss. Yes, that was my client."

Lyssa's eyes narrowed. "Okay, what happened?"

"What do you mean?"

"Don't you dare stonewall me, Kat. This is your best friend you're talking to. You know darn well you can't pull the wool over my eyes. The other night he had you creaming your thong. Today he's 'my client'? What gives?"

"Hello, do you remember exactly what transpired that night?"

"Oooh, yes, I almost jumped Savidge after watching you two in action. It was only after you introduced me to Savidge that I understood what the Platinum Society is all about. It's not dirty. It's a turn-on."

Kat's mouth curled up in a parody of a smile. "Tell that to the guest of honor. He thinks I'm a whore."

"Kat, no! How did you ever reach that conclusion?"

"What he *said*, not what he did. He said, and I quote, 'I primed the pump for your Platinum friends.' He was showing me just what he thought of me, of us."

Lyssa sat a hip on the desk and leaned toward Kat. "And what did you do?"

"Good grief, Lyss, I don't want to relive that debacle! You know damn well what I did. I begged him! And what did he do? He threw it back in my face!"

"Get a grip, girlfriend." Lyssa stood and plunked her hands on her hips. "He showed you something about yourself."

Kat buried her face in her hands. Her voice came out muffled. "I know. He showed me just what kind of a floozy I really am."

"Well, I never thought I'd see the day."

Reluctantly, Kat looked up. "What?"

"The day that you wimped out."

"What do you mean?"

"The Kathryn Ondov Donaldson I know would fight for what she wanted. This one is just giving up—" she snapped her fingers " —like that?"

"You didn't see the expression on his face. He couldn't even look at me!"

"Did you ever hear the saying, 'you can't see the forest for the trees'?"

Kat nodded. "But what's that got to do with anything?"

"You don't have a clue what you learned about yourself that night?"

"I told you—"

"Think, girlfriend, think! You learned that you didn't want to diddle with Savidge after all those years of trying to grab his cock."

"Well, sure, he's your—"

"But you also didn't want Jules."

"Lyss, he's so submissive, I could never—"

"And," Lyssa rode right over Kat's words, "you didn't want anyone else, either." Her eyes sparkled. "What does that tell you about yourself?"

Kat fidgeted. She didn't want to admit what her friend was driving at, because it was too painful to contemplate.

"You finally met your match!" Lyssa crowed.

"For all the good it did," Kat said morosely.

"Then you agree?"

"I repeat. What good does it do me to find out I'm hooked on Magnus when he doesn't want anything more to do with me?"

"Wait. You said he's your client. So he hasn't backed out, right?"

Kat nodded.

"So you have all that time preparing his exhibit, you have the cocktail reception to show him off to the art world, you have all those sales to report to him... Girlfriend, if you can't win him over in the next six months, you aren't the Kat Donaldson I think you are!"

Chapter Sixteen

෪

Magnus set down the 320-grit sandpaper and reached for the sable-bristled brush. Almost smooth enough, he decided as he carefully brushed flecks of wood dust from the curves and planes of that face that continued to haunt him. He angled the gooseneck lamp one way and then another, studied the smooth cherry surface as light and shadow played over her cheekbones, eyelids, mouth.

Oh, that mouth. He knew he'd never be able to capture the full sensuality of it, the feel of it milking his cock of every drop.

"Shit."

Annoyed at himself, he tossed the brush onto the worktable. He'd vowed not to think of her in a sexual way again, of the way she puddled all over his fingers, the way her eyes glazed over when near a climax, the rosy glow on her satin skin. The way she'd been helpless against the restraints but yearning from his sensual onslaught.

The way she'd begged him for his cock.

He pushed himself off the stool and began pacing the limited width of the workroom.

"Double shit." What the hell had he been thinking? How could he have thought it a good idea to have her handcuffed and helpless, then done what he'd done to her in front of an audience? No matter if they were jaded rich folk who swapped partners. What kind of man was *he*, to take out his frustration on her like that?

More to the point, how could he purge the maddening Kat Donaldson from his mind?

The woman bedeviled him. If he believed in witches, he'd have said she cast a spell over him. He'd never wanted a woman the way he wanted Kat. And, dammit, it didn't make sense. They were oil and water. Fire and tinder. She was promiscuous. He was a one-woman man.

But oh, how sublimely she fit against him! How she sparked a fire in him like he'd never experienced before. That soft, demanding mouth sucking his cock. That hot, wet pussy weeping for him. The fire in her hair, the sultry heat in her eyes. The damn woman had gotten under his skin like a tick in summer.

There was only way to get rid of her. He had to fuck her until the fever broke.

Hell, that was one image he could do without. He needed a cold shower.

"No, dammit. What I need is a brain transplant."

Shaking his head, Magnus studied the half-completed sculpture. He'd never exhibit this one. It was too personal. He'd poured every ounce of love and attention that he had into it. It would be like selling his firstborn child.

The image immobilized him. What would a child of his and Kat's be like? Would it have her fiery auburn glory or his blond hair? Her amber eyes or his blue ones?

One thing for sure. It would be stubborn.

"Jesus. Not a brain transplant. I need a lobotomy." He strode to the small mirror over the wash-up sink in the corner and stared at his reflection. Haunted eyes, with dark smudges beneath them. Two-day-old beard stubble. Rat's-nest hair that hadn't seen a comb since he'd made an ass of himself at Kat's gallery, offering to rescind the agency contract. Damn, he was still ambivalent, wishing she'd get out of his life at the same time he craved her like his next breath.

"I need a life." He turned on the faucet, ducked his head and splashed cold water over his face. Raising up, he glanced into the mirror again. Droplets of water clung to his eyelashes, his whiskers. "What day is today? I'll go to Soren's bar and drown my thoughts in a bottle of cheap liquor. And see who's playing tonight."

The thought of Dwayne's mellow saxophone playing bluesy jazz conjured up images of dancing skintight next to Kat.

Scratch that idea.

Hell. Speaking of scratch, he had a constant itch that only Kat could scratch.

"Dammit! Is everything I say or think going to be superimposed onto that she-cat?"

After a quick swipe of his wet face with a paper towel, Magnus took the stairs two at a time and headed for the shower. A cold shower.

He wondered if he had the stamina to go cold-turkey to purge a particular maddening woman out of his system.

* * * * *

"Okay, you're a professional. You have questions you have to ask the client. And they can't wait, because the show date is looming closer and closer." Like a mantra, Kat listed all the cogent reasons she found herself bumping down Magnus' rutted driveway at six-thirty on an already dark evening. She refused to articulate the one overarching reason that clung like a burr to the back of her brain. Magnus himself.

And the fact that he'd so effortlessly walked away from her after handcuffing her to the ceiling, the shit. Even though she'd begged him to fuck her. Even though the depth of his desire showed loud and clear in the size and hardness of his cock beneath his trousers. It was obvious to Kat that he was trying to prove a point—that he could arouse her as well as himself and still walk away.

"Well, not this time, buddy. If I have to handcuff you to that sleigh bed myself…"

She gasped as a big pothole caught a wheel of her Beemer and jolted some sense into her. "I will *not* initiate sex. I will just be *there*. In your face. Alluring. Available. Well, maybe not blatantly advertising that I'm available. I'll just be so goddamn innately sexy that you won't be able to resist my charms."

But the specter of being rejected by a man she'd come to care for and respect churned her stomach. She'd never before met a man who wouldn't say yes, and she didn't understand it. She *knew* he wanted her. Besides, she had so much to offer. She was attractive, witty, savvy in the art world, and deeply believed in his talent. Why wouldn't he accept what she was so willing to give?

She scrutinized the looming stone barn for telltale signs of life. The French doors in the upstairs office were dark, as was the rear window on the near side...his bedroom. Rounding the curve, she saw only darkness in the downstairs workshop, too, but a soft yellow light glowed from the two upstairs windows in the front of the apartment. The kitchenette and the bathroom.

A smile tipped up the corners of her mouth. Could she be lucky enough to catch him in the shower? Or maybe he was eating another lonely sandwich dinner in that primitive kitchen? Or were they simply night-lights for when he returned in the middle of the night after easing his itch with some other woman? *That* thought made her stomach clench. Quickly she shoved it to the back of her mind.

She couldn't see anything in the garage, but she knew he had several farm vehicles, so he could either be out driving any one of them or have them locked up for the night.

Turning the headlights down to parking lights, she slowly negotiated the half-circle around the barn. "I'm not trying to hide the fact that I'm here," she told the crisp, cold air around her. "I'm just being sensitive to the environment. I don't want to awaken any wildlife that's bedded down in the area."

Right. She wasn't sneaking, she really wasn't, but she figured she'd better park the Beemer so it wouldn't be readily visible by anyone driving down the driveway. When she got out at the office side of the barn, she quietly closed the door behind her. The half moon shed enough silvery light to allow her to find the hiding place Rolf had told her about. She lifted an innocuous-looking chunk of dead tree-root tucked under an evergreen shrub, turned it over, and extracted the spare house key from an ingenious jigsaw-puzzle opening that pulled apart easily.

Should she knock? Or just sneak in and hope to find him *au naturel*?

"Get a grip," she muttered. "This is strictly business." Why else would she be schlepping her attaché case containing the itemized list on which she'd made notes and questions?

Taking a deep breath, she lifted her hand and rapped several times. Waited. Rapped again. "Face it," she told herself. "Either he's not there or he knows it's you and he's hiding."

Dare she?

Oh, yeah, she dared. If he was in there, she wasn't going to let him get away with hiding. If he wasn't, no harm done. He'd never know his castle had been briefly occupied by an invading army of one spurned female. She shrugged then inserted the key in the lock.

At the exact moment she swung the door open, the outside lights flared into life. She let out an unladylike squeak of surprise. The attaché case slid from her boneless fingers. Light flooded through the uncurtained picture windows, illuminating a wide swath of Magnus' office.

Illuminating Magnus.

Magnificently nude, and dripping wet.

Holding a baseball bat in one hand. His other hand rested on a wall switch.

"Don't move or I'll smash your skull." His voice was a low, threatening growl. He moved forward like a lion stalking an injured gazelle, both hands now gripping the bat as he raised it to shoulder height.

Kat's vocal cords seemed frozen. Her boots felt nailed to the floor as she drank in the fluid movement of masculine muscle and sinew as Magnus came nearer. It occurred to her that he didn't recognize her silhouette, standing as she was in a swing coat, with her back to the outside light, her flyaway hair tucked underneath a knitted cloche.

"You!" Eyes narrowed, he lowered the bat, holding it loosely at his side. "I thought someone was trying to break in. How the hell did you get the door open?"

"Magnus." Her voice came out no better than a relieved croak at his recognition. She'd hoped he wouldn't attack first and ask questions later. The strength in her legs dissipated like fog in a breeze and she sagged against the French door, the key still in the lock. He looked like a primeval Viking chief, resplendent in his nakedness, beads of water shimmering on his eyebrows, his chest hair, his...

Good lord. Even flaccid, his penis looked at least a handspan's length, and his balls hung heavy and full amid the thick, wiry pubic hair several shades darker than elsewhere. His feet were planted in a warrior's ready stance, far enough apart that she could kneel between them and take his cock in her—

With an effort she shook the tantalizing vision from her mind and pulled her reluctant gaze from his groin to his face. And blanched at the thunderous expression there.

"I can explain, Magnus." She reached down to retrieve the attaché case that had fallen at her feet. "When no one answered the door, I thought I'd just leave the file with my questions..."

"How did you get in?" Another growl, like a Doberman preparing to attack.

"R-Rolf. He told me about the spare key." She cleared her throat, tried to preempt him. "You know, that tree-root hidey-

hole is a marvelous piece of work that should be included in—
"

Magnus flung the bat aside. The clatter made Kat flinch. The attaché case slipped from her fingers and bounced back onto the floor with a dull thud. He took another step closer. Kat stood her ground. She would show him he couldn't intimidate her with his overabundance of naked testosterone and male attitude.

"Pillow talk?" he murmured. "He's giving away family secrets to strangers? You fuck him silly until he doesn't know which way is up, and then pump him for information?"

"How dare you jump to conclusions!" Kat didn't realize her hand had come up until she heard the resounding slap of her palm against his cheek. Instantly she regretted her rash action. Horrified at what her unconscious mind had ordered her to do, she began to mumble an apology.

He didn't give her a chance. "So, you like to play rough, do you?" Grabbing both her wrists, he maneuvered them behind her back, held them in one massive hand while the other slipped her silk scarf from around her neck. In the blink of an eye, he'd double-wrapped it around her hands and tied a knot of some sort, immobilizing her arms.

"Jesus, not again. Untie me, you Neanderthal!" Her eyes flashed enough fire that he should have been burned to a crisp as she immediately tried to free her wrists.

Taking hold of her shoulders, he pinned her against the wall. "I can play rough, too. Do allow me to join in the fun."

Even with her three-inch boot heels, he was several inches taller, and Kat had to look up to glare at him. She wanted to push him away. She wanted him to kiss her. She wanted her hands free to touch him, dammit! How could he be so nonchalant about his nudity when he'd given her every impression of being a prude? "Why do you insist on thinking that I'll screw anything in pants?"

"Isn't that what Platinum Society people do?"

"I haven't done anything with anyone else since I met you."

"Is that right?" he murmured into her ear, his breath fanning the delicate shell of it. "Then tell me, please, what transpired after I left the party. After I left you wet and damn near naked and begging for a cock."

Kat resisted the urge to spit in his face. "I was begging for *your* cock, if your pea-brain can remember that far back."

"And who was the lucky guy who wound up giving you some relief from your craving?"

"Nobody, dammit. I didn't want anyone else."

"That's not what I heard."

"You heard wrong, buster. Yeah, sure, Savidge came nosing around, kissing me, stroking me. I thought he'd gone stupid, what with Lyssa keeping him so satisfied, and I told him so. Then Lyssa sandwiched me between her and Savidge. Tell the truth, I'm glad she's getting over her sexual hang-ups, but I didn't want a threesie. Especially with those two. I mean, she's my best friend. That makes him off-limits, because he's hers."

"Mmm. Such scruples. So they unlocked the cuffs and you went home right away? No one else sought to avail himself of your charms? Someone, say, with a cat-o'-nine tails?"

Kat narrowed her eyes. "Who's feeding you this stuff?"

"You mean I'm wrong?"

An exasperated sigh escaped her. She tugged her bound hands against the scarf again, but nothing budged. She tried to worm a finger into the knot. "No, you're not wrong. Jules Rubin wanted to help. You met him that night."

"Ah, yes, the young man who made moon-eyes at you. Who tried to come to your rescue when I pulled you aside and said we had unfinished business."

"Yes. Jules is a perfect gentleman, if you must know." She tossed her head with more bravado than she felt.

"A gentleman. Who flogs beautiful women with a cat-o'-nine tails."

"Dammit, nobody flogged me. I wouldn't allow it."

"But you were handcuffed to the ceiling." He all but crooned it. "How could you stop someone if he really had his heart set on a little S&M?"

"I made damn sure everyone remembered I was on the board of directors. Believe me, they listen when I give an unequivocal order."

"Mmmm. You're telling me that all the men in the Platinum Society jump to do your bidding."

"Well, no. Savidge never... I mean, actually, yes, he was the one with the key to the cuffs. So when I asked him—" She wasn't going to tell him how many times she'd asked. " —he set me free. I hope Lyssa wasn't disappointed that I didn't, you know, give her the experience of a typical man's ultimate fantasy."

"And that would be...?"

She threw him a withering glance that seemed to bounce right off him. "You know exactly what I mean. One man, two women. One pussy in each hand. Or licking one woman's cunt while the other sucks your cock." She made it as explicit, as raunchy, as she could, just to see if she could get his goat. He was provoking her, dammit, and she was mad as hell about it.

Provoking her in more ways than one. Her gaze hadn't left his during their verbal sparring, but she could see in her peripheral vision that his cock kept growing, thickening, as they talked. Good. Let him have blue balls just from talking. Men always talked dirty to women, thinking to make them hornier. Well, hooray for equal opportunity. She was living proof that women could dish out crude language with the best of them. And she hoped to hell she was making him hornier. Because she was getting wet just thinking of his big, hard, *naked* body only inches from her. In two minutes, whether she'd gotten loose from the damned scarf or not, she'd drop to her knees and suck him off, just to prove to him that he wasn't as strong, as unaffected by her, as he tried to pretend.

"What about when a woman wants two men? How did you go about setting that up?"

Kat wrenched her wrists against the binding. Had she loosened it a tad by working the knot with her fingernails? "None of your frickin' business!"

Relentlessly he kept up his attack. "Are you afraid of offending my tender sensibilities by telling me how you much you enjoy having something in every orifice at the same time?"

Her eyelids fluttered closed against the sting of tears. She did *not* want to be having this conversation with Magnus. She'd only done threesies once in her life, with twins, just for the novelty of it. She'd rate the experience a C-plus. Pleasant, like most of her sexual encounters, not at all like what Magnus had done to her the other night at the cocktail party, a ten on the Richter scale, and he hadn't even let her climax.

He'd made it obvious how much he despised her past. Why did he keep hammering at what she'd done before she'd met him? It didn't feel like he was doing it to titillate himself or her, more like punishing both of them for sins she'd committed during her butterfly days—punishing her for committing those acts, punishing him for still wanting her even though she'd sinned.

Butterfly days. Those were gone as surely as if she'd been exiled to outermost Mongolia. She wanted Magnus and only Magnus. She'd never be promiscuous again. She wanted him—to fuck him, yes, but also to be with him, to share things with him, to make him a star in the art world. God help her, to grow old together.

Something must have showed in her eyes, because Magnus bent his head a fraction, skimmed his mouth over hers, lightly, tantalizingly. "Penny for your thoughts."

Then he drew back, just as she felt the heat, the pressure of his rampant cock through the opening in her swing coat.

"I'm thinking you should untie me," she rasped, working the scarf looser another millimeter behind her back. *Because I'm going to come just thinking about you and I don't want to do it alone.*

He made a rude sound. "Just when you're becoming so biddable? I don't think so."

She switched gears. "Look, it's getting warm in here. Don't forget, I'm bundled up with a long woolen coat, hat, sweater, skirt, socks, et cetera. All you're wearing is…" she paused, a hitch in her throat, "…a smile."

"Why, so I am."

"So this isn't an even playing field. I'm sweating in here, and you're cool as a…" She gulped. Do *not* think of cucumbers, those firm, fleshy, thick… "as an ice cube," she finished lamely.

His smile stretched wider, until it was a full-fledged grin. "It's so nice to have the upper hand for a change."

With a triumphant grunt, she pulled one hand free of the silk scarf. "I'll give you upper hands," she retorted as she shrugged out of her coat and ripped off her hat to allow her wild hair to cascade down around her shoulders.

In three seconds she was down on her knees, her mouth hungrily devouring his cock while her hands, the scarf still dangling from one wrist, kneaded his ass cheeks and held him as close as she could without suffocating herself.

"Jesus, woman," he groaned. "Are you trying to kill me?"

She mumbled an indecipherable response around that formidable mouthful as she drank in the salty, soapy taste of him, the feel of his hot skin sliding in and out of her mouth.

Magnus felt his knees go weak as her sexy mouth closed around him. He refused to let her set him off like a short-fuse rocket, the way she'd done the other day, but he knew it was only a matter of seconds. Inside—he needed to be inside her. *Now.*

He reached down, anchored his hands under her armpits and dragged her to her feet. Her mouth, oh God, her mouth looked swollen and red from sucking on him. Quick change of plan. He hauled her tight against his naked length and plunged his tongue into her mouth, one hand behind her head to hold her captive, the other grabbing the hem of the fuzzy red sweater she wore. Like a clumsy sophomore in the backseat of a Chevy, he shoved it up over those glorious tits and fitted his hand around one of them.

The tiny part of his mind that wasn't thinking with his cock marveled at the fact that she wasn't wearing a bra. Her nipple was hard and tight under his palm. He bent down to pull that little acorn into his mouth with none of the finesse he'd displayed when she'd been handcuffed. He was starving for the taste, the feel of her naked against his skin. His hands were everywhere—skimming up and down her back, around her waist and rib cage, pressing her tits together with his face between them, suckling one, then the other, until he thought he'd go mad.

With an inarticulate sound of impatience, he yanked her sweater higher. "Lift your arms," he growled, and jerked the offending garment up and over her head. Her fire-lit hair cascaded down in wispy bunches, draping over one eye and pooling on her shoulders.

"God, you're beautiful," he rasped. For a moment he just stood there, voraciously drinking in every smooth inch of her skin silhouetted in the light.

The light.

Jesus, they were ready to fuck like rabbits and the front door stood wide open, the outer floodlights bathing the office—and them—as though it was Times Square on New Year's Eve. Yeah, they were in the middle of nowhere and yeah, it was dark, but holy hell, what if Rolf had come barging in on them? Brother or no brother, Magnus had no intention of sharing Kat with him. Or with anyone.

"Hold that thought." His voice creaked like a rusty hinge. He strode to the door, yanked the key out of the outside lock, and slammed the door. A snick of the lock from the inside, and he was back at her side in seconds, but seemed to him like hours of deprivation.

In one easy swoop, he lifted her, one arm around her bare back and shoulders, the other under her knees. Her long, billowy skirt wrapped itself around his thighs as he strode through the darkened office, into the kitchen and on to the bedroom, invading her mouth with fast, hard strokes of his tongue so she'd have absolutely no uncertainty about what he was planning to do next.

As if she didn't want the same thing he did. Jesus, she gave him back every torrid stroke, wrapped her arms around his neck, pressing her tits into his bare chest and damn near climbing up on his shoulders to get a better, tighter grip on him.

His muscles tensed to lift her high enough to toss her onto the bed when she spoke.

"Stop."

No way no way nowaynoway, his mind was shouting. Stopping was the very last thing on his to-do list between now and the end of next month.

"I just want to get more comfortable first," she murmured, licking the outer edge of his ear and making him damn near drop her from the pleasure rocketing through him.

He allowed her to slide down the length of his body, her naked tits plumping upward as they scraped against his chest, the delicious friction almost unmanning him. She took a step back from him, toed off her ankle boots. He knew what she was doing—paying him back for leaving her frustrated and handcuffed. The devilish gleam in her eyes told him that loud and clear.

Her skin was all rosy and glowing. Her mouth was pure sex, and her tits, her perfect tits were as swollen as her lips, the nipples pointing right at him. It took all of his control to allow her this moment in the spotlight.

Slowly, like a seasoned stripper, she unhooked the waistband of her skirt and slid the zipper down. Her gaze locked onto his as she let go of the fabric and the material slithered to the floor in a black puddle.

His eyes followed its movement. Naked. She wasn't even wearing a thong. The small fluff of hair at her crotch was the same color as the rest of her hair, flaming red.

All his control shattered. In one fluid movement, he lifted her by the waist, sat her on the edge of the high mattress, yanked those long, shapely legs around him and thrust into her. A primitive, guttural sound escaped from deep within as he felt her pussy closing around him, squeezing, milking him. Grabbing her hips, he slammed his cock into her again and again, needing to get closer and yet closer to her. Dear God, he'd never felt anything so good. She was warm and wet and welcoming, and he was going to come if he didn't —

Condom. Buried deep within her, his cock throbbing, he froze. Dammit, dammit, dammit!

"Don't stop," she breathed, digging her nails into his ass cheeks and clenching her legs even tighter around his hips. "I don't want you to ever stop."

"Kat — protection," he managed to gasp. Sweat popped out on his forehead from the effort of holding back.

"Got it covered." Her eyes glowed with feral lust as she contracted her inner muscles to hold him captive. "I was a Boy Scout in a previous life."

Magnus was too far gone to chuckle. All he could think of was the exquisite feel of her hot satin rubbing against his hard cock, flesh to flesh, without that intrusive latex membrane between them. Man, woman. Primitive. Visceral. Elemental. He moved again, wanting to slow down his pace, but she was having none of it. She egged him on, writhing under him, taking nips of his chest skin with her teeth, tilting her pelvis to guide him deeper and deeper into her, until he couldn't tell where he ended and she began.

With one last mighty thrust, Magnus exploded. Too soon. Way too soon. He let out a sound that was part groan, part triumph, all conquering male. He felt himself coming in an endless stream, as though he'd waited all his life for this one chance to shoot his life force deep into her. His legs felt like rubber retreads flung to the side of the highway, but he managed to stay upright with his knees braced against the mattress, her writhing hips held firmly in his grip. Kat was matching him, spasm for spasm, moan for moan. Through slitted eyes he watched the tension ratchet up in her face and then let go as she reached her own climax. Her beautiful teak eyes lost their focus and she shuddered and quivered and then went limp against his chest.

A long time later, after a half dozen more climaxes, they fell into exhausted slumber.

Chapter Seventeen

ಬಿ

Kat awakened to the unfamiliar sound of absolute silence. And to an unfamiliar, but pleasant, ache. She stretched luxuriously, a lazy smile on her face, as though she'd received the best Christmas present in the world. Her hands wandered down the length of her torso to the source of that ache. The muscles and tendons on her inner thighs felt stretched, almost bruised. Her pussy, too. Idly she stroked the slit with one long finger. Swollen. Damp. *Well used.*

The synapses in her brain finally fired. *Magnus.* Oh God, she was in Magnus' sleigh bed. Naked. With shafts of weak, early-morning sunlight making small rhomboids of design on the floor through the many-paned windows. She'd obviously fallen asleep at some point during the night, and he'd let her stay.

Images flooded her mind. The first mind-blowing fuck, neither of them able to wait until they were ensconced in the comfort of the mattress. The second time not much slower, both of them as hungry as if they'd been hermits for the past decade.

She swallowed hard. Now she'd done it. He'd really think her a whore, with his Puritan mentality and her uninhibited behavior. No one had ever tapped into her inner hunger the way Magnus had, a Viking chieftain in his prime. She remembered kissing, licking every inch of his magnificent body, looking and tasting her fill, with the bedclothes kicked to the floor and the huge mattress their playground. Sucking his cock ranked right up there with a private tour of the Louvre or the Prado. He was so huge, so damn responsive, she couldn't get enough of it.

149

But where was he now? With an uncertainty she'd never experienced before, she sat up cautiously, holding the sheet in front of her breasts in some unaccustomed attempt at modesty. She reached over to his side of the bed and ran her palm over the indentation in his pillow, then along the mattress. Both felt cool. He'd been up for some while.

Had he sat watching her sleep, reliving the earthquakes they'd created together? Had he been disgusted with himself for showing his own hunger and gone running away or chopping wood or otherwise letting loose some self-directed anger?

Had he been unable to face her and abandoned her to shift for herself?

Insecurity settled over her like a scratchy blanket. She'd always taken what she wanted sexually and thought no more about it than if she'd dipped out some ice cream. But with Magnus, it was anything but impersonal. She wanted him in her life, in her bed. She wanted to be embedded so deep in his mind that she was never far from his consciousness.

A soft *clink* caught her attention. A spoon in a coffee cup?

The thought of caffeine galvanized her. She needed a big dose of it this morning. Starbucks would be too much to hope for out here in the middle of nowhere, but any old kind would do for her first eye-opener.

Kat swung her feet off the mattress, then remembered the considerable distance to the floor. Leaning forward to peer down, she was unaccountably touched that the stepstool was right where her feet could land on it. She took the two steps down, suddenly aware of her nakedness. She glanced back at the bed. He'd straightened and tucked the bedcovers properly when he'd pulled the blanket around her. Should she mess everything up and yank out a sheet to wrap around herself?

Wait. Hadn't she dropped her skirt on the other side of the bed?

That still didn't produce the sweater, which Magnus had flung somewhere in a corner of the office when he'd ripped it off her. Well, she could always wear the skirt like a *serape*, draped over her shoulders. It was long enough and flared enough to cover what needed to be covered.

And she had to pee. She hoped he had a functioning bathroom in this Civil War-era barn. Outhouses weren't her style.

Indecision rested poorly on her shoulders. She stood, naked as a newborn, with her hand unconsciously stroking the curved scroll at the footrest when she heard the rumble of the barn doors opening. A moment later an engine fired up. From the heavy growl of it, she thought it might be his three-quarter-ton truck that Rolf had used to deliver the heavy carvings to her gallery. She followed the sound as it curved around the barn.

The coward! He was leaving her alone because he couldn't face the morning after. She hurried to the window in time to see the black truck raising one hell of a rooster plume of dust and gravel up the driveway. Then it disappeared from view.

Kat didn't know whether to laugh or cry.

That *clink* she'd thought might be a spoon against a cup was probably the front door latch closing. With a deep sigh, she arose and pulled her skirt on, then went searching for her sweater and boots. Suitably armored, warmer, and feeling less vulnerable, she wandered around, opening the few doors she found, finally finding the bathroom, a small space off the bedroom. She relieved herself, splashed water on her face. Picked up his tube of plain toothpaste with no bells-and-whistles additives, squished out a dab and finger-brushed her teeth.

Thus fortified, she glanced at the shower, wondering briefly how Magnus' large body could negotiate inside such a small space without banging elbows on the walls.

Not good. It conjured up images of a very nude, very virile Magnus standing arrogantly under a fall of hot water, washing his muscular body, reaching between his legs to soap his cock, his balls, stroking them lazily as he thought of her…

Not good at all. If he was afraid to face her in the morning, well, she'd gotten what she wished for, hadn't she? Magnus, all magnificent nine inches of him, banging into her like a finely tuned racecar piston, bringing her to orgasm upon orgasm, as talented and thorough as she'd imagined him…and then some.

Coffee. She really should be thinking of coffee, instead of following that dead-end.

After a cursory exam of his meager stock of foodstuffs on the haphazardly placed shelves and finding only coagulated dregs of instant crystals in the bottom of a jar, she settled for a swallow of orange juice, right from the half-gallon jug.

The unfamiliar sting of tears at the backs of her eyeballs irked her. "I will *not* cry. I'm a big girl. I can handle rejection."

If she thought about it, she'd say that most things came easily to her. The men, the education, the vocation. She'd even lucked into the gallery, buying at an opportune time and making a name for herself through a combination of her outgoing personality, knowledge of the art field, and sheer persistence. She hadn't really had to fight for what she wanted.

And she wanted Magnus.

So she would learn how to fight. With teeth bared and nails sharpened, if need be. If he didn't yet know they were meant to be together, she'd just have to show him.

Meanwhile, there was such a thing as strategic retreat, so she could live to fight another day.

* * * * *

Okay, he'd gotten Kat Donaldson out of his system. How many times could one couple have mind-blowing sex, anyway? They'd already had their allotment and then some. It was bound to be all downhill from now on.

Even his wannabe porn-star ex-wife hadn't had such expertise. But then, she hadn't belonged to a sex club of rich society types who could pay for any exotic or depraved experience.

And that was the thing Magnus couldn't get his mind around. Kat was no more than a whore, sleeping with anyone and everyone. It was wrong, no matter that she'd learned it at her mother's knee. To his shame, he wasn't immune to the allure of her. He was hardwired as a twenty-first-century man, dammit. And Kat was the sexiest, most beautiful, most satisfying woman he'd ever met. So he'd been thinking with his cock. Most men did at one time or another.

That was changing. Right now. He'd start thinking with his brain. He'd avoid her both business-wise and personally. He'd let Rolf be his intermediary—

Hell, he couldn't let Rolf within three miles of her. Not after seeing them together in his bedroom, Kat lying on his sleigh bed with a satisfied grin on her face, Rolf looking down at her with love-struck eyes. He couldn't do it. Couldn't take the chance. That lusty Valkyrie would chew Rolf up and spit him out. He had to protect his little brother.

Yeah, right. That excuse wouldn't get you an ice cube in heaven. He let out a raw oath as he took the last turn of the detour that had added ten minutes to what should have been a quick in-and-out to the local donut shop. "Who are you kidding? You know you need another night with her, just to be sure you've gotten over this sick fascination."

A few more anxious minutes behind a slow-moving tractor hauling a loaded hay wagon and he was screeching around the curve into his driveway. "Shit." Her BMW was doing an uphill slalom around his potholes. He spun the wheel to swerve diagonally, blocking her path, and braked to a gravel-scattering halt.

Shoving the gear into park, he jumped out and reached her car in three long strides. "I didn't think I'd be this long," he said as her window rolled down.

Her eyes were as huge as doe eyes, not quite afraid, but wary. Hell, it hadn't been his intention to scare her. He just didn't want her to maneuver that sporty car past his clunky truck without at least saying…something.

Damn. He ran a big hand through his blond hair. By now it probably looked like a compost pile, he'd done that so many times already today. "Look, I know it's not very civilized down there." He gestured to the vicinity of the barn. "I thought I'd be back before you woke…"

His voice was getting reedy just thinking of her waking up in his bed. He cleared his throat. "I ran into a detour on my way to Doylestown, but that's the only place I know of around here that has good takeout coffee. I didn't think that jar of leftover coffee crumbs was very appetizing." Talk about understatement.

She just kept looking at him. Obviously she wasn't going to make it easy for him.

"I figured you for a coffee person," he tried. "So I went out to get some."

"You went out for coffee? For me?"

Damn, she didn't have to sound so surprised. He'd learned good manners from his Mom and his Grandda. "Uh, yeah. I also got some breakfast. A selection of donuts and muffins. If you're hungry, that is. If you'd like to join me."

Something inside Kat melted. He had a gallant streak he probably didn't even realize. She'd love to stay with him, but they'd probably spend the day the way they spent the previous night, fucking until they were both exhausted. Because Magnus was like a potato chip…you couldn't eat just one. Or three. And his opinion of her would still be in the sewer. She wouldn't make it any worse than it already was.

154

"That's so sweet of you," she said. "But I really should be going. I have several appointments this morning."

"Right. Of course. I have a lot of work, too."

She smiled. "I wouldn't mind having one for the road, though."

For a long moment he stared at her, as if debating whether she meant a kiss or a coffee. "Oh yeah, sure. If you promise not to drive around me and hightail it out of here, I'll go back to the truck and bring you some."

He returned with a cardboard carton holding four white cups in heatproof collars. "I wasn't sure what you liked, so I got a couple of plain black — they're the ones in front — one black with French vanilla, and one black with hazelnut. Sugar and creamers on the side."

Choosing the vanilla, Kat stuffed it into the car's cup holder, flipped off the top, and added two creamers. As though reading her mind, he handed her a swizzle stick through her open window. After a slow stir, she took a long sip. And sighed. "Ah, heaven. Just what the doctor ordered." She turned her head to thank him.

And came within inches of his face. Magnus, right arm resting on her roof, left hand propped on her side-view mirror, head framed through the window opening, his eyes focused on her mouth. Heat that had nothing to do with coffee slithered through her as she watched his pupils dilate.

Oh yeah, he still wanted her. But Kat was realistic enough to know that he resented that desire. So she wouldn't give him the chance to surrender to it.

A sidelong glance to her car's clock showed it was about seven-thirty. She'd better move. Rice's was already open. "How do you get to Rice's Market from here?"

He blinked. "What's that?"

"You haven't heard of them? It's a famous flea-market kind of place off Aquatong Road. Draws hundreds of vendors. I go there to get my baskets."

"You go all the way from Bryn Mawr to Aquatong Road just to get baskets?"

Kat suppressed the urge to smile at his utterly masculine reaction to what he probably thought of as a female obsession with shopping. "Not just baskets. Sure, I buy my baskets there, but I also fill them with things and then distribute them to a group I work with."

"I see."

He didn't, Kat was sure of it. But she didn't have time to chat. "They're only open twice a week. From seven to one. I thought Rice's might be near here. I can always backtrack down Route 611 until I see something familiar…"

Magnus slapped a palm on the roof of her car. "Come back down to the barn. I have a big map of upper Bucks County. We'll find it." Without waiting for her acquiescence, he strode to his truck and, backing up a smidge, negotiated it around her car and down the driveway.

"Well, since you put it that way…" With a resigned huff, Kat maneuvered the Beemer in a series of K-turns until its nose pointed toward the barn, and followed him.

By the time she parked next to his truck at the upper level and entered the cavernous office, Magnus had unfolded a large map onto the conference table and was bent over it. "Show me how you get to this Rice's."

Coming alongside him, Kat became newly aware of his height, his strength. Snug jeans cradled muscled thighs. A University of Pennsylvania sweatshirt covered broad shoulders. His blond hair spiked in places where he'd run his hands through it.

Reluctantly, she drew her gaze to the map. Getting her bearings from Route 611, she traced a scarlet fingernail to Aquatong Road and then to Greenhill Road.

Magnus studied it a moment. "Here's where we are," he said, stabbing a long finger to a point marked with a hand-drawn red star. He stood to his full height and lasered a stare at her. "There's no easy way from here. Most of these are unmarked country roads. You'd probably get lost."

She opened her mouth to protest his blanket condemnation of women's directional failings, but he continued, "I'll drive you."

Her mouth stayed open.

"You have a problem with that?"

She unlocked her jaw. "No. I appreciate the offer. But I thought you had work to do."

Placing his large hands on her shoulders, Magnus turned Kat to face him. "Kat, we're both aware that everything that's happened between us has something to do with either sex or art. I'm willing to go to this place with you to see if we can stand each other in the light of day."

Swallowing hard, she said meekly, "Okay."

"I have only one requirement."

She bristled unconsciously.

"The requirement is that you eat one of these muffins on the way. I wouldn't want you to faint in the middle of five hundred vendors. They might think I beat you up or starve you or something."

With that, he hustled her through the French doors, locked up, and escorted her to his truck. She needed his help to climb up. "This thing needs a running board," she groused.

"Not when the view from here is so good," he murmured just before he slammed her door shut

* * * * *

Magnus' head was spinning. He was accustomed to early hours, but it was barely eight o'clock and he'd had to park the truck at the back end of the thirty-acre lot. The place was teeming with shoppers, browsers, buyers. Rows of tables, either inside a long building or under the cold blue sky, each with something different to coax a dollar or ten out of the eager or unwary. Clothing of all kinds, dolls, soaps and candles, hand-crafted aprons and quilts, lace tablecloths, fruits and vegetables, curtains, bird feeders, government surplus items, rocks, garden sheds, switchplates, old license plates, dog pillows and floor mats. And more.

Following Kat like a robot, he walked mechanically, head bobbing from side to side like a bobble-head doll as he tried to process the plethora of offerings. She seemed to know exactly what she wanted, slipping deftly between the press of bodies, haggling on occasion, at others looking like she'd just gotten a bargain at whatever ridiculous price marked on the item. And always, always with a kind word or friendly greeting. Many of the vendors seemed to know her by sight. These would fuss over her, sometimes reaching below the table for a package and saying, "I saved this just for you."

He watched Kat stuff her purchases into a canvas shopping bag. When that was full, she opened her purse to pull out a net bag, and proceeded to fill that one, too. Finally, eyes sparkling and face flushed, she turned to him and said, "Are you ready for some lunch? I'm starving."

It was eleven o'clock. In three hours she had purchased, by Magnus' count, forty-two packages, some by credit card, some by check, others by cash.

"You have this flea-market stuff down to a science, don't you?"

"I come here at least every other month. It's more fun than traipsing through a department store or a big-box store. You never know what's at the next table. It's like a treasure hunt. And the women are always so appreciative."

His radar went up. "What women?"

She waved the question away. "The basket vendor is on the way to my favorite food stand. I'll tell you while we eat."

If he had to guess, Magnus would have said two thousand different baskets and containers, woven from an array of raw materials, were hung overhead or displayed on shelves and tables within one interior stall. There were tiny ones that wouldn't hold more than a box of paperclips, nests of baskets in incremental sizes, big square ones like clothes hampers, sturdy trunks with fanciful animal heads on the lids, cornucopia and barrel shapes. As an artist himself, Magnus marveled at some of the more complex patterns of the weaves and designs.

He found himself carting a large shopping bag full of her baskets as he followed Kat to an old wooden barn operated by a Pennsylvania Dutch group, judging by the long dresses and white caps of the woman servers. She ordered a hot sausage hoagie with peppers and onions and a large diet cola. It smelled good, so Magnus ordered the same, with more coffee. She insisted on paying. "Since you spent gas money."

They settled on a picnic bench under a strong winter sun. *Fresh air suits her,* Magnus thought as he perused her rosy cheeks, her cold, red-tipped nose. The sun made long, feathery shadows of her eyelashes and threw red sparkles in her auburn hair. She looked…satiated. Like she did last night—

No, dammit. Don't think about how she looked after her third orgasm in his arms. The look on her face now had nothing to do with sex, with him.

Which brought him up short. After all, it was his idea to see if they had anything in common besides sex and art. He forced himself to switch gears. "Tell me about the women who are going to appreciate these goodies."

"Oh, it's just something I do on the side."

"For whom?"

She gave him a measuring look. "I have a particular interest in a local women's shelter. These women run from an abuser, sometimes with nothing but the clothes on their backs. Some of them have children they're trying to protect." She shrugged. "I just try to make them forget their problems for a few minutes."

Magnus gestured with his coffee cup to the packages stacked beside them on the picnic table. "I saw some of the stuff you bought—candy, sunglasses, hair thingies. What else did you get?"

Chewing the bite of sausage in her mouth, Kat took a sip of soda before she answered. "I have an idea. Why don't you help me sort and pack them into the baskets? That way you can see for yourself."

"Me? What do I know about sorting that kind of stuff?"

"Wasn't it the esteemed educator John Dewey who said, 'You learn by doing'? And I'll cook dinner."

"Fine." He stood abruptly. "You stay right here. I saw a couple of things I'd like to pick up. I'll be back in ten."

And he was gone.

Chapter Eighteen

ഇ

Kat glanced in her rearview mirror. Magnus had switched to his Jeep and was following her home. "Better gas mileage," he'd told her. "Besides, the black one is the farm truck, available to my brothers if they need to haul anything."

Had she gone overboard by inviting him to dinner? Did he think she wanted him to linger so they'd have sex again?

She did, of course. But she'd enjoyed being with him today, introducing him to something new, watching his eyes boggle as he tried to absorb the organized chaos around them. And they'd actually talked without fighting. She hoped things were looking up.

As she paid the turnpike toll, she mentally reviewed her food stock. She could whip up a quick shrimp scampi and risotto. Or maybe he'd like lasagna. No, that took too much preparation. She aimed the Beemer south on I-276, what locals called the Blue Route, making sure the Jeep stayed in sight behind her.

Steak. Men loved steak. She could stop at the gourmet market to get a couple of filet mignons for Tournedos Rossini.

Hey, it was just dinner, not a chef's competition. Face it, girl, to a red-blooded man, anything hot and home-cooked was probably better than an unchanging diet of cold cuts on pumpernickel bread.

By the time she pulled into her driveway on a quiet Devon street, she had resolved not to make a big deal out of dinner, but go with the flow. For all she knew, they'd wind up having mushroom omelets.

The Jeep came to a halt behind her and Magnus stepped out. "Nice place," he said, taking in the Tudor-style dwelling with pitched rooflines jutting in several directions, the still-green leaves of the rhododendron and native mountain laurel complementing the mellow brick-and-timber façade.

"Small but cozy." She was about to explain that "small" in this area meant "Only three bedrooms" but bit her tongue to keep from making any remarks about bedrooms. She'd keep this excursion platonic for as long as she could hold out, determined that he'd break first.

Gathering her purchases, she led him to the patio overlooking the in-ground pool and through the back entrance.

"I see you like French doors, too." Magnus set his shopping bag on the country table in the center of a homey great room that opened onto a spacious kitchen that was her pride and joy. He looked back through one of the many-paned doors, covered with sheer white curtains that let in filtered afternoon sunlight.

"I do. That's one of the things I fell in love with when I saw this house." Kat slipped off her swing coat and slung it on the arm of an upholstered side chair adjacent to the fireplace. Her long woolen skirt swirled around her calves as she moved. "Let me show you around."

"Wait." He walked up to the fireplace. "This looks like an Adams mantel. Is it an original?"

"Of course you'd recognize fine wood workmanship. Yes, it is an Adams. This was in a home that was targeted for demolition when they finally started constructing the Blue Route. I found it in an antique shop on Lancaster Avenue. I appreciate beauty in any form, not just what's in my gallery for sale."

He turned in a circle within the great room. "I can see that you do. Things look like they just happened to be scattered around, but a great deal of thought went behind the placement of each piece, each color." He turned his gaze on her. "You have a terrific eye. I'm glad I'm your next project."

More pleased at his praise than she wanted him to see, Kat led Magnus through a dining room furnished with a Duncan Phyfe table and six chairs upholstered with red crushed-velvet seats, into a small living room that nevertheless had room for an upright piano. Off the front hall she opened a door. "Here's a half bath if you need. I won't show you the upstairs—I want to get started on the baskets." *And I don't want you to think I'm luring you into my bedroom.*

Back at the country table, Kat moved a vase of ochre-shaded mums, unpacked her flea-market finds, and began arranging them into little piles. Magnus watched, fascinated. It was almost as if... "Do you *know* who these are going to?"

Kat looked up at him. "Yes. The woman who runs the shelter called me the other day to tell me who was there, what she thought they'd like. I just followed my instincts. This pile, for example." She pulled one batch toward her. "The woman is thirty-one, with a four-year-old boy who's too traumatized to say a word. The mother is a big woman, long brown hair, had a little garden in the backyard before her husband's pit bull dug it up. So I got..." She moved them as she spoke. "A long scarf with yellow flowers and green leaves. A couple of hair clips. An extra-large T-shirt with Little Orphan Annie and the opening line to the song 'Tomorrow'. A silk rosebud for her hair. A Hot Wheels car for the boy."

Magnus looked over at the piles. "Who's that for?"

"New-age type. Here's an aromatherapy candle, a macramé bracelet, tie-dyed cotton shirt. Herbal teas. Chamomile hand lotion. Homeopathic bone-set to help heal her broken arm."

Magnus flinched at the thought that a man would break his woman's arm. There was a world of difference between being a dominant male and being abusive. He hoped he'd never be that angry. If he didn't wring Lydia's neck when he found her making that porno movie, he probably couldn't ever be goaded into doing something so despicable as beat up a woman, no matter the provocation. He was, after all, bigger than most males, and certainly stronger than any woman he was likely to meet.

The other three piles, Magnus found, were just as thoughtfully chosen. How she did it in that whirlwind of hustle and bustle confounded him. He guessed some women were just born to shop. The only difference was, Kat shopped for others.

"Your turn."

Magnus looked up. Kat was gazing expectantly at him. She gestured to his plastic shopping bag emblazoned "Rice's Market". "Did you buy something for these women?"

He felt his ears turning hot. There was no reason he should be embarrassed at what he did. No, not embarrassment. It was an uncomfortable feeling that she would laugh at his choices, at his clumsy attempt to help, at his old-fashioned view of women.

After a moment, he reached for a smaller bag inside the carryall. "Hair brushes." He felt his Adam's apple bob up and down. "I like to see a woman brush her hair." *Or let a man do it for her.* But that didn't pertain to these women, he had to remember that. These women didn't have men in their lives who cared about them. Strangers had to help them.

"And mirrors. I haven't met a woman yet who didn't feel the urge to primp." He'd picked out a half dozen of them, some with enameled frames, some with silver backs, a couple with intricate handles, all of them a little out of the ordinary.

He chanced a look at Kat. Tears shimmered in her eyes.

"Magnus." The word was a whisper against his skin.

Clearing his throat, he pulled out one more bag. "You said some of them come with kids. I saw this cute little Raggedy Ann. It just looked so lonely on the table in the middle of kitchen junk, I thought it needed someone to give it a hug." He fought the urge to squirm at the look of compassion in her eyes. "The only things I saw for boys were things anyone would have. I remember my Grandda making all of us little pull-trains. I can carve a couple, they'd take no time at all. I can have them for you in a week."

For a long time neither of them spoke. The light outside the sheer curtains was fading. A dog barked somewhere in the distance. Nearby a car door slammed and laughing voices carried through the still evening air.

Suddenly a bright light flared through the French doors, breaking the spell.

"Oh." Kat jumped. "The floodlights are on a timer." She glanced at the clock over the stove, a black cat with its curling tail twitching every second. "Are you hungry yet? It's six o'clock. What time do you usually eat dinner?"

He shrugged. "Whenever I think of it."

"Are you hungry yet?"

His gaze burned into her. *You bet I'm hungry. Hungry for the taste of you, the feel of you wrapped around me, squeezing me, milking me dry.*

He ran his tongue across the edge of his teeth. "I can wait. I brought something for us to do. If you want to."

She cocked her head. "What's that?"

"A jigsaw puzzle. You're always so full of energy. I wanted to see what it's like when you have to slow down, to sit still. That is, *if* you can."

"That sounds suspiciously like a challenge." She narrowed her eyes. "Let's pack these things in their baskets first and we'll see who's better at sitting still."

"Challenge? I didn't hear a challenge. But if you're looking for one, let's see...how's this? Whoever gets bored with fitting puzzle pieces first has to cook dinner."

Kat laughed. "No way, José. Nobody cooks in my kitchen except me. And that means you clean up, so you just keep thinking of something else to challenge me with." She stood, holding the first packed basket and turning to put it on an end table.

When she turned back around, he was right there for her to bump into. Without prelude, he kissed her, an aggressive kiss of teeth and tongue and raw hunger, and hot hands roaming up and down her back, sliding down to grab the taut muscles of her ass cheeks and lift her into his instant hard-on. She moaned, melted into him like hot honey, and kissed him back, grabbing handfuls of his shirt in her fists. His kiss gentled into soft nibbles and licks and tongue-stroking, and she reveled in it, in his heat, his tenderness. She worked her hands up his chest and neck, then into his soft, wavy hair, bringing him even closer to her.

Suddenly he pulled away. "And we'll see," he said hoarsely, "which of us won't be able to wait to continue what we just started here."

Her eyes squinted at him. "Now who's challenging? You're on, buddy. And the loser has to follow the winner's instructions for three hours thereafter."

He gave her a devilish look. "It'll be my pleasure."

She couldn't tell if he wanted to win or lose.

Did it matter?

* * * * *

They'd compromised, after a fashion, agreeing to eat first and work the puzzle after the table was cleared, rather than have to eat in the dining room, which was too formal, besides which, it didn't have a fireplace. While Kat stir-fried shrimp with fresh ginger, red peppers and oyster mushrooms, Magnus set and lit the fire. By the time the fettuccine was cooked to *al dente* and a romaine salad tossed, he had also set the table at her direction and found a soft-jazz station on her radio.

The scene could have been pulled from the old movie *Tom Jones*. With a blazing fire illuminating them, Magnus deliberately licked the buttery sauce off his extra-large shrimp before taking little bites one at a time. Kat nursed her bottle of beer, settling her plump lips over the top of it as though it were his cock, tipping her head back for a sip then licking a drop as it dribbled down from the mouth. Magnus sucked one strand of fettuccine into his mouth slowly, deliberately, locked eyes with Kat's. She took a cherry tomato and meaningfully rolled it around in her mouth.

The game was on. Each instinctively teased the other with hot looks and provocative gestures. But at last their plates were empty and they cleared the table. Kat offered him an apron, which he disdained to wear while he rinsed the dishes and loaded the dishwasher.

Kat could feel her heart racing. He was a formidable challenge, but she was determined not to be the one to capitulate to the sexual heat raging between them. If he wanted to continue their pyrotechnics, he'd have to admit he wanted her more than she wanted him.

As if.

To derail dangerous thoughts, she pulled the puzzle out of the last plastic bag and felt a smile tugging at the corners of her mouth. How like Magnus. The photograph depicted a redwood forest, with a number of old-growth trees that had to be thirty feet in circumference, judging by the tiny human standing in a red shirt by one of them. Green and more green deep into the picture, myriad shades of the forest with benevolent rays of misty yellow sunlight piercing through the high branches, and lush ferns gracing the bottoms of the trunks like ballet dancers dipping in a bow.

Talk about a challenge.

She slit open the box with a fingernail, then rummaged through the five hundred pieces for the edges. One always needed to know one's parameters.

Engrossed in matching edges she'd arrayed before her, she saw in her peripheral vision that Magnus had sat down next to her and pulled the box in front of him. When next she looked up, he had sorted all the brownish pieces and had started constructing the tree trunks.

He must have had radar, because his eyes locked with hers. The lust in them almost knocked Kat off her chair. Unwittingly she slid her gaze to his mouth. He rubbed his tongue across it, leaving a slick trail that she wanted to follow with her own tongue. Then she noticed the small bowl he'd brought to the table, filled with vanilla pudding. Holding her gaze captive, he dipped his middle finger into it and popped a small mound of the dessert into his mouth, sucking juicily on his finger as he pulled it out.

Liquid heat shot through her. She could almost taste the tang of her cum on his fingers, could feel the slick slide of that finger as he glided it in and out of her pussy.

She swallowed hard. "Make sure you don't get any of that gook on the puzzle." The calm sound of her voice pleased her immensely. She stood up, her skirt swirling around her, to head for the fridge. She took out a small bottle, opened it at the counter with a soft psst, and came back to sit down.

"Cream," she said as she rolled the lip of the bottle across her mouth, then tipped up for a swallow. "This is the real thing, you know. Old-fashioned cream soda in a glass bottle. No fake additives." Before she sat down, Kat caught a glimpse of the bulge that strained the buttons of his jeans. Ah, how empowering to be a woman and to know that a man couldn't hide his desire as well as she could.

Except that her breasts were swollen and achy and she could see her nipples poking hard and proud through the soft knit of her sweater.

For all the reaction she got from Magnus.

Other than the hard-on.

She became aware of the plaintive voice of Little Jimmy Scott singing about a lost love, a heart-wrenching sob in every note. She'd been staring at a dozen greenish-brown edge pieces for an unknown number of minutes without fitting a single one.

"Tell me you can resist that." Suddenly Magnus had a grip on her upper arms and was lifting her to her feet. "This is dancing music." He swung her into his arms and cradled her close to his chest, one hand holding hers at his shoulder, the other spread across the center of her back.

Kat closed her eyes and reveled in the solid length of him against her, the masculine smell of him up close. His legs moved in slow cadence, one leg sinuously pushing between hers. His hand slid down her back to cradle her butt, aligning her even more solidly against him. She felt the unmistakable bulge of his cock rubbing against *that* spot, where she most wanted their clothes to disappear.

"You feel good in my arms," he murmured, his lips brushing against her temple as he moved slowly to the beat, his footwork a little more fancy than the uninspired one-two, one-two of most males.

Nestled as she was so intimately against him, Kat thought she could dance with Magnus Thorvald for the rest of her life. She felt safe, cherished, languorous. "You're a good dancer."

"Runs in the family, I think."

Jimmy Scott gave way to Houston Person's soulful sax blowing a very sexy, slow rendition of Cole Porter's "Night and Day". The soft music enveloped them in a sensual haze. They slowed, swayed in place then stopped dancing altogether. Magnus tucked a finger under Kat's chin and raised her head. Through downswept lashes she saw his face come closer, closer, felt the fan of his breath against her cheek. He touched his lips to hers, like the kiss of a butterfly on a rose petal. He held her gently, as though she were a fragile glass vase. His fingertips stroked her face as though committing her features to memory.

Kat forgot to breathe. She could have been an illuminated page from a tenth-century manuscript, he touched her so reverently.

Cupping her face in his large hands, Magnus returned to her mouth, dropped soft kisses from one side to the other then caught her lower lip gently between his teeth. Kat made an inarticulate sound in the back of her throat and tried to take the kiss deeper. Seemingly without effort, he held her just shy of full contact and teased her mouth again and again.

Kat surrendered to his leisurely pace. To the taste of him, the heat, the gentle probing of his tongue at the rim of her open, inviting mouth, an invitation he consciously ignored. This was not about control, this was about pleasure, about savoring the moment.

"Who won?" she murmured.

He lifted his head a fraction. "Won what?"

"You know. The loser has to follow the winner's instructions for three hours?"

With a sound that was half chuckle, half groan, he traced a path with his tongue down the long expanse of her throat. "How about if we split it?"

"Sounds like a plan," she said dreamily, cocking her head to allow him greater access.

"Here's what we'll do." He danced her inside the circle of heat emanating from the fireplace, lifted her into his arms and sank to his knees. Then he gently set her down on the thick Scandinavian rug and followed her there. "We'll just lie here in each other's arms and enjoy the fire."

"Mmmm." She snuggled into him, spoon-fashion, her ass tucked into the angle where his body met his legs. They faced the dancing flames, her head resting on the cradle of his outstretched arm. "Which fire?"

He nibbled on the tender skin just behind her ear. "Oh, there's more than the one in the fireplace?"

Kat reached behind her to place her free hand on the hard column of his thigh and stroked leisurely, up and down. "Don't know. But if there is, I'll find it." Her hand wormed its way in between where their bodies were sandwiched together, cupped his formidable bulge. "Correct me if I'm wrong, but I think I might have found another fire."

A satisfying hiss greeted her action. "There's probably one in here, too." He slid his free hand under her swing skirt, skimming her knee, to her thigh. "No pantyhose? Weren't you cold in that outdoor market?"

"I kept thinking warm thoughts." She adjusted herself to give his hand better access.

He took advantage of it. His hand moved higher, then abruptly stopped. "Jesus! You mean you spent the entire day without panties? I'm glad you didn't tell me."

"If you'll recall, I wasn't wearing any last night when I..."

In one smooth move, he flipped her onto her back and rucked up her skirt to her hips. "Still, you could have gotten frostbite. Let me check it out."

Gently he nudged her legs apart and lay down between them, the weight of his upper body on his elbows. He licked one inner thigh, then the other. He breathed on her vaginal lips, blowing puffs of hot air at the very core of her. Then he tenderly pried those lips open and upward to reveal the bud of her clitoris and blew again, softly, insistently.

Kat lifted her hips, silently demanding his tongue, his teeth, his mouth on her clit.

"You're beautiful. So rosy and swollen. So wet." He dipped his head and lapped at her slit with his tongue. "So sweet. You taste like honey."

"Magnus..."

"So hot." He inserted two fingers into her pussy as his mouth descended to her clit again. In a slow rhythm he licked and stroked until she was writhing beneath him, her hands clutching his head to press him even closer.

Her climax started slowly, softly, almost dreamlike. She could feel it building, feel the relentless touch of his tongue against the hard nubbin of her clit, the stroke, stroke, stroking of his fingers inside her, making her juices flow freely onto his hand. She saw no fireworks, no explosions, but rather a floating-on-a-cloud feeling that kept on going and going until finally she loosened her fisted hands from his hair and allowed herself to relax into a boneless puddle.

"I'll be right back. Don't move."

"As if I could," she murmured, suffused with a feeling of well-being and lassitude, the afterglow of the sweetest climax she could remember ever having.

"Here." Magnus knelt beside her, lifted her head, and guided the wineglass to her lips.

She sipped gratefully. He'd obviously found the opened bottle of pinot noir in the fridge. It tasted cool and refreshing going down. Idly she wondered if Magnus had washed away the taste of her cum with a sip of his own, but she was too languorous to ask.

"Let me make you more comfortable," he said as she felt his fingers working the button on her waistband. He lifted her hips and slid the skirt off her. She raised her arms slowly, to help him remove her sweater, but instead he lay down beside her.

Naked.

She could feel his hard cock pressing into her side as he ran the tips of his fingers over her belly, her hips, her thighs.

Her pussy twitched. Here she lay, wearing only red boots and red sweater, with Magnus naked and rampant beside her and the logs burning down to glowing red coals and falling between the andirons. What an erotic photograph it would make, she mused.

Magnus tucked his body behind hers so they spooned again. "Close your eyes and just relax."

His voice was low, hypnotic. She felt the utter need to comply. After all, they'd had very little sleep the night before, and she felt safe in her own home. In his strong arms. Her lashes fluttered closed. She was aware of the steady beat of his heart against her back. Of the heat of him almost matching the heat from the fire. Of the stubble on his chin as he nibbled on her neck.

She slept.

And fell into a delicious dream.

Magnus was fucking her from behind, his heat enveloping every inch of her, as if they were in a steam bath, his cock making long, slow, dreamy strokes into her pussy. The dream was so real, she began moving to its trancelike rhythm. Slow heat, sweet sliding cock, unhurried strokes, making her come alive again, building to a sleepy crescendo of wonder and delight.

"Magnus," she murmured.

"Shh, don't talk, just feel." The words rumbled in her ear.

Her eyes popped open. Not a dream. Oh God, not a dream. The real, live Magnus was sliding his humongous cock inside her ever so slowly from behind, deliberately holding back, and she was on the verge of coming.

And then it hit her, the spasms as her muscles clenched around his cock, the long, low moan that surged to a series of incomprehensible sounds in her throat. And then she felt him let go of his control, his strong hands holding her hips in a vise grip as his own spasms sent spurts of his cum deep into her pussy.

She was so involved in her own climax that she might have misheard… She thought she heard him say, rough-voiced in the heat of his climax, "You're mine, dammit."

Chapter Nineteen

৯০

Roses? In November?

Reality hit Magnus like a sawed-off branch crashing to the forest floor. His mind focused on the soft, silk-skinned woman lying naked in his arms. The tangle of fire-red hair tickling his chin.

Kat. His flaming, incendiary Valkyrie.

His.

After they'd made love by the fire, he'd carried her, sleepy and cuddly, upstairs to her bedroom. He remembered feeling unaccountably like a voyeur as he stepped inside to the faint scent of roses and the sight of utter femininity, a swath of red and pink roses edging the sheet on the turned-down bed. He'd set her on the mattress, removed her boots, her sweater and bra, and tucked her in. Then climbed in with her.

Tender, possessive feelings washed over him. She looked so fragile, so vulnerable in sleep that he wanted to protect her, keep her safe. Damn if she hadn't wormed her way into his heart with that unexpected soft side of her. She certainly hadn't struck him as a person who would care enough about others to make personal baskets for women who had escaped abusive relationships, most of them arriving at the shelter with just the clothes on their backs. He'd been appalled when she sketched some of their harrowing experiences. Never would he treat her, or any woman, that way.

Had she come to such empathy through personal experience? He didn't think so. Kat was too strong to allow a man to dominate her. Although she was so loving, so giving. Too giving. Magnus gritted his teeth. She had given too much to too many men. It still niggled at him, her promiscuity, her unabashed acceptance of casual sex.

On the other hand, he hadn't expected her to dive into something as mundane as a jigsaw puzzle with as much pleasure and concentration as she had. The woman was full of contradictions. He wouldn't have pegged her as someone who could sit still and silent for an hour at a time.

The way they fit together dancing had him wanting to take her to Soren's on nights when the bar offered a live band. And that slow, sweet sex in front of the fire was as satisfying as their first, highly explosive encounter. His cock awakened just thinking about it.

Kat stirred and sighed, her breath fanning across his skin, her fingers unconsciously curling into the hair on his chest. Brushing a strand of her wild curls behind her ear, he looked down at her face. Her skin was flawless, even from inches away. Her profile revealed a perfectly straight nose. Her thick lashes curled slightly upward.

Could she ever settle for just one man in her life?

He wouldn't think about that, wouldn't torture himself. He'd take it one day, one kiss at a time.

She rubbed against him, her leg moving across his thighs.

Awake or asleep? He couldn't tell if she was teasing him or merely dreaming.

Whichever, she'd done a hell of a job waking his cock to full mast. He gently eased her onto her back and slipped between her legs. Slowly, slowly he pushed his cock in, one hard inch at a time, almost groaning with pleasure at the feel of her warm pussy enclosing him, welcoming him. He'd never felt like this with another woman, as though he'd never get enough of her. Soft, hard, tender, explosive, it didn't matter. He could easily become addicted to Kat Donaldson.

He gazed at her face as he moved in and out, watching for that moment of wakefulness, of recognition of him, of what they were doing.

Her eyelids fluttered, but didn't open. She whispered his name. Her arms came around his waist, her fingers splayed downward toward the curve of his butt.

"Oh." She opened her eyes, suddenly awake. Then closed them as a smile tilted the corners of her mouth upward. "I thought it was a dream." She shifted her hips to invite him further. "I'm glad it wasn't."

"Look at me, Kat."

Languidly her lashes swept upward, her teak-colored eyes connecting with his. "Yes."

Something shifted inside Magnus. He felt as if he were looking into the deepest part of her soul as he moved his body slowly, deliberately, not fucking, as he'd so crudely told her a lifetime ago, but making love to her with every cell and fiber of his being. He wanted to tell her, without the words he couldn't say, what he thought of her, how sorry he was that he'd been such a chauvinist about her past lovers, how much he wanted her in his bed, in his life.

She raised her knees, her heels digging into the soft padding of the mattress, giving him fuller access to her sweet pussy, but allowing him to set the pace, a slow, maddening pace, but tender and full of unspoken meaning. Their soul-deep gazes stayed connected when Kat spiraled into a climax and Magnus fell into the same abyss of mindless pleasure only seconds after her.

* * * * *

"My wife was the sexiest woman I ever knew."

Wrapped in the cocoon of Magnus' strong arms, Kat tensed at the sleep-filled voice murmuring in her ear. Was he dreaming? Hell, was *she*?

"Turned men's heads, she was so beautiful. I was proud to have her at my side."

She didn't, did *not*, want to hear this. She gritted her teeth and tried to escape from his embrace under the rose-dappled sheets. They had dozed off after the most exquisite lovemaking she'd ever experienced. The sky outside the bedroom window was still dark except for a faint slice of moon.

"Hear me out, Kat." His arms pinned her to him, her back to his warm chest. "I have to say this my way."

Squeezing her eyes shut, she stopped fighting his superior strength and bulk. In addition to the pincers around her shoulders, he had flung a muscled calf over her legs, effectively immobilizing her. She didn't like being physically restrained, not one bit. And to have to listen to him lionizing his wife, she couldn't believe how insensitive he was proving to be.

"I loved the way she filled out a sweater, the short skirts that showed off her legs to perfection. Hell, I enjoyed the envious looks I'd get when we went out on the town. She knew how to make an entrance."

"Magnus, what's the point—"

"Please, let me finish." His voice had taken on a mechanical sound, without emotion. "Lucky Thorvald, that was me. Yeah, right. Until the day I came home unexpectedly, the proverbial clueless spouse, and found them."

Them. Kat stopped breathing. Waited for the shoe to drop.

"In our bed. Three of them. My beautiful wife, in all her naked glory. On her knees, with one naked bastard humping her from behind like a dog, the other holding her head to his dick, and Lydia sucking away like a pro."

Kat didn't know what to say, so she kept silent.

"As if that wasn't enough to piss off the Pope, you'll never guess what else."

She made a noise in response, sort of a cross between "What" and "Don't tell me".

"There was a third son of a bitch in the room. Also naked. Running the video cam."

"Oh, Magnus." She tried to turn to him, to comfort him. He tightened his hold on her, and she realized he was handling it the only way he could, refusing to let her see the emotion in his face, or hear it in his voice.

"The cameraman was a wimp. One shot to his kidney and he dropped like a rotten apple. I ripped the camera out of his hands and bashed it against the floor again and again, until I was satisfied they couldn't retrieve any of the tape. I didn't even feel the other two guys hanging onto my back like monkeys, punching me, trying to stop me."

He took a breath. Kat could feel the tremor in his muscles from holding himself rigid.

"And Lydia. Beautiful, blonde, built Lydia, just sat back on her haunches and watched. I think she was tickled that I fought over her. Boy, did she have it wrong. I filed for divorce the next day."

Kat bit her tongue to keep from offering unwanted sympathy. All she could do was lean back into him, snuggle into him, tell him without words that she understood, that she was sorry he'd had such a bitter experience.

Suddenly Magnus withdrew his arms, rolled onto his back, as if distancing himself from her. Kat felt bereft. But she didn't move. She sensed another shoe about to drop.

"So maybe now you can understand," he rasped, "why I reacted so negatively even as I was attracted to you. The last thing I needed in my life was another beautiful babe, sexy as hell in those red boots and tight jeans, tossing out double entendres the way a quarterback tosses a touchdown pass. From all I'd heard and seen, you were promiscuous as hell. A big honcho in a sex club. Not to mention your inviting Rolf to pose nude, or the blatantly sexual paintings you featured in your shop."

Kat swallowed hard. And she'd intensified those perceptions by blithely giving him a blowjob when he'd been trying to get rid of her. "I can't change who I was," she finally managed to force out past a knot in her throat.

"Neither can I."

They lay in Kat's queen-size bed, not moving, not touching, barely breathing. The moon had disappeared beyond the window and the room had turned as dark as her mood. She ached for Magnus and his hurt, but also for herself. She'd had a good life with enough money to indulge in material comfort or pleasure, but she saw now that they were poor substitutes for a love that would transcend mere things. If her mother had met a man she could commit to forever, would her life, and Kat's, have been different? Would she have bequeathed to her daughter a respect for the concept of one man, one woman instead of accumulating notches until her figurative bedpost had disintegrated to sawdust?

"Was?" Magnus' voice, though soft, echoed in the silence of the room.

"What?" She must have missed something. Had he asked her a question?

"You said, 'I can't change who I was'. Not 'who I am'."

"I did, didn't I."

"Does that mean…?" He stopped.

She rolled onto her side to face him, then slid her hand in his direction across the dark chasm of the rumpled sheet, cool now with their apartness. Her mother was wrong. She wanted to be with Magnus, only Magnus. "This is all new to me." Her fingers touched his forearm, brushed the silky hairs there. She breathed a prayer of gratitude that he didn't pull away.

"What is it that's new?"

Okay, so he'd make her work for it. She could do this. She needed to do this. "Commitment. The only thing in my life that ever received my full commitment was my gallery. Even my mother and I have such a loose relationship that I can't really call it commitment. You have something precious, Magnus. You have a set of values that I never learned. Honor.

Ethics. A sense of continuity. Of family history. I-I want to be part of your life. For the long term. Do you think we could let go of the past—yours and mine—and start from today?"

"Kat, I want—" He let out a long breath. "Don't jerk me around. If we're going to have any chance together, you can't be screwing around with other men."

"I don't *want* other men. After you did your studly thing at the cocktail party—I think your exact words were, 'I've primed the pump'—I had any number of offers to finish what you started. I turned down every one of them. Loud and clear."

"You did? I thought that pretty society boy you were with had the hots for you."

"Jules and I are old friends. Nothing more." Even though Jules had asked her a number of times to marry him, she'd never even considered him for the long term.

"And that Savidge guy, hovering around you, eating you up with his eyes."

"He was not!" Letting go of his arm, Kat pushed herself upright in the bed, the sheet dropping to her waist. Dawn was lightening the world outside the bedroom window, and she could see the tense set of his jaw as he lay on her pillow, staring up at her, arms rigidly at his sides. "Savidge is Lyssa's partner. There's no way I'd hurt my best friend by doing something with him."

Magnus sat up as well, turning to her with one bent knee thrust into the space between them, his foot tucked under his opposite thigh. His gaze bored into hers. "The men in that sex club, were they all single men?"

Kat could see the trap he was building. But she had to be honest. "No. Of course not. But all the married men were there with their wives' complicity. They had to join as couples. In fact, when I brought Lyssa to the Masquerade, I had several wives thank me, because they got turned on watching their husbands get hot and horny with her and then the wives got the benefit of all that foreplay."

She raised her arms to thrust her unruly hair off her face. It pleased her that his gaze snapped to her uplifted breasts. "But getting back to the subject, when you left me high and dry, you made me realize I've been marking time all my life, waiting for you. It's you I want. Only you."

He stared at her with unnerving intensity. "I want to believe that."

"Then give me a chance. Trust me, at least a little."

"Can you imagine how it hurt to find my wife making a porno movie in our own bedroom?"

"Please believe me, Magnus, I've never wrecked a marriage. I've never connected with a married man on the prowl. Meager though they are, I do have scruples. And if I make a commitment, I keep it."

The air around them grew fraught with expectancy. Kat held her breath. She could see the war within Magnus. The moment lengthened as dawn threw a swath of delicate pink across the bed. She had one last trump card to play. "I'll resign from the Platinum Club. Come on. I'll make some coffee and breakfast, and then I'll email my resignation to the president and the board."

His Adam's apple bobbed. "You'd do that for me?"

"Yes. It's a no-brainer. I want to be in your life."

"Kat." He leaned over to her, cupped her cheek with one hand, and gave her an almost reverent kiss that told her his answer.

They didn't get to the coffee for another hour.

Chapter Twenty

ဢ

"Holy shit! Who are you? What happened to Magnus?"

Standing before a small wall mirror in the sleeping area of his apartment, Magnus turned at his brother's exclamation. "Oh, good. I'll bet you know how to tie one of these damn things." He indicated the black bowtie he'd been fiddling with for the past five minutes. Then he took a good look at Rolf and narrowed his eyes. "Your chin is down to your navel. What's the matter, haven't you ever seen a monkey suit before?"

"Your hair. What happened to your hair?"

Magnus smoothed a big hand at his nape, still feeling a bit naked without the warmth and the weight he'd gotten accustomed to on his shoulders. His hair now barely touched his stiff white collar, with just enough curl so it didn't look like he'd been under the shears an hour ago. "I figured the Tarzan look didn't go too well with a tux. So I went to the barber."

Rolf sauntered farther into the room. "Did he faint?"

Magnus felt his mouth twitch. "You mean because he hadn't seen me in a couple of years and thought I was a ghost? No. He simply asked, 'Just trim the sides?' Pretty droll of him, don't you think? What are you doing here, by the way?"

"The real question is, what are you doing in a tux?"

"Do you always answer a question with a question?" Magnus was getting ticked. His little brother was as subtle as an avalanche.

"Where'd you get the dough to buy an Armani?"

"It's rented. Why anyone would want to buy one of these things is beyond me."

Rolf snorted. "Some people actually look good in tuxedoes. Too bad you—" At Magnus' glare, he switched gears in midstream. "To answer your question, I'm here to see my big brother. I left four messages on your answering machine over the past few days and I started to get worried when you didn't call back. Where've you been?"

"You know I don't answer the phone when I'm in my workshop."

"Yeah, but you weren't *home*, either."

Magnus pulled the strip of black silk from his neck and tossed it at Rolf. "Here. Make yourself useful and tie it for me. What makes you think I wasn't home just because I haven't called you yet?"

"I was here. Three times." Rolf turned Magnus toward the light from the setting sun streaming in through the many-paned windows and started fussing with the bowtie. "The Jeep was gone."

"Why did you need to contact me?"

"Just curious."

"About what? Am I in the Army and you're taking roll call?"

"Lift your chin. This isn't like you, Mags. Soren and I are worried about you."

"I can take care of myself." In a sudden swift motion, Magnus dipped his body and put a shoulder to Rolf's midsection, sweeping the younger man off his feet and hoisting him over his right shoulder like a sack of potatoes. Then, just as quickly, he set Rolf back down. "See? You didn't have time to blink. Soren should have remembered I'm a bouncer at his bar."

Rolf let out an exaggerated sigh. "Now I've got to start all over." He pulled the tie off Magnus' neck and began forming the intricate loops again. "That's not what I mean. You're seeing Kat, aren't you."

It was a statement, Magnus realized, not a question. He tensed. "Does it make you jealous?"

Rolf's hands stilled. He looked his brother in the eye. "I just want to be sure you know what you're getting into."

Magnus met his gaze calmly. "I know all about how her mother raised her and about the Platinum Society and what happened after I left the cocktail party."

"Hell, if you hadn't kicked me out the other day, I'd have told you that Kat refused any and all offers. Her friend Lyssa thinks she's going to get her heart broken. I just wanted to know your intentions."

"Are you done yet? I have a date an hour away and I intend to keep it."

"Mags—"

"Shouldn't you be worrying about me instead? Like, if I couldn't handle my wife, how could I handle a Valkyrie like Kat?"

Rolf held his brother's gaze a moment, then concentrated on arranging the tie to his liking. "I never asked you why you got a divorce. Neither did Soren. That's between you and Lydia. I wasn't comparing them. Kat's got an unorthodox past, I'll grant you that, but she's a sweet, vulnerable person for all her outward show of savoir-faire. I don't want to see her hurt."

"And you think I'll hurt her because…?"

"There. All done." He stepped away from Magnus. "No, I don't think you'll hurt her intentionally."

"But I will unintentionally?"

"Aw, hell, Mags, I didn't mean that."

"So what you're really doing is prying. That's why you came here. To dig around in the dirt, so to speak." Magnus turned back to the mirror. "Yeah. Looks okay to me. I have to go. Don't want to be late. I'm auctioning off a bowl."

"Huh?"

Pleased that he was able to shut up his inquisitive brother, whose big mouth gaped open again, Magnus grabbed the keys to the Ram. "After you, bro."

* * * * *

"Oh…my…God."

Kat blinked. The vision was still standing on her front porch.

"Magnus," she breathed, stepping back from the doorway to invite him in. Magnus the Magnificent. She didn't know why she hadn't come up with that appellation before. Because he certainly was. He'd looked good in jeans and scuffed boots. He'd looked even better naked in her bed. But now, now he looked to the manor born, the equal of any of her Fortune Five Hundred friends whose wealth harkened back to Robber Baron days. Her gaze unabashedly roved over him, reveling in the sight of his lumberjack shoulders under elegant black worsted, the taper of the jacket fitting smoothly over narrow hips, the strong thighs accented by a satin stripe down the pants leg.

She had splurged on a designer gown, a one-shouldered confection of white silk that clung to her curves, with a slit from mid-thigh down to her Manolo Blahnik stilettos that bared a length of leg when she walked. She'd piled her red curls into a topknot with loose tendrils escaping around her face.

"You look like a strawberry on top of a pile of whipped cream," he growled as he strode toward her, his intense stare weakening her knees. "Makes me want to take a bite out of you here…" His mouth found the curve of her ear and nipped. "And here…" His teeth grazed down her exposed throat. "And then…"

He dropped to his knees, gripped her hips in two strong hands, and buried his face in the vee that cradled her sex.

"Then I'd lick every mouthful of that white stuff off your body."

Kat backed up a step, grateful for the solid feel of the wall at her back. Without that support, she might well have buckled right to the floor at his tender assault. "Magnus," she whimpered, her hands fluttering to his head, unsure whether she was pushing him away or inviting him closer. "We don't have time…"

"A man can dream." Slowly Magnus rose to his feet, his large hands gliding upward over her curves, until he stood tall and proud next to her. "You take my breath away." He leaned forward, closing the inches-wide gap between them, and dropped a soft kiss on her cheek. "You're more beautiful than a sunrise."

Kat felt a cloud of butterflies swirling in her belly at the devouring look he aimed at her. Oh, man, he made her want a quickie right this minute, wanted him to hike up her skirt, bend her over the sideboard and slam his cock into her from behind. Judging by the lusty look on his face, it would be hard and fast, and mutually satisfying.

They had time for one kiss, didn't they? She lifted a hand to his nape and nudged his head down to hers for a kiss. Her fingers grazed the unexpectedly short hair where she had expected a neat ponytail. "Oh. What happened here?"

One side of his mouth quirked upward in that lopsided smile she was coming to love. "I joined the land of the civilized, thanks to you."

"Turn around." He obliged, and she ran her fingers through his short, wavy locks. "You clean up real good, Magnus. Like a *GQ* cover. I can see I'm going to have my hands full tonight, fending off all the women who will fall at your feet."

"Won't do 'em any good. I've got the woman I want." His intense gaze bored deep into her soul, staking his claim, branding her with his own stamp.

The grandfather clock chimed eight times, breaking the spell. She sighed. "We'd better go, or we'll miss the opening bid. If they put your bowl up first…"

"Say no more." He picked up the lined velvet cloak she had laid over the back of the nearby sofa and held it out for her. "Fair warning, though," he said gruffly as he wrapped it around her, holding her briefly, tightly, against him. "When we get back tonight, I'm going to show you no mercy. I hope you're taking your vitamins."

Her answer was a delicious shiver.

* * * * *

A half hour later Magnus pulled Kat's BMW to a stop under the porte-cochere of the Ritz Carlton Hotel in downtown Philadelphia and handed the keys to a waiting valet. He had easily acquiesced to her suggestion that the sporty car was more appropriate than his big truck, considering their formal attire. He checked her cloak and they entered a ballroom that looked like a summer garden, with huge baskets of fresh blooms under arbors and around gazebos. Kat had supplied the tickets, at five hundred dollars a couple, arguing that his donation of a sculpture more than evened the score. He wasn't too macho to rationalize she could take a tax deduction from her purchase.

Waitstaff wearing pleated white shirts, red cummerbunds and black pants weaved through the crowd offering hors d'oeuvres and champagne. The sounds of a string quartet in one corner drifted through the perfumed air. It seemed to Magnus that the women tried to outdo each other in the jewelry department. In contrast, Kat's diamond ear-studs, her only ornamentation, were understated yet regal.

And so was she. Pride surged through him at having this elegant woman on his arm. She moved through the crowd gracefully, introducing him to everyone as the soon-to-be-famous sculptor. Although the admiring glances and subtle visual invitations of the women bounced off him, Magnus found himself brooding over which of the many male hands he shook had touched Kat intimately at the Platinum Society. Then he saw the man who'd been mooning over her at the cocktail party. Jules something. The one who wanted to use a cat-o'-nine tails, according to Rolf. Magnus put his arm around Kat's shoulder possessively and nudged her in the opposite direction.

And saw a pair of familiar faces. He broke into a smile. "Mr. and Mrs. Peifer. Good to see you again. I hope you're enjoying your new table."

"I've gotten more compliments on it than I can tell you," said Charlene Peifer. "I want to bid on that swan bowl you donated. It's elegant, and so realistic."

"I'm sure the bidding will be spirited," Kat responded. "Thank you so much for telling me about him, Charlene. I don't know how you heard of Magnus Thorvald before I did. Now we both know that we're in the presence of genius."

Magnus swallowed. It was one thing to hear Kat tell him privately what she thought of his talent, but complimenting him so profusely in public made his heart swell. If he wasn't careful, he'd find his head swelling, too.

The lights flickered twice, the signal that the auction was about to begin. Clutching her numbered bidding paddle, Kat led Magnus to the rows of seating in front of the auctioneer's dais. He'd had no time—or, he admitted, no desire, since his bank account was minimal—to inspect the other items. He wondered if Kat would bid on his swan.

As if reading his mind, Kat said, settling into her padded chair, "You know it would be unethical for me to bid on you. It would look like I'm jacking up the price."

"Oh. Of course."

"Even though I wouldn't mind possessing it." She leaned close to him and dropped her voice to a near-whisper. "It's a stunning piece of work, and the people here have both artistic taste and deep pocketbooks. My educated guess is it'll go for more than a thousand dollars."

He swiveled his head around. "You're kidding."

Her smug smile told him otherwise. "I'm not. And again, on behalf of the women's shelter, thank you for donating it to the auction."

He stroked her cheek with his knuckle. "Glad to do it. For you."

She had no time to melt at his gentle touch, because the auctioneer launched into his complicated spiel, artfully urging higher bids. Magnus enjoyed Kat's offhand comments about various items, from a gourmet dinner cooked at one's home to a private performance by a classical guitarist, and about the winning bidders.

When the auctioneer held up the swan bowl, Magnus tensed. He felt Kat take hold of his suddenly clammy hand in her small, warm one and squeeze encouragingly. Gratitude swamped him at her instinctive understanding.

"You may not have heard of Magnus Thorvald yet," the auctioneer was saying, "but I promise you, you will. Most of you know our board member Kat Donaldson as an especially astute connoisseur of artistic talent. She will formally launch Mr. Thorvald into the art world with a one-man show this spring at her gallery, A Discerning Eye. One lucky bidder here will be able to say, 'I was one of the first to recognize his talent'."

Displaying the bowl in a wide arc so that everyone could view it, he continued, "If you've inspected it earlier tonight, you know it's made of burled elm. The artist ingeniously incorporated the nuances of the burl to add depth and dimension to the swan's feathers. It's an exceptional piece, and it's signed. Do I hear a thousand?"

By now Magnus was aware the auctioneer usually started the bidding at an exorbitant sum, then accepted a first bid at about a tenth of that figure. More often than not, it seemed to him, the fast-talking man on the dais came pretty close to the final bid with that first volley. He held his breath as the price on his carving went up by a hundred dollars a shot. Watching the auctioneer carefully, Magnus deduced that two people were bidding against each other. He wondered if Mrs. Peifer would be the winner.

"Sold, to the gentleman in the back, for one thousand, three hundred seventy-five dollars." The gavel slammed down.

Magnus felt as though a stun gun had hit him in the chest. His breathing turned shallow. Almost fourteen hundred bucks. For a wooden bowl. For *his* bowl.

"Take a deep breath, Magnus. Don't you go hyperventilating on me."

Slowly he became aware of the pressure Kat was exerting on his hand. He wanted to shoot up from his chair and punch a fist into the air. He wanted to catch her in a bear hug and twirl her around until they were both dizzy. Instead, he willed himself to relax, to breathe normally.

Her look of pride burrowed itself deep into his heart. "Thank you," he mouthed.

"This calls for a toast," Kat said, a huge smile on her face. "Let's get some champagne." She stood, and he followed.

They made their way to the bar, which was closed during the auction. On the counter they found an open bottle nestled in cracked ice and Magnus poured the bubbly liquid into two flutes.

"To the next star in the art world," she said, her eyes glowing with pride.

"To the woman who's putting him there."

They touched rims and sipped, gazing into each other's eyes for untold minutes while the auction continued around them. Finally the patter of the auctioneer penetrated his brain when he heard her name. He forced himself to focus on the words as he turned to the dais.

"We all know Ms. Donaldson as an expert in the fine arts, a first-rate tour guide, a connoisseur of good food and drink. A free spirit. A charming companion."

Magnus snapped his head back to Kat, narrowing his eyes as his gaze bored into her. "What's that all about?" he hissed.

Kat's eyes widened, a look of panic flitting across her lovely features. "Oh no, I forgot all about that!"

The auctioneer boomed, "One lucky person will spend a fun-filled weekend with Kat Donaldson at her *pied-à-terre* in Cancun during the height of Winter season."

"You offered to go to Cancun with another man?" Magnus put both contempt and disbelief into his voice.

"I've done this for years. It was no big deal. I just forgot—"

"No. Big. Deal." Magnus enunciated each word carefully. "Is what we had together no big deal, too? Just another poor slob who got suckered in by your charms?"

"Please, Magnus. Not here. Not now."

"You march right up to that auctioneer and tell him you withdraw your *donation*." He all but spat the last word.

"It's too late. The bidding is already in progress." Tears rimmed her eyes. "I'll work it out with the high bidder. I'll reimburse him whatever his bid is. Please believe me, Magnus. I never even thought about it. I was too busy with you…"

Willing his temper under control, Magnus looked around to see if he could spot who was bidding. He spied that Jules character making a sign.

"I have twelve thousand. Do I hear thirteen?"

Magnus' heart all but stopped. *Twelve thousand dollars.*

"The gentleman on the left bids thirteen."

Magnus craned his neck, but couldn't figure out who the other bidder was.

Fourteen, Jules nodded.

"Twenty thousand dollars." Magnus didn't know he was going to bid until the words came out of his mouth.

"Magnus, you don't have to…"

"Ladies and gentlemen, we have a third bidder for Ms. Donaldson's excursion to Cancun. Do I hear twenty-one?"

Jules' burning gaze shot across the room, sending daggers to Magnus. Then the playboy turned back to the auctioneer and stood in an arrogant pose. "Thirty thousand dollars."

Damn! Magnus knew he had no business competing in this high-stakes game. He'd have to take out a mortgage on the farm to pay even twenty thousand. But thirty?

Defeated, his chest feeling like a vise had clamped around it, he spun on his heel and stalked out of the ballroom. The announcement followed him like a curse. "Sold, to Jules Rubin for thirty thousand dollars."

His long stride propelled him down the fire stairs. He couldn't wait for the elevator, he had to get out into the open air or choke to death on all that wealth and snobbery and pretense.

Kat. *His* Kat, spending a weekend with another man in a playground of the rich. Whatever had possessed him to think he could be the equal of all those society types who had money to throw away on a whim? Ah God, and to think she'd be there with a bastard who wanted to use a cat-o'-nine tails on her soft skin.

At the porte-cochere he stopped short, remembering. They'd taken Kat's car. His Ram was parked in her driveway. Single-mindedly determined to get out of Philadelphia as quickly as possible, he strode to the street and hailed a cab. That, at least, he could afford.

Cursing himself for all kinds of a fool, he gave the cabbie her address and watched, numb, as the city lights flickered by his backseat window. Forty dollars later he was in his truck and pointing its nose to Soren's bar. Where not a single bottle of champagne would be in sight. Where everyday people congregated. Where he belonged.

Not at the Ritz Carlton Hotel, for crying out loud. And not, obviously, with Kat.

It promised to be a long night. He wondered if he could drink enough to forget.

Chapter Twenty-One

🙰

"Whiskey. And leave the bottle."

Magnus' terse order made Soren blink. Seeing him storm into the bar at midnight on a Saturday night hadn't done it. Noting he was decked out in a tux and short hair didn't do it. But whiskey? Leave the bottle? Something had happened, and he'd bet his next shipment of Amsterdam beer that a woman caused the pain he heard in his older brother's voice. Probably Kat. He debated with himself—to talk or not to talk?

Finally Soren simply shoved a shot glass and a half-full bottle of Crown Royal in front of Magnus and wiped down the spotless bar in the vicinity, close enough that Mags could talk to him if he chose to.

Seconds, minutes ticked by. Magnus had downed one glassful in a single quick gulp, had poured a second and sat, morosely staring at the amber-colored liquid. Soren realized he couldn't spend all night pretending to polish the bar in front of a silent man, even his hurting brother. But when he moved a step away, Magnus spoke.

"Teak."

"What'd you say?"

Magnus lifted the shot glass, holding it to the light and swirling the liquid around. "Teak. The color of this rotgut." He took a slow sip. "Ever see teak? Her eyes are the exact shade as teakwood."

"Her?" Soren encouraged.

Magnus lifted his eyes to his brother. Soren had never seen such pain, such bleak despair in them, not even when he'd announced the abrupt end of his marriage.

"I fought it. Fought the attraction to her. I knew she slept around. Hell, that Platinum Society shit all but guaranteed it. But dammit, she got under my skin. I *had* to have her." Magnus lifted the glass to his lips then set it down without sipping.

Whether Magnus had indulged in a one-night stand here and there in the past few years, Soren didn't know. But he knew his brother hadn't had a close relationship with a woman since Lydia. He snuck a quick look at his best bartender, who was working the counter with him tonight, and gave him a sign — *Take my customers, I have a crisis here.* Softly he asked Magnus, "And did you?"

A muscle worked in Magnus' jaw. Soren could tell how hard he was trying to hold on to his temper.

"Forget I said anything. 'Don't ask, don't tell' is a bartender's motto." He turned his back on Magnus, rearranged a couple of the bottles on lighted shelving in front of the huge mirror, nevertheless keeping a surreptitious eye on his brother's reflection.

Magnus sighed. "Yeah. I did. I couldn't stop myself. Just kissing her, I'd never experienced anything so explosive. I thought I'd screw her brains out, get it out of my system, and be able to walk away." This time he did more than sip. He swallowed the rest of the shot. His huge hand gripped the empty glass until Soren could see the knuckles turn white. He wondered how much more pressure it would take to shatter the glass.

"Then she went all tender on me. Showed me a side I'd never have guessed. It was like, I don't know, like a warm spring rain after an ice-bound winter. She was more than a sex symbol, she was a *person.* Funny, witty, charming, intelligent, a success in her chosen field. A woman who cared about others, who'd been giving her time and money to a charity over the years, to the point where she was on their board of trustees."

His bleak gaze turned to Soren. "I bought a jigsaw puzzle. I figured she'd never have the patience to sit with me and work it. But she did, dammit. And she enjoyed it."

Soren swallowed. He remembered when they were kids, watching their mother and father sitting with their heads almost touching, fitting tiny pieces of one puzzle or another together. This in a time when money was scarce and outside entertainment almost nonexistent in the rural area where they'd lived. To both Soren and Magnus, it was a litmus test of a relationship. That Magnus had taken such a step with Kat said volumes.

"So. What's with the monkey suit?"

"This charity auction we went to was black-tie. All the women dressed to the nines with false eyelashes and real diamonds. I mean, the kind of stuff you don't see in a jeweler's window. The stuff you look at in a locked, alarmed back room with a rent-a-cop outside the door."

Magnus poured a third shot into the glass. "Every man she introduced me to, I thought, did he have his paws up her skirt in the past? Should I even shake the fellow's hand?" He pushed the glass to one side with his finger, then back again, his concentration totally focused on the useless chore.

"Tonight she put me at ease, though. Introduced me to everyone who'd ever walked into her gallery. Touched me with little private touches as if to say we were more than just agent and artist. Talked me up to everyone so much that I wondered if my swelled head would be able to fit through the door on the way out."

So far, so good, Soren thought. *Keep him talking.* He washed a couple of empty pilsner glasses a waitress had dropped off, dried them and hung them upside down on the appropriate rack, careful not to seem too interested, but available if need be.

When he looked up again, Magnus was shaking his head, a look of disbelief on his face. "She told me that my swan bowl would probably fetch a thousand bucks. I thought she'd been smoking loco weed. But no, when they banged the gavel, some fool had committed to paying the charity thirteen hundred seventy five dollars for a signed Thorvald."

In spite of himself, Soren whistled softly. "You're on your way, bro." He leaned elbows on the counter and smiled, genuinely glad for him. "You worked hard for it. Your star is gonna shine big."

The pained look darkened Magnus' eyes again. "I don't know how I can keep working with her, Soren. Not after what she did tonight."

Soren straightened to his full height. "What did she do?"

Magnus rubbed the heels of his big hands into his eye sockets, let his head rest there. His voice came out muffled. "She auctioned herself off as a companion for a weekend in Cancun."

Stunned silence was Soren's only reaction. How could he comfort a man who had suffered such a blow?

"I bid on it, Soren. I'd have had to mortgage the farm, but God help me, I bid twenty thousand dollars to keep her." Magnus snorted. "But it was a lose-lose situation for me. The guy overbidding me lives off a hefty trust fund, and he showed no signs of stopping. If I'd've tried to scare him off, it wouldn't have made any difference. And if he'd dropped it on me at sixty grand or so, I'd have probably lost the farm."

"Mags."

Magnus lifted pain-drugged eyes at him.

"How did she react when the guy won the bid?"

"Hell, I didn't stay around to see. As soon as the gavel hit, I hightailed it out of there. I wasn't about to let anyone see me whipped."

"Did she give any explanation when the auctioneer announced the, um, item?"

Gnawing on his upper lip, Magnus thought a moment. "Well, she did pretend to be surprised. She said she'd been doing the same gig for years and had forgotten that she'd promised the same thing again."

"There you go." Soren leaned over the bar, making sure Magnus was looking him in the eye. "Could it be that she genuinely forgot? How much time have you spent with her recently? Did you maybe keep her too busy to think of other things, like what she'd agreed to auction off for her favorite charity?"

"But she didn't take it off the table when I asked her to. If she cared about me, she'd have considered how it would hurt me. She *saw* how I reacted. She was so damned concerned that they get their money, she didn't want to stop the auction."

"Give me your keys."

"What?"

"If you want to drink yourself to oblivion, I don't want you driving. You'll stay upstairs with me tonight."

Magnus stared him down. "I'll be all right."

They engaged in a staring duel. Finally Soren turned away. "If you make me lose my liquor license, I'll never forgive you."

"I'll be all right," Magnus repeated. Yeah, sure. He'd never be all right again. But he didn't need Soren worrying about him. He watched idly while his brother was called to the phone. He saw Soren glance at him, saw his expression go from cautious to inscrutable.

Then he turned his attention back to the bottle. The only thing he could hope for was that enough Crown Royal would ease the sting of pain, if not obliterate it.

* * * * *

"Dammit, where the hell *is* it?" Kat's panic mounted. She'd only been to Soren's bar the one time, when she'd shot some pool with Rolf, and she hadn't really paid attention to how they got there. She consulted the notes she'd hurriedly written down as Soren gave her directions over the phone. Had she passed it? Should she turn around and retrace her steps?

After Magnus stormed out of the ballroom, Kat had been torn between love and duty. But she knew she couldn't go to him with loose ends. Resolutely she shoved to the back of her mind the contretemps with Jules and the auctioneer. That was nothing compared to the frightful experience of trying to locate Magnus. First she asked the concierge, who simply shrugged. Then the doorman told her that a big blond man in a tux had hailed a cab. So she retrieved the BMW and raced home. His truck was gone from her driveway. Then she'd called Soren's bar, but they hadn't seen him. So she'd called Rolf, had gotten his answering machine. Of course. Saturday night. Then she called both the local and State Police to see if any black Ram trucks had been involved in an accident in the past hour.

With rising hysteria, she tried Soren's again. Relief had tears springing to her eyes when he confirmed Magnus was sitting at the bar getting slowly drunk. Her last resort would have been to travel to upper Bucks County. She hadn't been sure she could manage to keep her sanity after a long drive to Magnus' barn only to find the trip had been futile.

Kat squinted through the windshield. A quarter moon shed minimal light on street signs. Decatur Street. Where the hell was Decatur Street? She fervently hoped it wasn't in a poor section of town, because it was almost one in the morning, and she'd certainly stand out in her slinky white gown and red-lined black cape if she had to stop somewhere to ask. Briefly she'd considered, when at her own home, whether to change into jeans and sneakers, but decided she couldn't spare the time.

She slammed on the brakes. This might be the intersection, she thought, but there was no street sign. She backed up then aimed the car so the lights hit the signpost on the opposite side of the street.

Yes! She was almost there. She turned right on Decatur and drove down three blocks. There, near the right-hand corner, was a neon sign hanging over the entrance proclaiming Thor's Hammer. She parked too near a fire hydrant, got out and clicked the remote to lock the door. With a deep, calming breath, she prepared herself for…

Whatever would happen.

Gathering her dignity and her cloak around her, Kat took another deep breath and opened the front door. The smell of smoke and beer assaulted her nostrils. A hot jazz riff blared from numerous speakers. Every barstool was occupied, with more patrons congregating in groups in the aisle between bar and tables. Male heads swiveled her way, frank interest striking sparks in their eyes. For the first time in her life, she felt uncomfortable at the sexual awareness she seemed to elicit from the opposite sex.

Pulling her cloak more tightly around her, Kat took a tentative step inside. When she spied Soren working the tap — oh God, he looked so much like Magnus, she thought her heart would break — she wended her way toward the bar.

Then she saw him. At the far corner, head down, tie hanging askew around his neck, half the studs in his shirt unbuttoned. The splotch of his red cummerbund beneath the opened tux jacket conjured up the vision of a hemorrhaging heart.

"Magnus." The name came out half whisper, half prayer. Her blood thundered in her ears. He looked utterly defeated. And *she* had done that to him. Ignoring the come-hither stares and bawdy comments of the bar patrons, she fought her way through the raucous crowd. She saw the whiskey bottle and the empty shot glass before she reached him. How much had he drunk? Would he be belligerent? Make a scene? Or, worse yet, ignore her?

Hesitantly she placed a hand on his shoulder. "Magnus?"

Under her palm she felt him tense, but otherwise he remained as motionless and unyielding as one of his burled logs.

"Magnus, please. I'm so sorry this happened. Let me explain—"

He shrugged her hand off his shoulder and picked up the bottle, filling the shot glass with amber liquid. Setting down the bottle, he lifted the glass and held it toward one of the spotlights illuminating the rows of bottles, twirling the glass as if mesmerized by the shards of refracting light dancing through the liquid.

"I straightened out the mess. Everything is—"

The microphone on the stage boomed as a deep male voice announced the return of the live combo. The audience's applause momentarily drowned out Kat's words. When the noise died down, she continued, "Really, everything's fine. I've canceled the trip and settled things with the auctioneer."

"Hey, Red, let's see what you're hiding under that cloak."

Strong arms snaked around Kat from behind, pulled the edges of the cloak away from her front and over her shoulders. "That's better," a deep voice said as thick-fingered hands slithered across her waist.

She turned an imperial stare at the intruder. "I'm busy. Why don't you leave us alone?"

"You don't wanna hang around that dude. He drunk half the bottle already. What you want is a guy who can appreciate your many charms." He moved closer to nuzzle her nape, slithered his hands down to her hips. "Like me."

A fierce jab of her elbow into his midsection elicited a mild "Ooof" from the stranger, but he tightened his hold and thrust his tongue into her ear. "Oh yeah, darlin', I like 'em when they fight back. Makes the winnin' all the sweeter. An' I know you got fire in ya, with that red hair and them big tits."

"Get your dirty hands off me, you goon!" Kat tried to lift her foot to jab her stiletto onto his calf, but her leg was squished between the lecher and Magnus' barstool and all she could manage was a tepid punch on his instep. She glanced at Magnus for help, but he slowly, deliberately, lifted the glass and took a sip of whiskey, his eyes focused on one of the shelved bottles.

"Come on, sweetheart, let's you an' me dance. I wanna rub bellies with you in the worst way."

Kat began to squirm in earnest, elbowing him left and right, trying to dislodge the man's fierce grip on her hips as he ground his pelvis into her butt. "Let me go!" She groped behind her, found one of his ears, and twisted hard.

"Hey!" He loosened his hold and Kat spun out of his grip just as she felt him being yanked away from her.

"The lady said to get lost." Soren had him in an armlock and was easing him away. "We run a quiet place here. I suggest you go back to your table and calm down before I call the cops."

Even before the voices faded away, Kat put the incident out of her mind and turned her attention to Magnus. "I know you're hurt, Magnus. I don't blame you. We have something special together, and I almost jeopardized it tonight. Please believe me. I honestly forgot about that trip. To be truthful, everything else in my life is taking a backseat to you."

Magnus set down his half-drunk glass and swiveled on his stool. Relief washed through Kat—he was finally acknowledging her!

Not. He stood, dug into his trousers' pocket to pull out his wallet, and tossed a couple of twenties on the bar. Without a word or a glance, he strode past her toward the door. Under the weight of his glare, a path miraculously opened through the throng around the bar.

"Magnus! Wait!" Kat spun on her heel and ran after him. Several less-than-sober patrons grabbed for her, slowing her down, tossing out comments like, "What's your hurry, sweetheart?" and "If he don't want you, I'd be happy to…"

But she was out the door. Her panicked gaze darted around the street. His truck. Where had he parked it? *There!*

Damn. It was facing in the direction she'd come from, and he'd started the engine. She dashed for her BMW and jumped in. Revving up, she made a quick K-turn in the street and floored the gas pedal. She wasn't going to let him just walk out of her life. She'd make him look her in the eye and tell him he didn't want her anymore, that what they had together wasn't extraordinarily special. She'd *make* him believe that he was the only man she wanted, from now until forever.

Following the occasional flash of his brake lights a few blocks away, she drove through the town in an eyeblink. He was driving fast, probably exceeding the speed limit, but she knew her Beemer could keep pace. She wasn't about to lose him now.

Chapter Twenty-Two

∾

The farm. Magnus was heading to his farm!

Kat almost cried in relief. He was returning to the one place he felt safe, where he could hole up and hide. But she wouldn't let him hide from her. She'd make him face his own feelings for her. They'd work this out, even if she had to tie him to that sleigh bed of his for a week to make him listen.

She'd kept about a half mile between their vehicles, never quite narrowing the gap, partly because she was unfamiliar with these roads in the dark, and partly because he'd been traveling at such a high, angry rate of speed. At this hour of the night, it wasn't hard to keep his truck in sight. They'd encountered very little traffic as they headed into the rural area of upper Bucks County.

His headlights disappeared as he turned into his driveway. Kat warred within herself. Should she let her headlights blatantly announce that she was following him? Or should she creep up on him with only her parking lights to illuminate her way through the bumps and potholes?

Who was she kidding? He had to know she was behind him, had to have seen that the same configuration of headlights stayed in his rear-view mirror all these miles. Perhaps he knew it was her car, was even checking to be sure he didn't get too far ahead of her.

But maybe not. Maybe he was so mad at her that he didn't even bother to look. Maybe he was just hell-bent on getting away from her. The thought made her stomach clench.

In the end she opted to keep the Beemer safe from damage, and drove down the driveway with her running lights on. After all, it would only be a minute or two before she'd be knocking on his door anyway.

But no. His truck took the curve around the barn and continued down the driveway. Kat swallowed. She'd never been beyond his apartment. Where was he going? Was he luring her into the woods to harm her? Was this a shortcut to another safe haven? Another woman's home where he could be soothed and pampered?

Ruthlessly she stamped that image out of her mind. Magnus was *hers*. She'd scratch out the eyes of any other woman who tried to claim him.

The Ram disappeared behind another curve through the woods. Resolutely she followed the dirt path after him. Finally, through the trees, she saw the truck's lights illuminate another structure as he pulled to a stop.

A house. One of those two-and-a-half-story colonial-style homes constructed of native stone, looking like the same vintage as the barn where Magnus lived. Was this all part of his property? It looked forlorn and empty, its windowsills needing more than just a coat of paint, the roof over a decrepit porch sagging in spots, scraggly weeds leaning lopsidedly along the stoop.

She watched as Magnus cut the lights and got out of the truck. Slamming the door behind him, he took the three steps up in one long stride, unlocked a door and flung it back to crash against a wall. Rhomboids of light suddenly cascaded through the open doorway and adjoining windows. Kat let out a pent-up breath. At least the house had electricity. She wondered who lived there...or if, indeed, anyone did.

In the silence she waited to see what would happen next. The hoot of an owl made her jump. Then a light flared through an upstairs window. Kat pressed a hand to her thudding heart. Should she go inside? He hadn't so much as hinted that he knew she'd followed him, hadn't sneaked a look over his shoulder, hadn't uttered a word. Yet he'd left the front door ajar. In invitation? Indifference? Or in anger?

She couldn't allow him to stay angry. Sure, he had every right to be, but he still needed to show her a modicum of fairness and let her tell her side of the story.

"You can do it, dammit. You *need* to do it." Shoving aside her trepidation, Kat got out of her Beemer and softly shut the door. She picked her way gingerly across the unstable, broken slates that passed for a walkway and set her feet with great care on the edges of the uneven, unpainted steps, afraid to lean too hard on the rickety handrail.

The door opened onto a front-to-back hallway. A breathtaking, cantilevered stairway rose from the far side of the hall toward her in a graceful arc, and she realized she'd come in through the back door. A puddle of red—his cummerbund?—lay on the worn random-width planking leading to the steps. A pineapple finial crowned the baluster. In the dim light from the hall, she climbed the stairs with one hand skimming over the smooth rail. At the top, she stopped, cautious as a doe ready to enter a clearing. A hallway crossed the steps like the top of a T. On the right she spied the snake of his discarded bowtie. She turned in that direction and moved slowly toward the light spilling out of another doorway. His pleated white shirt lay in a heap just inside. She must have missed where he'd tossed the jacket.

Kat gulped, snugged her cloak around her as a shiver zigzagged its way down her spine, not all of it from the cold air inside the house. Would she stumble onto a scene she didn't want to see? Was he so eager to discard his clothing because a woman was waiting for him? Would he be even angrier at her for trespassing?

Hell. How could he get any angrier than he already was? She needed to talk to him, to diffuse his anger. To make him understand. And if a woman was with him, she'd scratch the bitch's eyes out.

Channeling some steel into her spine, she stepped into the lighted doorway. The scene that greeted her robbed her of oxygen. In the center of the large room, softly lit by a three-armed brass light fixture hung from the high ceiling, was a single item of furniture. A bed. Black bed linens covered the oversize mattress and fat pillows. Plain brass spindles like bars on a jail cell made up the headboard and footboard. Long red scarves were tied to the end-posts of the footboard.

A barefoot Magnus leaned over the mattress, one leg kneeling on the bed, the other stretched out to the floor, his pants tight against his magnificent ass and thighs, as he tied a similar scarf to one side of the headboard. The muscles in his bare back rippled as he worked.

Kat made an inarticulate sound in the back of her throat.

Acting as if he hadn't heard or seen her, Magnus walked around the bed, single-mindedly focused on the last scarf in his hand, and tied it to the remaining bedpost.

The chore completed, he finally turned and acknowledged her presence. The look he gave her—intense, all-consuming, arrogant—made Kat's insides liquefy. His voice thundered like a Viking's should. "What are you doing here?"

Kat had to swallow several times to bring moisture to her throat. "I—we need to talk. I need to explain."

With the proud bearing of a king surveying his domain, Magnus laid one hand on the brass headboard and lifted the other, palm outward, in a classic policeman's "stop" gesture. "Enter this room and you are no longer the queen bee."

Kat's eyes widened at his unexpected opening salvo.

"You will never again be a butterfly flitting from flower to flower."

Her heart beat faster.

"Enter here and be dominated."

She licked her lips.

"Enter here and give up your freedom."

"Magnus, I—"

"Silence! You will not speak unless spoken to."

Kat's first instinct was to bristle at his Neanderthal attitude. But love made her decide that he was testing her commitment to him. She lowered her lashes in a submissive gesture.

"Drop your cloak and step forward."

She undid the clasp and let the wool and silk slide off her shoulders and down to the floor. She took one, two steps into the room, her gaze still on the plank floor.

"Stop right there. How does that white thing come off?"

"A series of clasps."

"Undo them. Show me what happens."

With fingers that trembled slightly, Kat reached up to her left shoulder and fumbled until each of the three hooks had been released. The drape of fabric fell down and dangled across her left breast, exposing the soft mound plumped above the shelf of her strapless bra.

"Why didn't the whole thing fall off?"

"Zipper. On the side."

He smacked his palm against the brass headboard. "Don't play games! Open it!"

Kat bit the inside of her lip to keep from smiling. Who was the one playing games? She undid the hook at the armhole then slowly pulled the zipper down. The white silk gleamed in the creamy light as it pooled around her hips and exposed her merry widow to his view.

She thought she heard him gulp, but kept her eyes demurely downcast.

"Stop disobeying me and get rid of that dress."

"Sorry, I guess my hips are too big." She began to shimmy, allowing gravity and the motion of her hips to tug the dress down. As she moved, her breasts jiggled on their lace shelf and almost popped out of their minuscule restraints.

At last the gown puddled on the floor around her strappy Manolos. She visualized what he was seeing—her waist made even tinier by the snug-fitting merry widow, the white lace triangle of her thong, thigh-high stockings clinging by the lacy elastic at their tops. Her long length of leg in her stilettos.

"Step out of that thing and come here." His voice was gratifyingly hoarse.

She lifted her head high to capture his gaze and sauntered toward him, swaying her hips.

"No. You're not to look at me. Only I have that plea— freedom."

Quickly she lowered her eyes, knowing he meant to say "pleasure", not "freedom". She took a long, deep breath, straightening her spine and raising her breasts until her nipples broke free from their lace prison. With her demure pose she could see how hard they were, how puckered the areolas.

He spun her around and smacked her hard across the ass. "Don't try to entice me. I'm in charge here."

The tingle of his palm streaked directly to her clit. Yes, he was thawing. She smiled.

He whirled her around to face him again. "Take that lacy thing off. Makes you look like you can't breathe."

To show him that she could indeed breathe, she deliberately repeated the action that had caused him to paint his handprint on her ass. Her breasts rose and fell, elongating then plumping back into the demi-cups. Slowly she began the tedious process of unhooking the merry widow, from bottom to top, her gaze all the while on his crotch. She had to give him credit—either he was wearing tight shorts or he was keeping his cock under control. His bulge wasn't nearly as huge as it could be.

Or else he was still too angry to let himself go.

That thought sobered her somewhat, and she renewed her dedication to following his orders exactly. She had something to prove to him.

Cris Anson

"Toss it in the corner and come here. I want to see if your nipples can get any harder. Rub them back and forth across the hair on my chest."

He stood like a stone monolith, hands planted on his hips, waiting. She did as he ordered. The sensation was exquisite. She could actually feel her breasts swell with desire, felt her skin go rosy with heat.

"Close your eyes."

She did. And gasped when she felt him tug at her nipples. He rubbed them between his fingers almost to the point of pain. She thrust them further into his hands, wanting him to cup them, squeeze the soft mounds. Wanted his mouth on them, suckling them.

"No, you don't. I'm calling the shots." He released her breasts and she almost sobbed. "You might as well take that string thing off. It's so small, it hardly covers anything anyway."

Kat hooked her thumbs into the elastic of her thong and, bending forward with another shimmy of her unfettered breasts, skimmed it down her legs. Calculating exactly, she grazed her cheek against his cock at the same time. He stepped back abruptly. She schooled her features against a smile as she stood back up and stepped out of the "string thing".

Now she wore only her thigh-high stockings and stilettos, her diamond earrings, and the scent of her cunt juices. She hoped he was getting a good whiff of her.

He reached underneath the bed and pulled out a small carved box. "The hairpins. Get rid of them. I want to be able to do things with your hair."

Her heart stuttered. She remembered how he'd bared his soul to her, admitting that one of the pleasures of a relationship was to be able to brush the woman's hair. Gladly she complied, the tinkle of the pins audible in the quiet of the room.

"Climb onto the bed. Face first."

210

She did, crawling with her palms on the mattress, waving her ass in his face as she knee-walked to the center of the bed.

"Stop!" He jerked her knees apart, spread her ass cheeks, thrust a finger into her pussy. "You're dripping wet. That's got to be fixed."

Her eyes fluttered shut as his tongue reached into the crevice and lapped up her juices. She dipped her shoulders to the mattress, allowing him greater access to her pussy. He took it, burrowing deeper between her legs and sucking her swollen lips until she was ready to come.

And dammit, he must have been attuned to her rhythm, because he stopped suddenly and slapped her on the ass again, harder than before. "Lay down on your belly. Arms stretched over your head."

When she obeyed, he tied her wrists, then her ankles to the brass bedposts with the red scarves. She tugged her arms, testing. No give. She wondered if he'd ever won a Boy Scout merit badge for knot tying. Her silk-sheathed legs were stretched out wide almost to the point of discomfort, leaving her pussy and asshole available to his gaze...or his hands. She tucked her head into the sheet to hide a smile as she thought of the picture she made—a rosy X in the middle of an acre of black, the juncture of the X being his personal Ground Zero.

"One more scarf," he purred as he climbed onto the bed and straddled her torso with his knees. "Lift up your head."

A blindfold. Kat caught her tongue between her teeth. She didn't like that. She wanted to see what he was doing, wanted to have some control of this erotic dance.

But she had to prove to him that she trusted him, that he could trust her.

Thoroughly in the dark now, she settled down, her right cheek on the mattress, and adjusted herself to as much comfort as she could on the black sheets. They smelled like the outdoors, as though they'd been hung on a line instead of stuffed in a dryer. The room was fairly cool. Goose bumps raised on her bare skin. Her unfettered hair tickled her shoulders, her back whenever she moved. Which wasn't very much, she discovered, spread-eagled as she was on the bed.

Moments passed with no hint of movement, no air being stirred by human activity. She heard nothing but the occasional clink of ancient pipes as heat pulsed through them. Her stomach tightened. Had he left her like this, a prisoner in an unoccupied home? At last she could stand it no longer.

"Magnus?" She didn't like the plaintive, tentative sound of her voice.

She flinched at the whoosh of…something, then the stinging of many tongues on the naked portion of her thighs between stocking top and ass. "What are you doing?"

Silence.

"Magnus?" Nothing. "Who's there?"

Another lash, this one spread over the expanse of her ass cheeks. Multiple whips. Her breath stopped. A cat-o'-nine tails? Good God, had Magnus turned her over to Jules? She fought against the impulse to cry out in protest. He couldn't, wouldn't do that to her. Would he?

No, of course not.

Jules had been livid when she'd reneged on her offer after he'd eagerly stepped up to the cashier with his checkbook in hand. He'd threatened to go to the newspapers with the accusation of a fraudulent auction. She thought she'd calmed him down enough to see reason, but underneath the veneer of sophistication, Jules was a spoiled rich kid who had never grown up.

A third swish jolted her with a hard sting to her exposed, vulnerable slit. The others had been administered across her body, but this one was done vertically, with a heavy hand, as if Jules was punishing her for her deceit. And it had landed dead-on. Her pussy lips stung hotly.

Against her will, tears sprang to her eyes at the pain. It couldn't be Magnus. Magnus wouldn't consciously cause her pain. But how had someone else found this place? How had anyone known she was imprisoned here? She tugged futilely at her silken restraints.

"Magnus, please."

It was so quiet in the room, Kat could hear wind kicking up outside, swirling dead leaves around. "Magnus, where are you?"

He was testing her. There was no one here except Magnus and herself. She was letting her mind get out of control. She willed herself to think pleasant thoughts—of how well Magnus filled out a tux. The power of his talent. The way her knees buckled when he kissed her. The mirrors and hairbrushes he'd bought for the women in the shelter. *That* Magnus would never hurt her.

He *had* to be testing her.

She must have dozed off, because she hazily became aware of the most delicious feeling sweeping over her, a feeling of well-being, of floating on a cloud. The fog in her mind lifted and she realized what it was. Tender kisses, soft licks being dropped on the stinging strips of skin of her thighs, her ass. "Magnus," she murmured, involuntarily lifting her hips to meet his mouth.

A finger slipped into her pussy, glided in and out, rousing her, exciting her. A second finger joined the first and the tempo of the stroking accelerated. Her breathing did, too. A callused thumb found the nub of her clit and massaged it. She couldn't help it. She started wiggling her hips, wanting more, wanting him. "Magnus, please."

He stroked her to a fever pitch. The accumulation of sensations from the evening washed over her, the kick of stripping for him, of obeying him. The pleasure-pain of his palm snapping hard on her ass cheek. She could feel the climax building, tension making her body go rigid. So close, so close, just another stroke, just one more...

The hand withdrew.

Kat's breathing was labored, but as she strained against her bonds, she managed to gasp, "Magnus, you bastard, don't do this to me again! Don't you dare bring me to the verge of coming and then leave me alone."

She felt the bed dip. A moment later her left foot was freed. And then the right. Instinctively she pulled her legs together. And came up against a set of muscular calves between them. Big, strong hands lifted her by the hips until she got her knees under her, shoulders still pressed into the mattress to form a haystack. In seconds she felt a huge, burning-hot cock slam into her pussy from behind. Again and again her body shook under his onslaught, hard and fast, almost punitive in its ferocity.

"Magnus. Oh, Magnus, yes! Please, Magnus, more…" The rest of her litany got lost in a powerful climax that ripped feral sounds from deep in her throat, like a wolf growling a warning to an intruder. Her inner muscles pulsed and contracted seemingly without end, squeezing around a cock that kept on thrusting into her in a glorious freight-train rhythm until another savage climax left her weak and gasping for breath.

And still he fucked her, his tight balls slapping against her wide-open slit, his pelvic bones slamming into her ass cheeks with sledgehammer blows, fingers digging into her hips that would no doubt blossom with ten small bruises.

A third climax exploded within her, a blast of figurative dynamite that shattered her world into a million pieces and left her a mass of tingling neurons. If she hadn't already been blindfolded, her world would have gone black with the power of it. She struggled to remain conscious, to revel in the build-up of energy in the cock, in the man still fucking her like it was the last five minutes of life before the earth was annihilated by a giant meteor. And then he detonated inside her, his climax shooting his cum into her pussy with the force of a fire hose that went on and on until she felt full and replete.

It wasn't until he'd withdrawn and she'd collapsed face first into the mattress that she realized it. He hadn't made a sound.

* * * * *

Every muscle in his body trembled to the point of collapse. He'd damn near killed himself holding off his own climax, but he had something to prove. He wanted to tuck her safely inside the curve of his body and fall asleep with his arms around her. But he wouldn't. Not until he'd gotten what he wanted out of her.

He put his feet up on the low table, rested his head on the back of the chair, and set his inner clock for an hour's catnap.

Chapter Twenty-Three

ဆာ

"Good God, what happened to your butt?"

Kat roused at the welcome sound of Magnus' voice. She could have slept five minutes or five hours, she couldn't tell, the damn blindfold still clung to her eyes. Her arms ached from being stretched upward like a weightlifter hoisting a barbell. Her neck felt stiff from the angle of her head as she'd slept on her stomach with no way to flip over. Surely the backs of her thighs were bruised from his punishing thrusts, for they throbbed still.

But that rough-timbred voice. Like raw honey gliding over her.

Then his surprised comment penetrated her hazy mind and her senses jolted as though someone had thrown ice water over her naked skin. Did that mean it wasn't Magnus who had laid down the marks from the cat-o'-nine tails and subsequently fucked her silly?

No, her mind screamed. No one but Magnus could have made her come so violently, so many times in such quick succession.

Still, her silent lover hadn't given her a clue to his identity, except for the quality of his lovemaking and the strength of his grip. Then why didn't he know how she'd gotten those lash marks?

"Magnus, didn't you—?"

"Let's get you a little more comfortable." His voice sounded hoarse, as though he was reining in some unfathomable emotion.

Kat felt the warmth of his big hands as he untied the silken scarf from her left wrist. With a deep sigh of relief, she swung her arm down to cradle it at her side, feeling phantom pins and needles pricking her as circulation returned.

The mattress dipped as he kneeled on it, knees straddling her hips and pinning her arm to her body. Disappointment speared through her to feel the rough texture of jeans grazing her bare skin. Gently, he smoothed her tangled hair to one side and began to massage her neck and shoulder muscles. "Oh, that feels good," she murmured. Soon his mouth began tracing the same path as his hands, dropping soft little kisses and tongue-licks to ease her pain.

"My right hand, Magnus, you forgot to untie my right hand."

"No, I didn't." The words were muffled as his lips skimmed over her spine. He knee-walked backwards on the mattress, pressing his mouth over each vertebra in turn, until he reached the top of her crack.

She tried to turn under him, to offer him access to her mouth, her breasts, her pussy, but his big hands settled at her waist with casual strength. "Stay."

"I've had this blindfold on for too long," she complained. It drove her crazy that she still couldn't see him, didn't know whether it was day or night. "I want to look at you."

"Soon." His fingers lightly traced over the welts that still smarted on her ass cheeks. "Nasty-looking marks."

"It hurt when you made them."

He withdrew his hands, his mouth from her skin. "Do you really think I would do something like that to you?"

Kat stilled. "Who else would it be?"

"Or would you rather believe I'd willingly share you? That I'd let another man see you naked, with your legs spread wide open to advertise your charms?"

"Dammit, Magnus, are you playing head games with me? You stripped me in front of a whole roomful of people! They saw me begging for your cock. You can't have it both ways. Either you flogged me or someone else did, whether you watched or not."

"Let's table that for now, shall we?" His voice was low, hypnotic. "Will you do something for me?"

Kat took a deep breath. "What?"

"The answer to my question is 'yes' or 'no', not 'what'."

You want to please him, she reminded herself. "Yes."

"You'll do what I ask?"

"Yes." No prompting, no hesitation this time.

"Good. You will only move when I tell you to."

"Yes."

Kat felt him slip off the bed. A moment later she felt the binding on her right wrist loosen. Fighting the instinctive urge to bring her arm down to ease the stiffness, she forced herself to remain motionless.

"Good. You've earned a reprieve." Gently he grasped her arm at wrist and elbow and swung it down to her side. Then with one hand at her shoulder, the other at her hip, he rolled her over onto her back. Kat let out a small sigh of relief.

"That was cheating, but we'll let that one little sigh go without penalty."

The muscles in Kat's mouth twitched, but she held back a smile.

"I'm going to help you sit up now." With one arm under her shoulders and the other under her knees, he lifted her, turned, and deposited her with her feet dangling down the side of the mattress. Her hands instinctively gripped the edges to steady herself.

"Comfortable?"

"Yes. Thank you."

"Can you see anything through or around that blindfold?"

"No."

"Good." She heard clinking sounds, then the most welcome smell of fresh coffee wafted to her nostrils. Kat almost cried with joy.

"Open your mouth."

Like a baby bird, she did, and was rewarded with the rich taste of cream- and vanilla-flavored coffee. She took several greedy gulps before he withdraw the cup with a droll, "Easy, now, there's plenty more."

A minute later, "Open."

She did. And her taste buds jumped at the tart flavor of a strawberry. Savoring it, she chewed slowly.

He repeated the ritual with bite-sized pieces of toast spread with apricot jam, seedless grapes, small chunks of tart cheddar cheese, chunks of chocolate croissant. And coffee. As much coffee as she wanted. Kat couldn't help but compare the scene to Mickey Rourke feeding Kim Basinger in that movie, what was the name? *9½ Weeks?*

"Had enough?"

"Yes, thank you. I'm full."

"Good. Just sit still while I get rid of this stuff."

Kat envisioned him whisking a tray away, his shoulder and back muscles rippling, his ass cheeks in snug jeans bunching and relaxing as he walked. The sound of his footsteps diminished into silence.

She desperately wanted to rip off the blindfold, wanted to see the sun or the moon, or whatever was outside the bedroom window. But he'd said "Sit still" and he was obviously testing her. Making a decision, she tucked her fingers under her thighs and sat on them for a minute. Two minutes. Three. Five.

Her skin puckered in the cool air. Her scalp itched underneath the knot in back of her head. The elastic of her stockings bit into her thighs. She wished he had put something under her feet so the circulation wouldn't be impeded as it was with them dangling, her stilettos still strapped to her feet. In the utter silence she could hear her own breathing, an occasional bird-style sound—the hoot of an owl? A dove cooing? If she was going to live here, she'd better learn some things.

"Cold?"

Kat jumped. She hadn't heard him return. "A little."

"We'll fix that." His big hands grabbed her at the waist and lifted her off the bed and onto the floor. Her nearly nude body brushed against his body. His *nude* body, warm as a rug in the sunshine. Suddenly she didn't care if she was disobeying, she leaned into him, her breasts pillowing into his hard chest, her thighs pushing against his. And between them, her hips cradled the raging furnace of his cock. His arms closed around her.

She couldn't stifle a soft sigh as she rubbed her cheek against the ridge of his collarbone, pressed her lips to the taut skin on his shoulder, inhaled the unique male scent of Magnus Thorvald. *This* was where she belonged. Skin to skin with him.

"I'm going to walk you into another room."

Kat felt herself being twirled around then her back snugged into his chest, his big hands resting on her shoulders. With slight pressure he directed her forward, then to a right turn then a left, his long legs skimming hers from behind as he matched his stride to her hesitant one.

"Stop."

She felt his fingers and knuckles at her skull. In seconds the blindfold fell away. Blinking hard against the sudden brightness, Kat looked around the royal blue-tiled room. A bathroom. Sunlight streaming through a many-paned window. A large ball-and-clawfoot tub. Vintage pedestal sink.

He nudged her another step forward, spun her to one side. Reflected in a full-length mirror was one magnificent Viking and one bedraggled odalisque. Her hair looked like a couple of porcupines had taken residence in it. Still, she fancied that she looked rather sexy in nothing but high heels and stockings.

Her mouth was swollen and red, her wrists marred by faint ligature marks. Small reddish-blue bruises dappled her hips from where his fingers had gripped her so securely in their fucking frenzy the previous night. She resisted the urge to turn her ass cheeks to the mirror to see what kind of damage the cat-o'-nine tails had inflicted on her skin. She knew she'd better wait for him to bring up the subject.

From somewhere behind him Magnus produced a hairbrush and began to brush out the knots in her hair. Slowly, carefully, taking hanks of auburn snarls in his hand so as not to pull her scalp, he brushed and untangled and brushed some more. Kat noted the flashes of silver as his hand moved. This one looked more intricate than the ones he bought for the women at the shelter. Had he had this—her—in mind when he bought it?

She found herself being lulled by the calm, methodical stroking. Her eyelids drooped. A dreamy smile softened her face as she reveled in this intimate grooming, in the utter surrender to his will. When all the snarls had been detangled, still he brushed, from the crown of her head to the ends of her curly tresses.

"Let's get these things off." He tucked his fingers inside the elastic and tugged her stockings down to her ankles.

"Sit." He indicated the closed toilet seat. She sat.

He knelt at her feet, unbuckled the ankle straps of her heels then removed them and the stockings. And then…heaven…he massaged her toes, her ankles.

"Okay, get up. It's your turn to work now." Magnus moved to the opposite side of the bathroom, where Kat noticed the walk-in shower. He turned the water on full-force. "Come here and bathe me."

"With pleasure," she murmured. She followed him inside the tiled cavern. The warm spray hit her like hundreds of caressing fingers. She grabbed a bar of soap and lathered her hands. She washed his face, feeling the pleasant rasp of his stubble against her palms. Washed his neck, shoulders, arms, the muscles flexing and rippling as her hands moved against velvet over steel. She paid special attention to the flat brown nipples half hidden within the tangle of his chest hair, and smiled at the way his cock jerked when she scraped a fingernail over the tiny buttons.

She moved around him to lather his back, the trim waist, that marvelous tight ass. She insinuated the fingers of both hands inside his crack and rubbed up and down, feeling the edge of the tight hole close instinctively. Then down the thick columns of his thighs, the rough hair making swirling designs under her touch, and to his calves, then his toes.

"All done," she said sweetly.

"Not on your life, woman." He grabbed for her, swung her back around to face him. "On your knees, and be thorough."

"Oh, my, how could I have forgotten this big thing? It's sticking right out into my face." Kat closed her soapy hands around the long, thick length of his cock and slid her palms up and down, up and down, then reached below for his balls. "Please, master, open your legs so I can be as thorough as you require."

With a growl, he complied. Head bent, Kat allowed herself a smug smile. Two could play this game of dominant-submissive. Lovingly and lavishly she cupped and soaped his balls, heavy and taut now, then slid her hands back to his cock, then around to where the base of it attached to his torso, swirling his groin hair with the soapsuds until it made a bull's-eye.

When she thought she had tortured him enough, she nudged him a quarter turn so the water could slide over his belly, his cock, washing away the soap until his skin shone tan and hard. She lifted his cock, rubbing a gentle finger across the thick wet ridge of the head, and made a small sound of displeasure in the back of her throat. "Needs more washing." She grabbed his shaft at its base. Her tongue lapped at the ridge, all around it once, twice, then her mouth closed around the whole of it. She had the satisfaction of feeling his knees buckle until he stabilized himself with his hands braced against the tile wall.

"Enough," he growled, hoisting her by her upper arms to stand on her feet. He looked magnificent, all wet and aroused male, water droplets catching in his thick eyelashes, dripping down from his stone-hard nipples, his long, heavy cock.

Magnus stepped out of the shower with a terse order. "Now wash yourself."

Disappointment speared through Kat. She had been so looking forward to his hands on her, to the teasing, the anticipation.

"Be as thorough as you were with me," he growled. "I'll watch to make sure."

So Magnus handed her a lemon? *Wait until you see the lemonade I'll be making.*

Reaching again for the soap, Kat began to lather herself, her eyes willing him not to look away from hers. She smoothed the suds over her throat, her arms, her breasts. Paid special attention to the nipples, rubbing, stroking, pulling them until they were hard as rocks and red as her cunt lips. Then dipped to her waist, her navel, her hips. She lifted one leg, set her foot on the recessed seat, and stroked the soap across one side of her slit and then the other. She set down the soap and dipped two fingers into her cunt. As she washed her inside passage with slow, sultry strokes, her eyes dropped down to his mouth, then to his cock.

It jerked upward as though she had touched it.

Wait until you see my next move. Kat turned her back to him, soaped her hands, then bent forward to thrust her ass into the air. Reaching behind her, she ran her soapy fingers up and down her crack, then dipped a lathered finger into her asshole.

In and out, deeper and deeper, her legs spread wide apart for maximum effect.

"Dammit!" Magnus shot back into the shower, grabbed her hips from behind, and slammed his rigid cock into her pussy with one mighty thrust. Kat had to slap her palms on the wet tiles to keep her balance.

He withdrew his cock until just the tip was inside, then shoved brutally into her once more. "You're mine!"

Withdrew and slammed. "Mine!"

Stayed buried inside her cunt. "You hear me?"

"Yes," she whimpered.

A few more savage strokes. "Only mine."

Then he withdrew totally, his breath rasping in the steamy air. Fumbling at the controls, he turned off the water. "Bend your knees."

She did. And felt him push into her soapy asshole, his cock hot and hard and slick with her juices, slowly deeper and deeper yet, until he was seated to the hilt. "Mine," he gasped.

"Only yours." She was sobbing now with the savagery of his emotion.

"No one else will ever touch you."

In response, her hips pressed upward into him, welcoming him, urging him to move.

"Say it, damn you."

"Magnus, I swear, only you. No one else."

"Will you say it in public, after the heat of the moment? Or are you just saying it so I'll fuck you blind until you come a dozen times?"

Her temper flared. She leaned forward, bent her knees further, pulling her body down until his cock popped out of her asshole. A pugnacious look settled on her face as she got to her feet, turned around and faced him. "I'll say it until I'm blue in the face." She poked an index finger into his sternum. "No one else will touch me. Only you." She emphasized the last word with another stab at his chest. "Yes, I'll say it in public." Slam with the finger. "And you'd better wash off that slab of oak between your legs so you can fuck me blind until I come a dozen times. Or else."

Magnus couldn't help it. He tossed his head back and roared with laughter. "My blazing Valkyrie. Be my guest." He handed her the soap. As she attended to his cock with exquisite attention to detail, he mused, "Living with you will never be dull, will it?"

The air between them suddenly seemed to shimmer. She dropped the soap and looked into his eyes. "Is that what you want?"

He cocked his head, his gaze tender on her. "Yeah. I could get used to waking up with you in my arms."

Kat felt her eyes go all soft and teary. "I'm so glad. I never knew it could be like this, needing someone more than my next breath. Please believe me, Magnus, I totally forgot about that Cancun thing. I'm going to sell the condo there, and from now on the only thing I'll auction off is tickets to opening night of the annual Magnus Thorvald exhibit."

He pulled her tight against him. "My Kat."

They stayed that way for a long moment, the fire of sex subdued by the glow of something new, something precious. Magnus buried his face in her riotous wet curls. Kat snuggled closer to his chest.

"I promise you, Magnus. I'll never do—" she bit her tongue before she could say *what your ex-wife did* "—anything to hurt you."

"And I promise not to be so domineering."

She reared back. "Don't be silly. Dominate me all you want. When I get tired of it, I'll let you know."

"If that's what you want—" he swooped her up in his arms and strode back to the brass bed, "—I'm going to see if you can really come a dozen times."

And damn if she didn't.

* * * * *

"That *was* me, you know."

Kat turned her sleepy head to her man, her body sated as never before. "What was?"

"With the cat-o'-nine tails."

"But you sounded so surprised when you asked what happened."

"I'm sorry for being so devious." Magnus tightened his arms around her. "I think part of it was that Rolf goaded me into thinking you might like it."

"How did you know where to get one?"

He looked sheepish. "I—"

"Never mind, I don't want to know." She snuggled closer to him, buried her face in the hollow between his shoulder and neck.

"Actually, Savidge got it for me," he admitted. "When I agreed to go to the auction with you, I concocted a grand plan to take you here afterwards and make love to you twelve ways from Sunday. To do all the bizarre and depraved things I imagined you wanted, like being tied up and flogged. And, selfishly, I tried not to give you a clue as to who was doing the flogging. I guess deep down, I wanted to see if you'd call out someone else's name."

Kat rose to one elbow and captured his gaze. "Oh, Magnus, by that time I knew I didn't want anyone but you."

"I can't believe I hurt you."

"I understand, really I do. You were furious with me, Magnus, I could see it. But you still wanted me—thank God." She snuggled back into the warmth of his embrace. "I just couldn't see you giving another man permission to do anything to me. I knew it was you. You needed to exorcize the demons both of us had."

"And are they gone?"

"Mine sure are. My mother was wrong. One man and one woman—the right man and the right woman—can move mountains. Just think what a Viking and a Valkyrie can do together."

He rolled on top of her. "Make a little red-haired Viking?"

Kat's eyes glimmered. "Or maybe a blonde Valkyrie."

"Then we'd better get married, don't you think? So we can start making one of each?"

"Yes, Master. Oh yes. We'd better."

Enjoy an excerpt from:
DANCE OF THE SEVEN VEILS

"Like him. That gladiator. I'd like to be the one to turn *him* on."

Lyssa's heart skipped a beat, then thudded back to catch up. About six feet tall, dark hair curling around his ears and nape, a narrow black mask that accented the sharp cheekbones and square jaw, the gladiator leaned negligently against the jamb, arms crossed, one leg casually crossed over the other. A gold medallion glowed against a thatch of dark chest hair overlaying well-sculpted muscles. Sandals were laced up his calves, and his thighs under the short Roman tunic looked strong enough to hold him over her in a variety of positions for hours.

She blinked. *Where had that thought come from?*

The gladiator inclined his head slightly, raised an eyebrow. In invitation?

Lyssa swallowed hard. Her heartbeat accelerated. She realized she *wanted* to go to him. But her feet felt rooted to the parquet floor. Lingering doubts about her femininity choked her.

In the background the music shifted. The frenetic opening strains of Richard Strauss' *Dance of the Seven Veils* wafted through the hidden speakers, tympani pounding, a haunting oboe solo connecting to her synapses. Her heart stuttered. It was as though fate had stepped in at this singular moment in time, sending her gaze to this particular stranger across this crowded room, the music reminding her of her costume of seven diaphanous veils tenuously held in place by a golden waist chain. In her eyes, the gladiator morphed into the lascivious, depraved Herod that the voluptuous Salome would entice into granting her deepest, darkest wish.

The gladiator moved languidly to a pile of plush cushions on the floor of a dimly lit alcove and reclined on his side, one knee upraised, leaning on an elbow. He swept his other arm out in a gesture of "The stage is yours" and waited, his mouth curled upward into a slight smile of anticipation.

You're Salome, a voice said inside Lyssa's head. *Amoral, decadent, willful. Dance for him. Seduce him.*

She thrust out her chin and posed like a dancer, the toes of one foot pointed out, one arm across her torso. She scribed a graceful arc up and over her head, then down to one hip, allowing her fingers to skim lightly up her thigh and between her breasts, as if calling his attention to the charms within the circle, ending with a graceful *salaam* gesture at face level.

Taking a deep, fortifying breath, she grabbed the edge of one veil, removed it from around her waist and dropped it to the floor at his feet. The sensuous music slowed to the *leitmotif* that was Salome's signature, infusing her blood with fire. She locked gazes with him—with Herod—and tugged another veil free. Raising it high, she allowed it to float down over her hair, then dragged it down peekaboo fashion until her eyes showed, then her nose, her lips. He transferred his intent gaze to her pouting mouth, and licked his lower lip. Lyssa felt a shock of pure lust course through her. She wanted him to kiss her. Everywhere.

The music shifted to a faster tempo, compelling her to rotate her hips, to bend and sway to the music. Her hair sifted over her face in a golden curtain. She gripped the third veil and trailed it over her breast until the sensitive peak tightened and tingled, then flung the veil aside.

Faster still, the music urged Salome to tempt King Herod to his limits, to hypnotize him, to make him *want* to grant her most perverse wish. Another veil slipped from her body, baring both her breasts. She bent toward him, teasing him, offering her hard, pink nipples to his view but just out of reach. She spun around, undulating her arms and shoulders with her back to him, then removed the veil that covered her ass cheeks. The languid Salome *leitmotif* recurred, relentlessly ratcheting up the tension. She rolled her hips in a slow front-to-back motion, imitating the sex act, as she turned slowly, slowly to face him.

The lust in Herod's eyes, the pupils so dilated they looked black, almost brought Salome to her knees. Absently she noted that his tunic tented up almost to his upraised knee. And *she* had done this to him. King though he may be, Salome knew she had spun a carnal web of obsession around him.

Frenzied now, the exotic music rushed to its climax as Salome divested herself of the penultimate veil across one restlessly moving hip, flinging it into the alcove, where it landed on Herod's muscular shoulder and slid down unnoticed. The last long obbligato sounded, the oboe trill drawing out the tension to an almost unbearable level. Salome ripped off the veil covering her golden thatch and stood before her King, triumphant, panting, exquisitely naked but for the waist chain and golden sandals, the veil in her raised fist fluttering with her harsh, hot breaths.

The music ended with a turbulent cadenza punctuated by three furious chords. Salome fell to her knees and collapsed, legs on Herod's lap, arms flung above her head, her naked skin sheened with perspiration, thighs spread apart without thought to modesty, open to her King's lustful gaze.

Panting, Salome slowly became aware of the flickering candlelight, of the muscular legs of King Herod under hers. Through lowered lashes she could see her flushed breasts rise and fall with every deep breath, the pink nipples standing erect, the areolas puckered and tight. Became aware that every nerve ending cried out for his mouth, his hands, his cock. Anywhere, everywhere, just satisfy this…this *craving*, this need for release that she'd never experienced before.

He shifted her so she lay on her back and he beside her, his leg slung over her thighs, his hard cock pressed against her hip. Bending forward, he captured a nipple in his mouth and suckled. No tender touches, no coy foreplay, his mouth felt as though he was starving and she was nectar for the gods. Her back arched upward violently, offering herself to his greed. Her hands swung down to grab his head and keep him anchored there, feasting on her breast, her nipple, her very soul, willing him, no, *demanding* that he relieve the relentless itch in her other breast.

When he did, she groaned in relief and pleasure. Carnal need spiraled higher and higher within her, infusing every nerve ending with electric current. The heat of his cock against her hip made her twist her body so that it would touch her where she burned the hottest, between her thighs. She wanted him to bury that fiery sword inside her, wanted him to pound his body into hers, fuck her until she ached, and then fuck her some more, until she melted into a puddle of warm honey in his arms.

From somewhere far away, she heard a deep chuckle, felt the vibrations from his chest to hers. "Not yet, temptress," he whispered into her ear.

"Yes," she hissed, squirming to get closer to the thick, hot cock that was driving her crazy.

Ignoring her demand, he inched his way down her torso, licking, nibbling, suckling on bits of her skin. He paused a moment to dip a hot tongue into her navel. She twitched, pressed his head down into her belly, wanting more. Her crotch burned for him. She wanted to feel his weight pushing her deep into the cushions, wanted to feel the rasp of his chest hair rubbing against her aching breasts. She wanted to wrap her legs around his hips, crush him to her as he pounded her. Her breath came in great, wrenching gasps, the oxygen in her lungs having been consumed by this fire inside her that burned hotter and hotter with every stroke of his tongue.

She writhed under him. Needed him. *Now!*

"Please," she begged, almost incoherent with passion.

Why an electronic book?

We live in the Information Age—an exciting time in the history of human civilization, in which technology rules supreme and continues to progress in leaps and bounds every minute of every day. For a multitude of reasons, more and more avid literary fans are opting to purchase e-books instead of paper books. The question from those not yet initiated into the world of electronic reading is simply: *Why?*

1. *Price.* An electronic title at Ellora's Cave Publishing and Cerridwen Press runs anywhere from 40% to 75% less than the cover price of the exact same title in paperback format. Why? Basic mathematics and cost. It is less expensive to publish an e-book (no paper and printing, no warehousing and shipping) than it is to publish a paperback, so the savings are passed along to the consumer.

2. *Space.* Running out of room in your house for your books? That is one worry you will never have with electronic books. For a low one-time cost, you can purchase a handheld device specifically designed for e-reading. Many e-readers have large, convenient screens for viewing. Better yet, hundreds of titles can be stored within your new library—on a single microchip. There are a variety of e-readers from different manufacturers. You can also read e-books on your PC or laptop computer. (Please note that Ellora's Cave does not endorse any specific brands.

You can check our websites at www.ellorascave.com or www.cerridwenpress.com for information we make available to new consumers.)

3. *Mobility.* Because your new e-library consists of only a microchip within a small, easily transportable e-reader, your entire cache of books can be taken with you wherever you go.

4. *Personal Viewing Preferences.* Are the words you are currently reading too small? Too large? Too... ANNOYING? Paperback books cannot be modified according to personal preferences, but e-books can.

5. *Instant Gratification.* Is it the middle of the night and all the bookstores near you are closed? Are you tired of waiting days, sometimes weeks, for bookstores to ship the novels you bought? Ellora's Cave Publishing sells instantaneous downloads twenty-four hours a day, seven days a week, every day of the year. Our webstore is never closed. Our e-book delivery system is 100% automated, meaning your order is filled as soon as you pay for it.

Those are a few of the top reasons why electronic books are replacing paperbacks for many avid readers.

As always, Ellora's Cave and Cerridwen Press welcome your questions and comments. We invite you to email us at Comments@ellorascave.com or write to us directly at Ellora's Cave Publishing Inc., 1056 Home Avenue, Akron, OH 44310-3502.

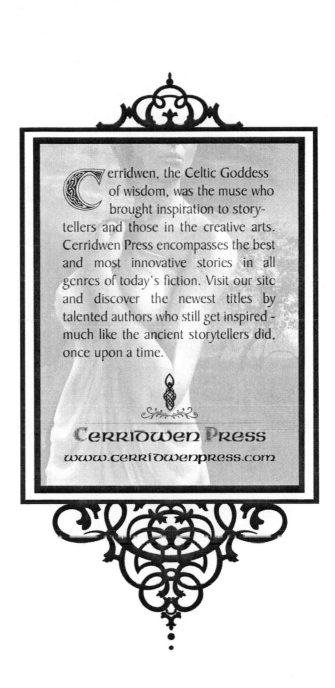

erridwen, the Celtic Goddess of wisdom, was the muse who brought inspiration to story-tellers and those in the creative arts. Cerridwen Press encompasses the best and most innovative stories in all genres of today's fiction. Visit our site and discover the newest titles by talented authors who still get inspired - much like the ancient storytellers did, once upon a time.

Cerridwen Press

www.cerridwenpress.com